CHILDREN
OF
DYSPHORIA

BOOK ONE: FALL OF HAVEN

RUDITH MOORE

Children of Dysphoria Book One: Fall of Haven

Published by Rudith Moore

Cover and artwork by Rudith Moore

ISBN: 979-8-9926147-0-1 (Paperback)
ISBN: 979-8-9926147-1-8 (Hardcover)

Children of Dysphoria

Kim Hae-Sol

Characters

Chio? Kyun-ho

Choi Tae-Kyun

Ages

Kyun-ho - 30
Tae-Kyun - 24
Hae-Sol - 30

4

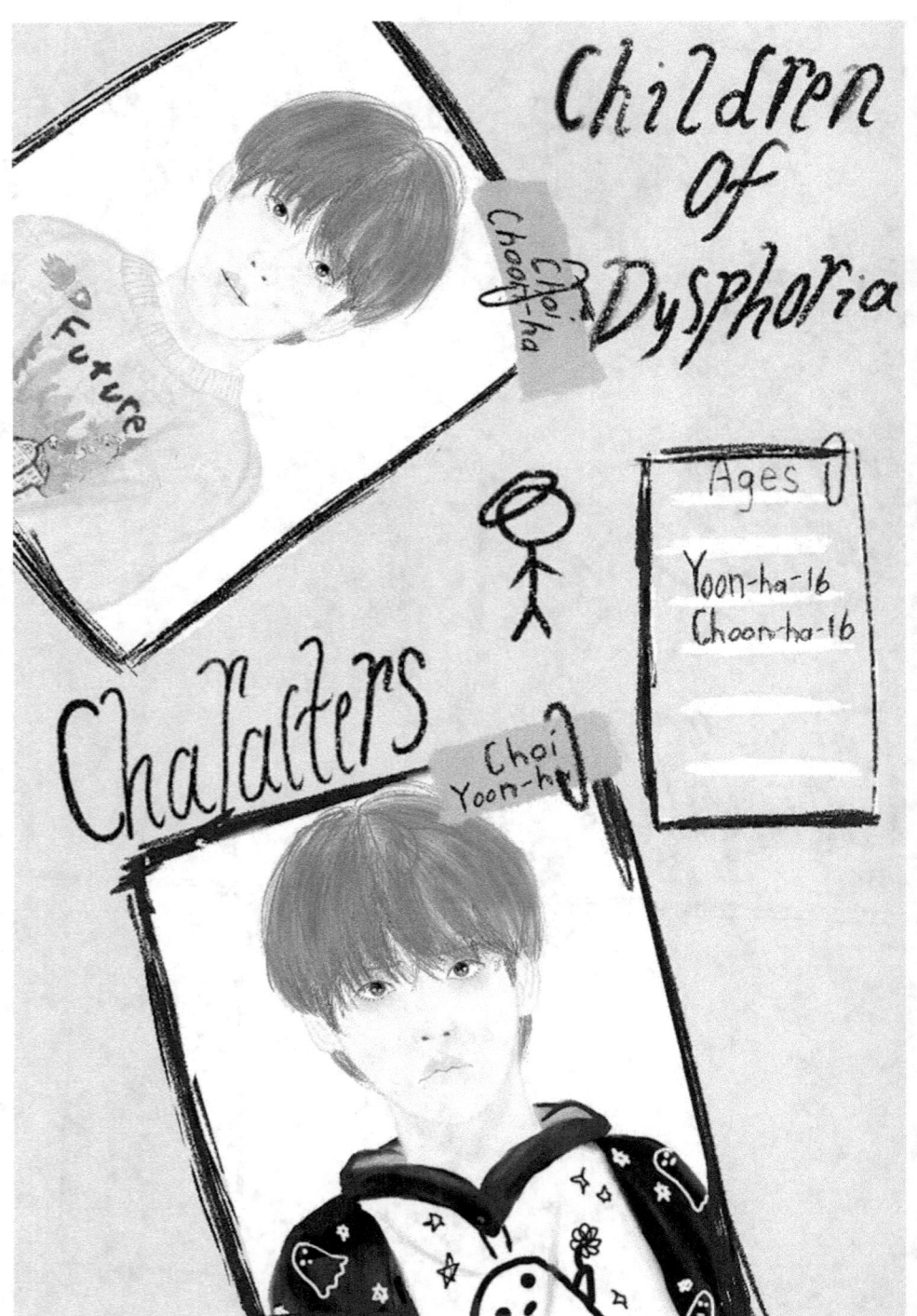

Children
of
Dysphoria

Choi
Choon-ha

Future

Characters

Choi
Yoon-ha

Ages

Yoon-ha-16
Choon-ha-16

- Prologue -

Start of Dysphoria

Part One

It occurs to Kyun-ho, that the longer he stares into his friend's frantic eyes, and the harder he tries to rid this knife from his crimson hands… that he could easily be killed by him.

Because to Hae-sol (the boy drenched in the rain despite his yellow coat), it's Kyun-ho's fault he wants to kill himself now.

To Hae-sol, the only reason any blood has been spilled at all, is because Kyun-ho failed to help him in the way he needed.

As Hae-sol struggles to pull the knife back, pushing the weapon deeper into the wound he's already created on his chest, Kyun-ho realizes just how frightening their friendship has become, what little control he has over Hae-sol, and how suffocating it feels to be wrapped so tightly in a situation he never thought would happen.

They're thirteen years old, these friends.

Alone and secluded in the forest behind Kyun-ho's home while the rain outside argues violently with the wind outside this treehouse, both children's heartbeats audible to each other because they're both very scared.

Of course, they're scared.

Something happened inside Hae-sol's house.

Something dark and cataclysmic Hae-sol refuses to voice.

Police sirens can still be heard even with the rain pouring down atop this treehouse, and Kyun-ho can still see the blood that littered the floor of his friend's home... can still see his friend sitting in it, crimson coating his face, hands, raincoat.

He's still experiencing the shock that threatened to asphyxiate him when Hae-sol softly told him while gripping his brother's shirt, *"Hae-yon's outside, now... I think it's raining because the clouds didn't want to see me bury him."*

"Hae-sol, w-why won't you just tell me...? You didn't really hurt anyone, d-did you?" Kyun-ho's voice is laced with the fear shaking him as he tightens his grip on the knife, biting his tongue to withhold the urge to scream when Hae-sol merely laughs, emerald eyes fervent beneath long, raven-colored bangs as he pulls the weapon toward him, tears continuing to streak his face despite his smile as he quips rapidly, *"Nothing! Nothing!"* more laughter falling from his lips as he yanks the knife's handle harder, nearly escaping Kyun-ho's grasp.

"This isn't funny, Hae-sol! W-why was there s-so much blood? Why did you say that about-about- H-Hae-yon, a-and why are you trying to hurt yourself if nothing—!?"

"WHY ARE YOU BOTHERING ME?"

All at once, the knife is free from Kyun-ho's grip, and a blur of silver flashes in Kyun-ho's eyes before pain erupts from beneath his bangs and warm crimson runs down his temple.

"WHY ARE YOU BOTHERING ME WHEN IT'S TOO LATE AND EVERYTHING IS RUINED!? THEY'RE DEAD BECAUSE OF YOU! THEY'RE DEAD BECAUSE OF YOU!" Hae-sol's audibly crying now, stabbing the knife over and over again into the wooden floor as he shouts, tears breaking his voice, *"You never fix anything, Kyun-ho. We're doctors! We should be able to fix ANYTHING, ANYTHING!"*

The rain outside seems to sigh at Hae-sol's tears, gradually slowing until eventually, all that's audible is the dull sound of water hitting the roof as a crimson swirled puddle climbs up the material of his wet jeans, beads of water dripping from his inky hair and onto the floor beneath him.

Kyun-ho can't speak.

He can't stop shaking, and he can't stop the panic coloring him the more his mind reiterates everything Hae-sol said and everything he saw before fleeing his home.

He doesn't want to believe his friend is a murderer, and he doesn't want to believe he's been a murderer for several years now.

After all, he still refuses to think he was the culprit behind the abrupt passing of the neighbor's child two years ago and refuses to believe these things have anything to do with Haven.

"It's not fair, *it's not... fair!*" Hae-sol whispers, emerald eyes seeming to glaze as the knife he was holding falls onto the floor, and he tugs in growing frustration at the hair beneath his hood while Kyun-ho dives to retrieve the weapon, standing to move away from his friend only to stumble into a shelf at his abrupt scream, countless jars of Hae-sol's medicines shattering around him as he shouts, rage reddening his cheeks, "*IT'S ALL BECAUSE OF YOU! DOCTORS AREN'T SUPPOSED TO GET RID OF PATIENTS! THEY CURE THEM!*"

"G-get rid of? What-what are you talking about? W-we aren't really doctors, Hae-sol— we only pretended because-"

"*HAVEN WAS WORKING BECAUSE OF ME, AND NOW, IT'S BROKEN BECAUSE OF YOU!*" Hae-sol has stood up now, advancing towards Kyun-ho, who acts on impulse and tries to run away, forgetting the wreckage beneath him and falling on his knees upon slipping, several shards of glass penetrating his skin as he emits a shrill cry and drops the knife in a failed attempt at ridding the irritants from his knees.

"*You make me feel like I can't fix anyone, Kyun-ho! Not your brother, not the children that beg for my medicines, or even my stupid, stupid excuse for a father!*" Hae-sol's tone is filled with such a sorrowful amount of frustration that guilt feels as though it's hugging him too tightly.

"*That's why my medicine isn't working, that's why...*"

"Y-You gave someone else your medicine?"

The treehouse falls silent. The rain outside gradually escalates as several claps of thunder give the lightning illuminating the windows of this treehouse an audible voice...

It was Hae-sol's idea, Haven.

Always been obsessed with medicines and the idea of healing those he deemed broken, perhaps because of the cruel way he was raised and the trauma that's festered because of it... or perhaps because inwardly, he's struggling to maintain his sanity, refusing to admit it until he can find and secure a definite remedy.

Haven, the small group they created when they were eleven for Kyun-ho's younger brother, Tae-kyun, was made to disarm the fear society had installed in the boy regarding his schizophrenia.

Haven was made to help him forget the cruel way he was treated by his father and those around him, because with Hae-sol and his brother, he was loved.

He was happy, and almost never afraid of himself.

For several years now, Haven has been there to reassure Tae-kyun that he isn't falling apart like the people around him claim. Not harboring the demon his father says is controlling him or shaming his family and those around him with his presence, because in Haven, his presence is special, and they would constantly remind him not to forget that.

Haven meant safety.

Haven meant pretending to be doctors and creating special medicines only Tae-kyun could take, medicines that made him cry with euphoric laughter because sometimes he'd be given ten candies and a side of tickles, or different toys and games in place of his real medicine, things his real doctors or father would never do.

Haven meant drawing pictures of Tae-kyun's stars and pretending they could see them when they didn't, as murmuring stars and incoherent whispers were the most prevalent symptoms of Tae-kyun's illness, and they were the most troubling—especially on the days the stars grew tired of being on earth and resorted to hurting the child because he was unable to send them back to the 'world' they came from…

Tae-kyun was so happy with Haven then, and yet now, its name alone will scare him. There are too many horrible things woven into that word that will never leave his mind.

How is one to know such a purposeful game of pretend would result in several tragedies?

"Y-you gave your medicine to our neighbor's son, didn't you...?"

Hae-sol emits a deep sound of frustration before practically throwing himself at the wall of their treehouse, pressing his head against it as he shouts, "I GAVE HIM MEDICINE BECAUSE YOU WOULDN'T LET ME GIVE IT TO TAE-KYUN!"

"I-I couldn't! I-it was making him sick—it's not safe!"

"BECAUSE YOU NEVER HELPED ME FIX IT!"

"But-but that means y-you *killed* him, though!" The medicines—we shouldn't have even taken them from your father...!" Kyun-ho utters weakly, eyes beginning to water as Hae-sol swiftly turns to retort, emerald eyes gleaming with rage, "I didn't kill him. The medicine was an anesthetic used to numb him during my surgery. You don't know these things, though, because YOU DON'T CARE!"

"I-I do care, Hae-sol, that's why I'm here...! I don't want you to believe that you've hurt people, that's not what Haven was for! Haven was to help people like Tae-kyun feel safe, not scared because we're trying to fix them!"

"If we can't fix them, there's no point in keeping them. Either the world will kill them with harsh judgment... or we kill them by accident through a series of surgeries made to heal them. It's not our fault if their bodies aren't strong enough to withstand any healing."

"Hae-sol, what are you saying?" Kyun-ho struggles to withhold the evidence of tears in his voice, gripping the rain-soaked hem of his school's sweater vest, several drops of water puddling to the floor, as he looks at his friend in bewilderment.

This isn't Hae-sol. This can't be Hae-sol. Why is he acting s-so scary? Hae-sol's not scary. Why is he scaring me?

"Why… can you not understand the reason I created Haven?"

"I-I do understand your reason, it's just y-you're not making any sense because you're not acting right, Hae-sol…! W-what happened?"

"WHAT HAPPENED!? WHAT HAPPENED!?" Laughter fills the air. Dry, sardonic laughter accompanied by several glances towards Kyun-ho when he bends to retrieve one of many broken medicine bottles scattered across the floor, the sharp edges penetrating his skin because he's gripping it too tightly, though his mind has yet to register it.

"You… you know all about what happened, Kyun-ho. Why… why do you continue to act as though everything is shocking and mysterious… when nothing at all should surprise or allude to you the way you claim it does?"

Kyun-ho opens his mouth to respond, but Hae-sol silences him with a dismissive wave of his hand, a dark crimson ribbon trailing down his wrist as he says, straightening up and whispering down at the broken bottle, "It didn't work… you know it didn't work… you know… because you lied and said we could do anything as Haven's doctors… you said our medicine would work… because—"

"Hae-sol, we were pretending, though!" Kyun-ho's voice heightens an octave as tears flood his eyes and cause him to waver, his light brown hair falling into coffee-colored eyes as small drops of water run past his temple and down his chin.

"Y-you can always do anything when you're pretending, that's why it was fun…!"

Hae-sol lifts his head slowly to lock emerald eyes with Kyun-ho, that broken bottle of his getting spotted with blood because he's still holding it too tightly. The soft beige color of the remaining concoction leaks from the glass and onto the floor as a terribly uncomfortable silence swallows them. Though it lasts no longer than a minute, Kyun-ho feels as though he's lived through several thousand.

"Pretending… why… do you think… I would pretend about something so serious? You weren't the one who created Haven. You only knew what to do because I told you. You… you never even asked about my medicine's ingredients, but you blamed me continuously for making Tae-kyun sick… when he would take them. But… it was you who made him sick… because you never asked me what the dosage was or how to take it."

"You don't need to when you're pretending, though! That's why Tae-kyun liked it! You never even said we weren't pretending! That's why Tae-kyun doesn't like Haven anymore. Y-you scare him now because you're using strange medicines, and *all week you've been acting—!"*

"It's because you haven't been attending Haven's meetings!"

Hae-sol shouts, sounding like an angered toddler as he pulls at his hair. *"You've been avoiding me, and so I've had to use other clients for Haven's surgeries and recruit different—!"*

16

"Y-you... used other... y-you-you..."

"We know everyone in this neighborhood, Kyun-ho, there's no one here who could possibly have any information regarding such crimes. It would be a shame if it was your friend's father, though, wouldn't it? You keep painting him as such a bad person. Why don't you go and ask him?

What a twist it would be if it was someone you really liked, though. Someone like his first son, perhaps you wouldn't be so quick to judge people, then."

The words feel like needles in his mind, the irony of his father's words nauseating him to the point of dizziness as he chokes out, *"D-dad was right about you! Y-you were the reason those kids were on the news. Y-you killed them, your dad and-and Hye-yon—"*

"I PUT HIM OUT OF HIS MISERY! OUR FATHER WAS BROKEN, AND NONE OF THE MEDICINES WORKED FOR HIM! THEY'RE DEAD BECAUSE YOU DIDN'T—!"

A deafening shout of thunder mutes the volume of Hae-sol's words as the wind outside rocks the tree holding them, the rain falling so hard it's beginning to sound as though little bullets are showering the roof of this small house; the police sirens are no longer audible in this storm.

"—There's no point to YOU, Kyun-ho! There's no point to ME if I *CAN'T MAKE THE RIGHT MEDICINE TO FIX PEOPLE!*" Overwhelmed with his emotions, Hae-sol thrusts himself back against the wall while yanking vigorously at his hair, the storm outside continuing to try to drown out his words.

"It's not *ME!* It's *YOU* who's ruined Haven! It's *YOU* who is killing everyone because you aren't helping me when they need Surgeries!"

"We can't do surgeries, we're not real doctors! You're hurting people for *no reason!*"

Hae-sol's face pales. His wet and dripping inky hair falls into dismayed eyes as he turns and whispers in a tone that instantly guilts his friend, "Kyun-ho... you.... you think I didn't have a reason for hurting my father...?"

"N-no, I'm sorry! That's not what I meant, Hae-sol, it's just...!"

"You don't think I've tried... other ways to help us...?"

"I-I know you have, but your medicine—"

"I'm going to kill Tae-kyun." Kyun-ho's face pales as his heartbeat seems to slow, and Hae-sol, no longer against the wall but standing directly in front of him, glares with eyes he never thought could look so cruel.

"Because you think I'm a baseless murderer. I'm going to kill Tae-kyun, and then I'm going to kill myself, and you'll be all alone... with nothing but Haven's failure to comfort you."

"Hae-sol you can't! Y-you're not like that, you wouldn't...!" Kyun-ho's voice breaks with the abrupt onset of tears as he shakes his head hurriedly while attempting to back away, his body tensing when Hae-sol grips his arm to stop him, his voice, normally low and feathery, so full of hurt and the intent to make Kyun-ho feel the same.

"I'll kill Tae-kyun, your stupid parents, and Tae-ho.

Then you'll be just like me... alone and empty... because *nothing* worked."

It feels as though fear has restricted his breath, Kyun-ho's mouth ajar with words too frightened to voice as Hae-sol's eyes continue to devour him with his glare.

"Or maybe… maybe I'll just kill myself… and make every-one think you did it. Then they'll think you're broken… just like me and just like… Tae-kyun…" Hae-sol's grip on his friend is loosening. His fingers are trembling too much to hold on. "And I bet you wouldn't stop me… because you didn't stop me from hurting Hye-yon, o-or…"

"Hae-sol, I'm sorry! I didn't know you were going to—"

"*HOW COULD YOU NOT KNOW I WOULD KILL THEM WHEN NOTHING I DID FOR THEM WAS WORKING?*"

"But I did try, Hae-sol—that's why you live here, in the tree-house, instead of-!"

"I LIVE HERE BECAUSE OF FEAR! YOU! YOU'RE TOO AFRAID TO DO ANYTHING, SO ALL YOU COULD DO WAS TRY TO LOCK ME AWAY IN THIS STUPID, STUPID TREEHOUSE BECAUSE YOU *KNEW* I WAS GOING TO HURT THEM! YOU *KNEW I WAS GOING TO HURT THEM, AND THIS WAS ALL YOU DID!*" He's cursing now, jumping up and down while yanking at his hair so violently I'm sure it must be hurting him, frustrated tears flushing his cheeks as Kyun-ho, feeling sick with the amount of guilt drenching him, closes his eyes and tries to steady his breathing, repeating over and over again in his mind,

It's not your fault, you really did try to help him. It's not your fault— there was nothing else you could do. You really did try to help him!

But it's not working because a large part of Kyun-ho still believes Hae-sol wouldn't have deteriorated this far if only he could have prevented Haven's falling… if only he could have changed the way Hae-sol's family was before it was too late.

But fear has such an interesting way of hindering us… such an interesting way of making nothing seem possible at all.

There are so many different things that complicate Hae-sol and Kyun-ho's friendship. So many things that brought them together, even though they're breaking apart now.

Despite the many things Kyun-ho has told himself to get rid of the feelings of guilt and uncertainty towards the events that have caused both their friendship, and Hae-sol's mind to drift, there are also several reasons why some things are his fault. Because Hae-sol is right, he truly is afraid to make things change because change has been the antecedent of too many beatings from his father, too many beatings from peers at school, and his older brother.

Change, at times, can be the trigger for a war to rage, not just inside one's mind, but in others, too.

"Leave things alone, Kyun-ho. That's what's wrong with you and your mother: you never want to leave things the way they are, and in turn, you make things worse than they were before.

I don't beat you for nothing, you put yourself in ridiculous situations that force me to. LEAVE THINGS THE WAY THEY ARE."

"Why… why won't you just stay with me in Haven?" Hae-sol breathes, exhausted from his abrupt display of emotions and visibly suffering because of it, his emerald eyes fluttering with fatigue as he leans into Kyun-ho's shoulder, gripping his arms as if to steady himself as he says, "I-I'm sorry, I won't hurt anyone again, Kyun-ho. Just stay…! Don't leave Haven. We can… we can make it better, I'm sorry!"

"You said that last time, though, Hae-sol…!" Kyun-ho forces out, tears audible in his voice as violent tremors run throughout his body. "H-how can I trust you when you said that last time… right before you hurt Tae-kyun… and right after y-you… right after you killed…?"

"You're supposed to be a Christian." His tone is so venomous, this child, emerald eyes glinting with the anger shaking his voice as he shouts, "You're supposed to be a Christian *just* like my *stupid parents who messed up our LIVES! FORGIVENESS IS THE BASIS OF YOUR STUPID RELIGION! YOU'RE NOT CONSISTENT! YOU'RE NEVER CONSISTENT IN WHAT YOU BELIEVE BECAUSE WHAT YOU BELIEVE IS—!"*

Kyun-ho feels his body stiffen with fear's paralysis as Hae-sol starts cursing, pulling at his hair and pacing the floors as a new group of tears gathers inside Kyun-ho's eyes, forcing him to blink rapidly as his mind blanks with what to do.

He really is a murderer. Hae-sol's a murderer—what should I do? He couldn't have killed those other children, though. He-he didn't even know them. Oh, no…! What if he hurts me because I—!

"*Kyun-ho, please!*" All at once, Hae-sol sounds so pitiful… so, so pitiful as he grabs onto Kyun-ho's arm again and says, "*I'll kill myself if you tell them. I'll kill myself, Kyun-ho, please!*"

"T-tell who?"

"*The police, Kyun-ho, those stupid, stupid officers!*" He's crying so much, Hae-sol, terrible tremors wrecking his frail body as his fingers dig into Kyun-ho's skin. "*I won't do it again. I'm sorry. Don't leave me there, Kyun-ho. Don't leave me!*"

21

Kyun-ho's heart stutters in his chest as Hae-sol's words float and spiral in his mind...

I... don't know what to do. Hae-sol's weird—he's been weird all week, so what if he isn't lying? But how can I get out of here? How can I go home and still be his friend when he's.... he's...! No, Hae-sol couldn't have done that; he's never hurt anyone like that. Maybe-maybe someone else did it—maybe none of this is really happening and...!

"Kyun-ho, my heart hurts...! It hurts, Kyun-ho...! I feel like... I'm dying!" Hae-sol's voice wavers as he grips his friend tighter, pressing his head into his shoulder and struggling to breathe through the tears choking him.

"I-I'll die if you leave, Kyun-ho. Tell me you won't leave!"

I don't know what to do.

"The police officers will get you if you leave! They'll suspect y-you too! Wh-who will take care of Tae-kyun-a-and Haven? You're my only friend, Kyun-ho, my only friend...!"

I don't know what to do.

I don't know what to do.

It's very dark outside; it must be close to midnight.

The police sirens are gone, but the evidence of Hae-sol's crime remains in dark and prominent stains all over the wooden floor of their treehouse…

"You didn't really kill them, though, did you, Hae-sol?"
"If I said I didn't kill them…
Would that prolong your stay…?"

Kyun-ho tried multiple times to convince himself that Hae-sol was lying or perhaps in shock from witnessing someone else commit such a crime. But every time he tried, Hae-sol convinced him again and again that it was him, for he wouldn't stop weeping about it before fatigue closed his eyes, just as the rain wouldn't stop falling outside.

"Why did the medicine fail? Why wouldn't it work, Kyun-ho? Why did they make me do that to them…? How can they ever wake up now…? Hye-yon… Hye-yon…!"

Minutes are beginning to churn into hours, and Kyun-ho still hasn't moved from his huddled position beside the fallen shelf. His body is shivering from his damp clothes because the air has yet to dry them.

He's sleeping now. I should run before he wakes up. Kyun-ho thinks, a thin trail of blood trickling down his chin from the force of biting his tongue, because he's desperately wishing this is merely a dream he can wake himself from, no matter how painful the escape is.

Tae-kyun's probably worried. What if dad's hurting him…? I should go. I have to go. But what will I do after I walk home? What will Hae-sol do once he notices I've left?

There's no explanation he can think of to explain this situation to his father.

No lie is big enough to cover the worry Tae-kyun has brought and his mother, even though she has been rather indifferent towards him lately…

He's picturing a very colorful map of bruises adorning his body after he enters his house, and an even darker depiction of his brother when their eyes meet.

It's three in the morning, and Kyun-ho is not prepared to bear anything else the world has to throw at him.

- Prologue -

Enter Part Two of Dysphoria

It's very hard to tell yourself you'll be okay when all the evidence around you tells you won't.

It's even harder to convince yourself of the Lord's presence when it seems as though He's moved quite far away.

As Kyun-ho stands in the doorway of his home, his hand sits paralyzed on the light switch. All hope for happiness slips as though a drop of water down a drain, and his heart seems to hyperventilate inside his chest.

He wasn't prepared for what he was seeing now, what he was staring at… But then again, how can one prepare themselves for a tragedy like the one hanging from the chandelier in his own kitchen…?

I don't suppose you've ever visited the Chois', so I'll take this time to introduce you to their home and Kyun-ho's family, which in turn should prepare you, the reader, for what's about to happen next in Kyun-ho's life.

Kyun-ho's father comes from a long line of prestigious doctors and college professors, so when he told his family of the dream he'd been harboring, he was not well received.

Sung-ho aspired to become a pastor and build his church from nothing at the young age of eleven. And although his family was, and still is, a very religious family, though a bit on the extremest side, his dream seemed like a threat to them. They said it would not work because he was too young to know if he was called for such, but he ignored them. By the time he was twenty-five, he was married, had bought the land he needed for his church, and had a son shortly after.

And for a while, everything was fine.

His wife got pregnant with Kyun-ho when Tae-ho was five, and his church was built within a year.

His church was popular, even for non-religious people, because of his family's reputation.

But after nearly four years of wealth and a growing church, another child was born. Tae-kyun.

Now, Tae-ho, Kyun-ho's eldest brother, already bore the reputation of an odd and complicated child, but he was also a successful student in his school and a family gem. He was and still is a very clever and smart boy, with no dips in his grades and perfect attendance that Kyun-ho would never come close to, for Kyun-ho is often too lost in his thoughts or the clouds above him to pay any mind to the time slipping away from him.

But even though Tae-ho was academically perfect, at home, he was anything but.

He showed little to no emotion towards those around him and was a dangerously extreme attention seeker, rushing into streets on purpose to force his parents to come and rescue him and basking in their tears when he would harm himself on purpose to gain attention that was already his, for Kyun-ho has always been overlooked in his short years here on earth and has never once forced his parents to notice him, even on the days it seems as though no one has noticed him at all.

Tae-ho pocketed money from the church offering plates and flushed it down the toilets, growing elated when caught and corrected.

He flirted with all the mothers as though he was much older than twelve, was rude around the fathers, and went to sleep during services.

And when Tae-kyun was born, he announced to the church that his mother gave birth to a demon who would take your soul and destroy the church.

No one thought anything of it at first; they all knew Tae-ho was academically gifted and dismissed his disruptive, attention-seeking behavior because of it.

But Tae-kyun, however, was not as easily dismissed at three.

They complained to his father, saying he was always frustrated and looked as if he was glaring at them and never responded right to their children when they would play in the nursery.

He would sit completely still at times and stare, only moving when moved and growing agitated and tearful when awakened from the spell.

His dialogue was less developed than most three-year-olds and was mainly a messy compilation of noises and strange gazes.

He rubbed anything within reach against his head as if soothing a painful headache, and kept to himself most of the time.

Sung-ho dismissed the complaints, saying that Tae-kyun was just more shy than his other children and often got lost in daydreaming. But Kyun-ho always knew there was something peculiar about his younger brother because Kyun-ho spent the majority of his time with him.

The possibility of a mental peculiarity didn't bother him like everyone else, though. It merely aroused his curiosity as to what could possibly be making Tae-kyun's mind work so differently than himself and the other children in their church.

"They say daydreaming is supposed to be fun. It seems that Tae-kyun is never happy and is not at peace with himself."

Sung-ho refused to believe them, though, afraid of discovering something he did not want to know about his child.

Tae-kyun's illness only progressed. His behavior got more and more disorganized as weeks and months inched by. It seemed as if his body could not keep up with his mind.

He would engage in completely inappropriate behavior in the middle of a service, only to laugh when corrected, as though thinking it was a game.

He would forget who his family was and follow families he didn't know to their car, smiling when they tried to kindly reject him.

He could look at things no one else could see for hours at a time and was able to switch between laughing at those things and screaming at those things in an instant.

He got agitated by seemingly nothing, and his odd habit of rubbing things against his head would sometimes turn into violent scratching at his neck and face as if there were millions of tiny insects trapped under his skin he was desperate to get free.

He developed an unhealthy obsession with anything involving pianos, and by the time he was five and a half, although his speech was still suffering, he was telling anyone who would listen that the piano music was conversing with him, and so were the hymn books at the church.

This was too disturbing for Sung-ho to ignore because contrary to his belief that Tae-kyun was shy, he wasn't. He tried to tell everyone about the extraordinary abilities he had involving music and how he was sure he was a famous piano player from France because he would often wake up there and have people ask to attend his concerts.

Tae-kyun was taken to the doctors, and it took more than five months to get a real diagnosis.

At first, the doctors said he was too young and was most likely just suffering from anxiety and an overactive imagination.

"He's such a bright child, he has many opportunities ahead of him…" They would say, offering him many candies and hugs and disregarding the odd way he had looked at them when they called his name, the odd way he had stated he wasn't Tae-kyun but another boy who was very, very famous and lived very, very far from there.

"What a wonderful imagination you have. What is the other boy's name?" one doctor had asked, her long, toffee-colored hair matching beautifully with her wide and earnest eyes as Tae-kyun frowned a little while rubbing anxiously at his head again, that strange and intimidating gaze of his traveling the hospital room as a stream of unintelligible words poured, as though a faucet with no intention to cease, out of his mouth and into the air

that had gone silent after he had tried to explain to them he wasn't familiar with their language.

"Ohhhh...." She had said after a while, writing something down on her clipboard before telling Tae-kyun's father she had scheduled his child another appointment with another doctor, giving Tae-kyun more candy and ushering him a little hesitantly out the door.

Months later, Tae-kyun was seen by another doctor who claimed Tae-kyun had a mixture of Attention Deficit Disorder and autism, a diagnosis that displeased and caused much gossip to surround the Choi family, as any sort of handicap was, and has been, anathema to them.

The last week of May, when Tae-kyun had his first noticeable hallucination involving piano notes in the doctor's office, he was diagnosed with 'Childhood Psychotic Disorder Not Otherwise Specified' and was sent away with various medications that only seemed to make him worse.

The year after, Tae-kyun snuck out of the house after cutting his neck badly with a pair of scissors due to the fear that he had ants stuck inside him that were trying to inwardly strangle him. He left to follow the stars that had told him about the ants and was almost run over by traffic after walking blindly across a busy road. This was something Tae-kyun's father couldn't ignore, and he was forced to have his son hospitalized due to his mental instability.

Shortly after, though he was still young, he was proclaimed to be an autistic, disorganized schizophrenic, words that made his church and his success fall apart.

Sung-ho's family cut ties, saying he ruined their reputation and his son was demonically possessed and in need of exorcism.

His church began to do the same for all the same reasons, most, if not all, not even possessing any real knowledge of Tae-kyun's condition, only the rumors that had been so cleverly sewn into the church by Tae-ho, who found the whole thing rather amusing.

They told Sung-ho his child was damaging his church and that his illness wasn't biblical.

His wife was avoided for giving birth to him, and within three months, the church that he worked in so hard for over sixteen years was desolate.

That was almost three years ago, yet the impact has shadowed them as though the aftereffects of drugs.

And ever since, Kyun-ho's parents have not been the same. His father has found that using abuse for Tae-kyun is the most efficient way of dissolving his frustration towards him. His mother has been neglectful, frequently turning her head the other way when she sees any hint of physical harm done to her children.

She no longer tells Tae-ho not to push Kyun-ho down the stairs or smack Tae-kyun's head while he's eating to make him choke. She no longer tells Tae-kyun to stop playing with his food and eat because he's getting too thin and needs to grow. She no longer tells Kyun-ho not to worry too much about school because he's perfect the way he is, and she'll love him regardless of the grades he brings home. She doesn't read them Bible stories anymore, and she won't even stop Tae-ho from cursing or watching things he knows he shouldn't in front of Tae-kyun just to see his and their mother's reaction.

Over time, their parents became completely useless. And while Kyun-ho has never been particularly close with either of them, as they always favored Tae-ho more, he would often pretend he was with his mother, for he desperately wanted her to approve of him the way she did Tae-ho and would follow her around wherever she went to try to ensure that.

He didn't use to like gardening, but his mother loved it, so

When he turned four, he started following her outside more to help care for her plants, forever glowing in her praise because it made him feel just as important as Tae-ho.

He learned the art of crochet because she did it, too, and though his care for it frustrated his father because it's often viewed as a female's hobby, just as gardening, the more his mother smiled and clapped when he accomplished small things like creating a square or filling up the watering can without spilling it, the more his passion for things now labeled as his hobbies grew.

And though he knew his mother was depressed with the way Tae-kyun turned out, he never once thought she would do this.

He never once pictured her hanging here, turning in slow circles beside the kitchen table as the chandelier holding her begins to whine at the amount of pressure she's putting on it, the thick brown rope around her neck, wrapped so tightly she's bleeding…

Gasping at the sight, Kyun-ho falls backward onto his bottom as the light in the kitchen begins flashing on and off, jovial laughter from his brother filling the air as he says, making his presence known from his sitting position at the table, "She asked me to help her up an hour ago. Do you think you could have prevented this if you weren't running away from our dad?"

Dread and disgust both erupt at once within him and within seconds, he's covering his mouth because he's close to vomiting, round cheeks drained of their usually flushed pink color as dark coffee-colored eyes stare in utter horror at Tae-ho's face.

32

"You should really stop running away. It only makes dad hurt Tae-kyun and mom more because you're not there to play savior. He took Tae-kyun to another ritual, by the way. This one was held at our church, funnily enough, but it's odd they haven't returned yet."

Her eyes are still open.

Their mother…

Hanging.

Each time Tae-ho flicks the lights on, she stares at Kyun-ho, and each time he holds her gaze, he's caught by the urge to run, for he's never been good with confronting the things that happen in his life, Kyun-ho, and I dare say he mastered the art of escapism the moment so much abuse darkened his home.

He loved his mother, he knows he must. But why is there this feeling of wanting to escape instead of crying…? Why has fear taken refuge in his heart when he knows his heart should be stuttering with shock and despair?

"You're no fun, Kyun-ho. You can't even entertain me with your emotions— are you even surprised she's dead?"

The lights flicker off, and this time, Tae-ho doesn't turn them back on.

"You don't even want to know why I helped her? Or even what her last dying words were? This is weird, to say the least."

His voice… Why does it sound like it's so much closer?

"You really only care about Tae-kyun, don't you? And even then, you suck at protecting him. You always want to run away when dad comes home. I never run away."

Kyun-ho presses himself against the door, his heart seeming to stop a few seconds when Tae-ho's warm fingers find his arm, and he's pulled into the kitchen, where the light is turned on again, and Tae-ho forces Kyun-ho to stand right under his mother's body.

"Wow, you're covered in blood... I was going to make you stand here so I could cut her up a bit and let the blood soak you, so dad would definitely know you killed her. But it looks like you've already dressed up. What even happened? Are you the reason there was so much commotion next door? Did you fight your friend and take it too far? Play some naughty games and..."

"Tae-ho, stop!" Kyun-ho shouts, backing away from his brother and squeezing his hands to try to stop them from shaking. "I-I'm not a murderer like you! I-I'm not— I-I didn't—"

"Murderer? Mom was already suicidal. The pills didn't work, so she asked me to move the table so she could hang off the chandelier thing. If anything, I assisted her in a better life. Our lives, as you know, suck."

Shaking his head, Kyun-ho swallows the bile, threatening to climb out of his throat before sprinting on impulse away from his brother and out of the kitchen, reaching for the front door only to fall backward on his rear when it's flung open. His father, drenched with the presence of rain, ignites the fear he's feeling into pure panic.

"WHAT DID YOU DO?" dropping his bag to the floor,

Sung-ho nearly trips over Kyun-ho's body trying to get to his wife, Tae-kyun, such a tall yet infantile-looking seven-year-old swaying in an absent sort of fashion outside the door while he rubs a fisted hand beneath his long, wet bangs... his pale blue dinosaur-printed sweater revealing multiple wounds on his body as it hangs limply from his thin frame, because it's ripped and torn in several places.

It's hard to tell whether he's conscious or not of what's before him, or even what's happening, as his father turns to grab him roughly by the shoulders to shake him violently, screaming, *"It was you! Demons have killed your mother because you refuse to leave them!"*

"T-Tae-kyun didn't do it! Tae-ho—!" Gasping from the abrupt impact of his father's foot against his side, Kyun-ho screams inwardly from the pain spreading through him, for there are so many places on his body that hurt already because of his father, so many bruises that have yet to heal because he's been too furious these days to care.

"Stop lying, idiot! Don't you know that the Lord has failed us tonight? There's a demon in that boy, there's a demon, and it's getting stronger each time we try to extract it!"

Tae-kyun merely smiles, looking over his shoulder and into the rain as Kyun-ho scoots back till he's pressed against the wall, the room around him growing distorted as his consciousness begins to fail him.

Kyun-ho is unsure of how to stop the room from spinning, how to withhold the bile crawling up his throat as his thoughts seem to flicker between his mother's body and the bodies on the floor of Hae-sol's living room.

"If I said I didn't kill them, would that prolong your visit...?"

"Why did you kill her? Why?" Their father is crying, large, anguished tears leaving red eyes as he drops to the floor. He's almost hysterical, and Kyun-ho wonders absently if that's how he would be if Hae-sol did such a thing to Tae-kyun...

Why am I not like that now, though…?

He's shocked that she's dead; of course, he's shocked.

And for a while, he did feel rather guilty he hadn't arrived sooner to prevent such a thing from happening, but other than the shock he feels now. Kyun-ho feels nothing.

He's crying now, but not for the same reasons as his father.

He's crying because this night that has continued into the early morning is utterly and terribly traumatic, and he doesn't know what to do about any of the events that have or are happening now.

Is it strange to be sitting here while your mother's body has just fallen along with the chandelier holding her to the floor, thinking thoughts like this instead of letting the shock and depression that would normally occur take you…?

Is Tae-kyun feeling sad, or is he having trouble feeling anything at all…? He doesn't look very bothered, but perhaps he's not even here. Perhaps his mind has taken him elsewhere, or perhaps he's just having trouble picking out and wearing whatever emotion he's feeling now.

"Piano… piano stars, piano stars… haha fwo shim… haha fwo shim…" He's not making any sense, and his face is a blank canvas towards whatever emotion he may be feeling. This is the thing about Tae-kyun that worries and upsets their parents the most.

Tae-kyun could watch the saddest cartoons with a smile and the funniest movies without ever emitting a laugh or expressing any sign of enjoyment.

He could be yelled at and hit by their father or other children at church, but after the initial shock, he would go about his day as usual, even if he did start crying, and would sometimes even laugh and try to repeat the actions done to him, as though confusing the abuse for a game, which in turn would only injure him more.

Tae-kyun's emotions are there, but it's almost as though they're stuck in certain moments because he doesn't know how to use them.

Blunted affect is the term his doctor used. Not being able to properly express your emotions and having little to no reaction to emotionally stimulating situations, while flat affect, the bitter brother to blunt affect, is the inability to express any emotion at all…

So perhaps he is here, in this moment… perhaps he wants to cry like their father, or drop next to their dead mother and mourn the loss of her. Or… perhaps he just wants to escape the cold of the rain because that's what he's doing now, stepping into the house and teetering side to side while drops of water drip cautiously onto the floor.

"No one can know. Absolutely no one can know Tae-kyun's done this!" Sung-ho's voice is trembling as he quickly shuts and locks the door, his heartbeat almost audible to Kyun-ho as he turns swiftly to say, "Turn off the lights. Turn off all the lights, Tae-ho. We're sleeping. No one can disturb us if we're sleeping." the look of insanity in his eyes causing Kyun-ho to laugh, because Tae-kyun, no matter how the world views him, has never worn that look before… yet he's supposed to be the crazy one…

The lights go off one by one as Sung-ho travels anxiously down the long hallways and up the stairs, cloaking their home in darkness and shutting all the open windows.

He's muttering to himself, muttering prayers for his children and damnation to the ones that have troubled him so, all these years…

*I have to keep them away from Tae-ho. He's the only one I can use,
the only one who can help us rid the world of this terrible plague.*

"I-I don't want to clean anymore, please!" Kyun-ho pleads
into this darkness, wiping up the last of his mother's blood with the
sleeve of his shirt before gripping tightly onto his knees, suddenly
overtaken by the urge to vomit as Tae-ho, looking up from his pile
of crimson spotted towels, scoffs and says,

"You can't go anywhere, even if it has been an hour. Daddy
said we have to keep cleaning. The floors wouldn't have been that
dirty if the glass from the chandelier hadn't shattered and impaled
our mother the way it did. Poor, poor lady, forced to—"

"WOULD YOU SHUT UP, TAE-HO!?" Their father cries,
throwing down a soiled rag and pointing an accusing finger at
Tae-ho through this darkness. "Everyone here just needs to shut
up. Do you think it's fun for me to wipe up my wife's blood off the
kitchen floor?"

Tae-ho, finding this rather amusing, smiles and says, in an
overly positive tone, "Well, at least it wasn't Tae-kyun that died.
That would have given us so many more issues, right?" to which
Sung-ho stands to smack the boy before pouring more alcohol
onto the floor, Kyun-ho, still sick over the decisions looming over
his mind, watching absently from a distance as the storm outside
thunders ferociously…

He has to get away and escape this place before Hae-sol
wakes up and realizes he's gone, but he doesn't know how and
doesn't even know where he'd be escaping to.

"Older brother~ older brother~" Tae-kyun calls, teetering over to his brother and crouching on the floor in front of him while rubbing anxiously at his head, the dim glow from the candles their father is lighting illuminating the child's skin of winter peach as he says, in that light, breathy voice of his,

"Play... play with the rain...?" A deep frown darkening his face as he blinks up at Kyun-ho.

He doesn't look or sound very happy about the rain, but Kyun-ho knows he is because he's always loved playing in such cascading drops of water.

Nothing is making a lot of sense in Kyun-ho's mind as he looks past Tae-kyun to ensure their father's busy before taking the child's small hand and standing to lead them away from the dim light of the candles and deeper into the shadows the rest of their house casts upon them.

"Tae-kyun, we're going to play outside in the rain..."

Kyun-ho whispers this right as their father starts yelling about them leaving, careless laughter from Tae-ho causing Tae-kyun to shrink a little into himself as he breathes, "Awake...?" while a slow yet hesitant smile spreads across his face.

"Yeah... It's been bedtime for a long time, but you don't have to go to sleep, Tae-kyun. I'm not even sure there's enough time to sleep now." Kyun-ho's voice sounds like it's running instead of walking to Tae-kyun, just as his father's voice often does on the days he makes him go to those scary gatherings with the chanting that so frequently gets stuck inside his mind, but he doesn't question Kyun-ho. He would much rather play outside in the rain with his best friend than watch his brothers and father clean the floor or be banished into his dark room where his father won't even allow him to play with his toys. So he only nods and keeps rubbing his head, teetering alongside his brother as they walk their way to the back door.

A bright flash of lightning startles Tae-kyun into a quiet chortle, and he sways in a rather rhythmic motion as he waits patiently for his brother to slide open the large glass doors.

Kyun-ho stares at Tae-kyun closely as he fiddles with the doors, wondering, for the millionth time, why his father and those around him want to harm this boy.

He's so good, Tae-kyun, and hardly ever gets into any trouble, rarely disobeys, and always wants to play.

What makes him so afraid of you...?
What makes him see a monster...?'

"Rain!" Tae-kyun laughs as he steps outside, removing his hand from under his bangs to feel the cool drops of rain bounce on and off his skin as he jumps excitedly up and down in the water.

"Rains in the other world, too~!" Tae-kyun smiles, clothes already dripping again from the rain as he returns his hand under his bangs to rub his head.

"What other world, Tae-kyun...?" Kyun-ho asks softly, stepping off the porch as Tae-kyun teeters in place under the rain, his wet hair pouring more water down his face as he strains to hear his brother whisper,

"Another world... that sounds nice... I wish... we could go to that other world together, Tae-kyun..."

"Sake…? World…? Mmmh-hmm, nahw…?" Confused, Tae-kyun starts rubbing his head harder as a low rumble in the clouds teases the visit of lightning. " Nef-fwoh… na nef-fwo…"

Sometimes, it's best to pretend we have never inhabited any dreadful thoughts at all regarding where we are in life.

And for Kyun-ho, the boy feigning a smile while tears and rain blur his vision, that's exactly what he does as he begins chasing Tae-kyun, around and around in the beautiful backyard their mother had transformed into a garden.

They trample the resurrection lilies beneath their feet, rush over the beds of cosmos flowers, and tumble into the pink muhly grass bordering their yard, laughing into the cascading rain and splashing mud onto each other's faces.

Oftentimes, the most beautiful moments in life are found through pain and sorrow, though it takes a while to acknowledge that without such troubles, such beauty would never exist.

Hae-sol didn't really kill anyone, right…? Games of pretend can't possibly kill someone. Maybe he'll be better tomorrow, and mom will be better too because she didn't actually die, and we can all just be happy, and no one will have to cry, ever again, for a very long time…

End of prologue

- One -

Hidden Medicine

(Seventeen years later, October)

"You won't even taste it. You'll be fine."

Yoon-ha's hands shake as his pale fingers enclose the small pills his brother placed in them, his heart stuttering at the thought of poison entering his body as his mellow brown eyes begin to fill with silent tears.

"You won't die, I promise." Choon-ha's wide eyes are earnest as he watches Yoon-ha hold the medicine to his small pouted lips, his expression radiating fear as Choon-ha glances about impatiently.

Choon-ha knows he's not supposed to be giving Yoon-ha his medicine. Yoon-ha has his own, and he's unsure if mixing theirs would cause something troublesome to occur.

But bipolar disorder and schizophrenia seem so similar in Choon-ha's mind that he feels it shouldn't matter; besides, it's not as though he wants to take it. He couldn't think of any other reason as to why the medicine from this morning was found falling out of his pocket before they left school.

So this is why he told Yoon-ha it was saved for him.

"Wh-what if it doesn't hurt-hurt you because yours is f-for-for you…?" Yoon-ha's monotone voice whispers, his lifelong stutter making his dialogue seem even more off-tuned as his twin brother stares at him blankly, blinking back what looks like irritation as he calmly says, "Well, that doesn't make any sense because it can easily be for you now. You'll be fine, I promise." Then, seeing the anxiety overshadowing Yoon-ha's face, he quickly smiles and says, "I mean, people all over the whole world use the same medicine, so anyone can take it. And besides, if you don't take it now, you won't have enough energy to do your healing powers on mister daddy, and he's been super stressed these days because of Tae-kyun, so you have to use my medicine in addition to yours to power up…!"

A cold breeze ruffles the children's fawn-colored hair as the trees around them begin to shed their leaves, painting the surrounding scenery in warm autumn colors as they dance playfully in the air before descending gracefully to the ground in an ending scene.

Yoon-ha looks close to releasing tears as his eyebrows furrow secretly under his long bangs, trembling slightly as his large head begins shaking unwillingly as if repeating the notion of 'no.'

It's never been one of his favorite symptoms of Tourette's, but it's less painful than some of his other motor tics and less annoying, he thinks, than his shrieking, which, contrary to his flat, whisper of a voice, is very loud.

"Mister daddy will be really happy if you heal him…" Choon-ha throws in, his oval, elfish face expressing great sincerity as he clasps his hands behind his back and kicks at a fallen leaf. "And if you take my medicine, you won't be afraid of your own tomorrow or the day after," He adds, proudly acknowledging his twin brother's daily fear of poisoned medicine as a crimson-colored leaf drops onto his head.

Yoon-ha is momentarily distracted by the brightly colored leaves as his head shaking falters, light brown eyes mesmerized by their performance as each one falls perfectly at his feet as if inviting him to pick it up, which he does, because this boy, as you'll soon see, is quite fond of leaves.

This bothers Choon-ha, though, because he needs him to hurry, so he takes the leaf from his grasp and moves the hand gripping his medicine towards his mouth as a reminder of their conversation.

"Hurry, mister twin buddy, you have to swallow it before mister daddy sees it," Choon-ha urges, expression dark as his round cheeks flush when Yoon-ha shakes his head and pushes the medicine away.

"N-no, we'll be in trouble...!"

"Mister daddy will be cursed again by his PTSD if you don't take it. I'm telling you, his health is up to you now."

Yoon-ha returns his brother's dark gaze, blinking furiously to keep up his facade. Eventually, it dies, though, and like most battles he has with Choon-ha, he loses silently.

They look so similar to each other. If not for the apprehension permanently etched on Yoon-ha's face and the color of many sleepless nights beneath his eyes, there would be no distinguishing features between the two. It's as though they're cookies cut from the same batch of dough.

They both look like they're closer to twelve instead of sixteen despite their tall height, share the same softly hooded, wing-shaped eyes with much aegyo sal beneath, and even have the same small and pouted lips that, in Choon-ha's case, curl at the corners with boundless mischief, adding to his elf-like appearance.

They tend to enjoy each other's company as long as Choon-ha doesn't get too competitive with their favorite video games or as long as Yoon-ha isn't too absorbed in his leaf creature fantasies to remember there's a world outside his hallucinations, as he often forgets because he's so frequently visited by them. Plus, the delusion that he was born to be his leaf creature's god makes him very busy, as gods have many duties, especially when there's a war going on because you've created the wrong creature or let the wrong one live inside your home...

"W-we have n-no-no water...!" Yoon-ha says in his last attempt at fighting, wringing out his wrist and sharply exhaling as he looks at Choon-ha pleadingly.

"Let's just use the pond," Choon-ha's lips turn up into a rather jovial smile as he edges closer to his brother, adventure bubbling up inside him, as it usually does before he creates his mischief.

And this, he knows, is very much mischief because he knows, like Yoon-ha, that they're not supposed to be dilly-dallying on their walks home from school because their father always gets paranoid at them when they do. After all, he's always worried about someone hurting them, which is why he tries his best to meet them before they start heading home.

There has been quite a bit of chaos going around their usually serene neighborhood, though.

It's the frequent protesting, or maybe the frequent gossiping about why his family isn't protesting, that has made Kyun-ho more stressed than usual.

The protests have all revolved around the same thing: the oppression of the mentally ill and disabled, the way the government treats them, and on the opposing side, the threat they pose to society and the need to better facilitate them.

And here is the crime that sparked these protests.

Five days ago, a man with Down syndrome suffering from psychosis escaped the facility he was being held and shot three officers.

The man was killed in self-defense, and with him, two of the three officers lost their lives as well.

No one knows how the man escaped.

No one knows how he obtained the gun.

No one knows why he targeted those police officers.

All they know is what the police released to the public: A deranged man attacked three officers, killing two, and in the span of five days, crimes involving those with disabilities and illness have increased significantly.

This has caused a tense division among those who think it's the government's fault for never treating those with peculiarities right and those who think anyone who has a diagnosis involving their mind should be sent away.

This, of course, has made all of dalkomhan even more afraid of Kyun-ho and his family than before.

But Choon-ha is used to the stares, crude whispers, and people visibly avoiding him and his family, just as Yoon-ha is, so besides the protesters that gather near his school at times, the news that frequents anything electronic and occasional physical altercation from those who deem him scum, he feels quite normal about this situation.

Besides that, it's Friday, and what's a Friday without a little mischief?

Yoon-ha doesn't look too pleased by Choon-ha's grand idea but follows his brother anyway (as he's always compelled to do) back up to the path they use to walk to and from school.

This path is lined with pleasant rows of Maple trees, various shades of yellow and orange coloring their leaves over the last few weeks of November, so it's always very pretty in fall.

In the center of this path sits a small clearing containing a deep, stoned-in water well that Choon-ha calls a pond, mostly due to the small amount of goldfish that preoccupy its waters.

Their father had once said it was built for historical purposes to remind the students of something or other on a day that was also something or other, but because it wasn't a very peculiar day, it's easy to see how his children have forgotten about its past purposes.

"Just take one handful. Goldfish need water, too." Choon-ha murmurs softly, carefully watching the way his brother obeys and dips his hands in the cool water, only to pause upon realizing its living conditions, for he's very conscious of the dirt that grows disturbed with the movement of the water, and worries about all the bacteria his skin could be absorbing.

A frantic goldfish darts past his fingers as Choon-ha looks at him expectantly, placing his elbows on either side of the well to prop his chin up on his hands, most likely displaying this pose because people are walking past them, and Choon-ha, being the vain boy he is, is probably thinking doing such will make him look more cute and innocent, though he's not in the slightest bit innocent and hasn't been called cute since kindergarten because it goes to his head and makes him behave quite rudely.

"The w-water-water is terribly dirty…" Yoon-ha says in shame, his whisper of a voice nearly lost in translation as Choon-ha sighs before telling his brother (as kindly as he can) to get over it because their father would be here any minute.

"S-Sash-aro says it's d-dirty, too…!" Yoon-ha persists, emitting several shrill shrieks before his head pivots violently backward and forward.

Sash-aro is one of the first hallucinations Yoon-ha's schizophrenia produced when he was four.

He's a small and sorrowful-looking creature made of leaves and shaped like a raindrop, with a large pink flower turned upside down atop his head.

He's in charge of the other leaf creatures because he's Yoon-ha's first friend, but he's frequently overlooked and abused, as apparently, the other creatures have never been too friendly to him due to such favoritism.

There's much more to know about Sash-aro, but I'll tell you more about him later because he's very small, but his life is very big, and only Yoon-ha can see him anyways.

"The wa-water is dirty…" He repeats, gathering his required 'handful' and examining its contents closely as they slip rapidly through his fingers, dampening one of his Pokémon band-aids and causing it to lose its grip on his skin and slide off and into the water, which only worsens the paranoia that had settled in Yoon-ha's stomach because now *he knows* he's bound to get infected…!

"All the water in the world is dirty," Choon-ha lies, chasing a pale, red, and black goldfish with his eyes, as Yoon-ha's face displays an array of offended confusion and disgust.

"N-no-no, it tried-tr-tried to get inside my-my body... It—" Yoon-ha pauses to sigh simultaneously with the trees, wiping his wet hands against the light khaki material of his pants and momentarily losing himself to the whispers in his head because they're warning him about the sickness that's seeping into his skin.

'Choon-ha is trying to kill you. He knew the water was poisonous, and that's why he wanted you to drink it. If someone is pouring poison all over the water, it might be under your skin right now...'

"Oooh..." Yoon-ha shakes his head a bit to and fro, stepping away from the water well and whispering," What kind of poison...? Ch-Choon-ha wouldn't do that..." to which Choon-ha, who had been watching his brother rather closely, frowns and inquires impatiently, "Yoon-ha, why are you like this again? You can only talk to yourself when I'm not around. Remember?"

"Y-you're always... a-always around... so are-s-so are the voices, and no one... n-no one leaves..." Yoon-ha breathes, much truth to his words, as he can never truly get away from his brother without some sort of guilt, just as he can never truly escape all the commotion in his mind without sneaking his father's sleeping pills and waking with a horrible headache.

"I'm better than your voices, though, they don't even... Fine, whatever, just take the pills." Choon-ha frowns, looking slightly upset with his brother as he folds his thin arm over his knitted, cream-colored vest while pouting indignantly. "If you die now, it will all be your fault. I'll laugh at your funeral."

Yoon-ha doesn't respond to his brother. He responds inwardly instead to his mind, agreeing that the poison was, indeed, put there to kill him and that Choon-ha may just be the culprit. This means he'll have to go through the trouble of phoning the police to have him taken away. But what if he breaks out of jail with even stronger intentions to murder him? What if he's already dying because it got into his skin?

No, no, why would Choon-ha want to kill him?

It's silly to think your own brother, who is also your best friend, would ever want to kill you, right...?

"O-oh, no..." Yoon-ha says abruptly, shaking his head side to side as he inquires, in a rather flat tone, "Did you tr-try to... kill... k-kill m-me, brother...? Y-you're not like that." before adding, as though an afterthought, "I-I've lost your-y-your medicine, brother."

Yoon-ha would like to apologize to his brother for losing his medicine because even though he wasn't going to take it, he knew it was still an important pill for Choon-ha.

He can't find the right words, though, and it's hard to hear himself think with such a loud conversation Sash-aro and his friends are having inside his mind regarding the poison that may have snuck into his body.

"That was dumb, what if the fish swallow them?" Choon-ha sighs, shaking his head at his brother before grumbling, "I didn't want to take my pills anyway, but how could you lose them...?" And then he adds, because this makes him feel proud, "I'm getting better, mister twin buddy. So I'll just say I lost them and no one will have to take them." he smiles that sneaky smile of his as he says, rather mischievously, "You can do it too, you know. Just put the medicine under your tongue or flush it down the toilet. I think the medicine actually makes us worse, because—"

"O-oh, look, it's daddy, and-a-and Tae-kyun, too." Yoon-ha says, relieved to be free from his brother's attempts at possibly killing him and hurrying over to greet his father.

He opens his mouth to do so, but no words come out once he sees the disappointment in Kyun-ho's face, the gray beneath sleepless eyes, and Tae-kyun, who pulls him this way and that, emitting sounds of discomfort despite the stillness of his expression.

"Yoon-ha, was Choon-ha doing something he shouldn't have?"

- Two -

Waiting for Happiness

"Dad... daddy seems sad today..." Yoon-ha exhales quietly, a soft chortle falling from his lips as he shakes his head back and forth while Choon-ha, who looks slightly suspicious, falls in step with him from behind their father and Tae-kyun, who doesn't seem to be listening at all today.

"Maybe it's because I didn't take the medicine, but honestly, I don't need it anymore. I'm fine..." Choon-ha murmurs, a brief smile revealing his dimples before vanishing into a rather child-like pout.

"Also, I guess it's not a secret anymore, but don't tell mister daddy...! I'm doing something that will help me, and it's been working. I just didn't tell you because you're too paranoid and stuff. You better not tell, Yoon-ha. If you do, you'll be cursed. I'll make sure of it."

"N-no... I won't t-tell, but-but only because it wouldn't m-matter..." he exhales deeply, shaking his head back and forth before saying quietly, "Y-you'll do it anyway because you want to. That's h-how the mind works. It is, I-I promise…! It's true for him…"

Choon-ha, realizing Yoon-ha has started conversing with himself, heaves a heavy sigh before reaching out and smacking him lightly on the head, an action that causes the boy to jump, wide eyes looking even larger than they were before as he exclaims, as much as one can with his whisper of a voice, "W-what was th-the reason for that…?" to which his brother glares at him and bluntly states, "Because I hate it when you talk to yourself. It makes you look dumb. Also, you were supposed to be talking to *me*. Your real brother, who's right next to you."

"O-ohhhh… ohhh… Well, sorry, b-brother, it's so sp-spontaneous, I can't a-always t-tell them to…"

"Whatever. Let's just go back to our mister daddy conversation." He says begrudgingly, kicking a small rock out of his way as Yoon-ha, apologizing to those only he can hear in his mind, lifts a hand to his mouth to begin biting his nubbed nails, his monotone voice nearly blown away by the abrupt wind as he whispers, "Daddy… Oh yes, h-he was sad when I woke up… when I-when I woke up this m-m-morning. Daddy-daddy was sad yesterday, too. He's been sad these days." Yoon-ha, unsatisfied with the inability to bite what's not there, moves on to a different nail while blinking excessively, inhaling shakily as Kyun-ho, who's failing to find any positivity in this day, pulls Tae-kyun (who had thought it funny to try to sit down while his brother walked) up from the ground while scolding him with silence.

"Mister daddy, Min-ho's school isn't this way. You took a wrong turn again," Choon-ha calls, just as Tae-kyun decides to sit down once more after giving his brother that silly doodle-like smile of his, which confuses Kyun-ho because he's making sounds of frustration while furrowing his brows beneath his long bangs.

"Tae-kyun, that doesn't make me happy with you. We already took our walk, it's time to go get Min-ho so we can go home…" Kyun-ho sighs, frowning at Tae-kyun, who begins to whine as he tries to lift him off the ground again.

"Tae-kyun, why are you mad?" Choon-ha inquires, looking innocently at his father, who sighs again and murmurs, his small, hesitant voice sounding close to breaking beneath so much stress,

"Uhm… Tae-kyun is upset because Tae-kyun doesn't want to listen. He was playing his piano too loud, and he didn't want to turn the volume down, so I took it before we took our walk. Then, he tried to run into the street, so I brought him home, but then I remembered we had to get you guys and Min-ho, so, we're here."

Tae-kyun emits another sound of discomfort, picking up his toy to rub it violently against his head as Kyun-ho continues, a bit more quietly than before, "All day long… he's been… doing things that make no sense…"

Choon-ha wants to question what he did that would bother their father so much, but he already looks so exhausted with his life, he places the question in his back pocket instead.

"Tae-kyun, get up. We're going home. I-I mean to get Min-ho, please…!" Tae-kyun chortles despite his flowing tears and pulls away from his brother, that strange smile of his doodling onto his oval-shaped face again as the bright sun casts an angelic radiance against his light, peach-colored skin.

"No home, no home, no home for Kyunie…" He breathes, standing to teeter side to side as he eyes the people that have gathered around them with that strangely intimidating gaze of his before dropping back to a cross-legged sitting position on the ground, which only frustrates Kyun-ho further as the people edging away begin exchanging loud whispers.

"That's the same man that scared my granddaughter... I could easily picture him being the next perpetrator."

"He's the one that was possessed by demons when he was younger. I heard the exorcism left him brain-dead or something..."

This is how it's been now.

Kyun-ho will dare to leave his house, and people will either whisper about him and his family and avoid him or follow to ask why he's stayed in this neighborhood when so many families have moved because of his own.

This is the result of living the lie Kyun-ho's been living, with the children he didn't initially want, for the past sixteen years.

The result of being unable to cut ties with the past even after advancing forward in the future.

Not much has changed about Kyun-ho. He's still awkwardly tall, still looks as though he's cringing when he forces a smile and still wears the same worried yet apologetic expression on his face (which he's often insecure about due to the baby fat that has yet to leave his cheeks, a feature that makes most believe he's lying when he says he's thirty), and continues to sweep his thick, light brown hair over his troubled, coffee-colored eyes.

Tae-kyun's changed, though. He's much more engrossed in his delusions than he was before, needs more care than Kyun-ho ever imagined providing for him, and is still heavily confused over the basic things in life, such as dressing and bathing himself at twenty-six, growing frustrated and inconsolable when Kyun-ho is forced to help him or continuously repeat instruction, as he's always forgetting or mixing up the steps to complete such common things.

He takes showers with his clothes on and uses his towel to dry the wet floor instead of himself.

He refuses to wear anything but Kakao's friend's pajamas.

He doesn't speak as much as he did before their father was imprisoned but still talks in that strange language of his, often avoiding using Korean or even what little English Kyun-ho taught him at twelve, and has kept that alarming gaze of his to this day.

He knows every police officer in their neighborhood because he keeps escaping his home at night to wander the streets until he's taken home by force.

His hair has grown significantly longer because he never sits still long enough for a real haircut, falling past his shoulders, while his long bangs are like smooth, inky waves swept over either side of his face and tucked behind his ears.

He strongly believes he's a time traveler or 'time manipulator' (as they're two different things in his mind) who's also a famous piano player from his old, yet futuristic, world of 1976 and is overly obsessed with his piano, spending hours, days, and even weeks sitting on the floor of his and Kyun-ho's room with an electric keyboard across his lap. And while Tae-kyun can play very beautifully when he wants to, he can also play very badly on the days his mind is racing too much to concentrate on his melodies. Once Tae-kyun's focused on doing something, the only way to remove him from that something is by force and physical restraint, options Kyun-ho has dreaded after Tae-kyun cried and ran away after announcing no one loved him the first time it happened.

"Maybe *we* should just get Min-ho, mister daddy..." Choon-ha says carefully, watching him pull Tae-kyun up from the ground by his arm only to have him pull away to stomp, in a rather exaggerated fashion, away from his brother to lean against a tree, still rubbing his head as he shifts those still eyes of his over to Kyun-ho.

Kyun-ho wishes he could just leave Tae-kyun home.

Tae-kyun's been so upset with his brother today; all day, he's been silently expressing his anger over such by refusing to acknowledge Kyun-ho's presence and hiding himself behind their bed in their room.

He's been getting like that more and more frequently for reasons that make less and less sense the more often they happen.

Kyun-ho tried apologizing multiple times for upsetting him, but each time he opened his mouth to do so, Tae-kyun would turn away from him or roll himself under their bed, dragging his Kakao toys with him and noodling when Kyun-ho was forced to pull him out from under the bed to try to get him to change his clothes, which never happened because he remained limp each time Kyun-ho would attempt to help him do such. And while he still would have been in pajamas, at least they'd be clean instead of the ones he's been wearing for five days.

He can never leave Tae-kyun alone, though; leaving him alone only gives him the opportunity to sneak out of the house and walk for hours without direction in mind, making Kyun-ho paranoid of both Hae-sol finding and killing him or someone else finding and hurting him, as he's gotten beaten up more than Kyun-ho would like to remember just for being Tae-kyun in the wrong place at the wrong time. The police are always the ones to rescue or escort him home, never happy to do so and always threatening to take him to a hospital next time instead of his home because the *'inappropriate behavior he displays to the public makes the public feel intimidated.'*

So no, unfortunately, Tae-kyun can't be trusted to be alone just yet, and Tae-ho, who often *is* at home on the days he's not getting drunk with his friends in the bar he owns, can't be trusted to watch him because he gets too much joy out of abusing him while Kyun-ho's away at work or getting his children and Min-ho (who Tae-ho, like Kyun-ho, hadn't planned on bringing into the world) from school.

"Hey, Tae-kyun, come here," Kyun-ho calls with little enthusiasm, stepping over to take the sleeve of the Kakao Friends pajama shirt despite its dirty appearance and pulling him along even with the angry sounds of resistance he makes as he moves his toy down from under his bangs to rub over his closed eyes, something he's started to do more recently as a sign of annoyance.

"Tae-kyun, you're not making a lot of sense today! I only took your piano because you wouldn't turn it down, and I had a terrible headache from not sleeping, and…"

"Mmm!"

"Yoon-ha, please don't bring any more leaves home, we have to get Min-ho," Kyun-ho pleads after seeing him crouch to gather the autumn leaves, tightening his grip on Tae-kyun as Yoon-ha stuffs the leaves in his pants pocket before falling in step behind Choon-ha, who inquires innocently, "Are you mad at me for giving Yoon-ha my medicine?" clasping his hands behind his back as his large eyes search his father's frustrated ones intently.

"Honestly, I didn't even know you did that." Kyun-ho sighs, ducking his head to avoid all the looks of so many people passing by.

"Is that the reason you guys were over there? You know Yoon-ha has his own medicine, Choon-ha; why would you do that?"

"No, but hypothetically, if I were, I would be doing it because the medicine would no longer be needed. Not that I'm…."

"Mm, I don't think that's a choice you can randomly make with your condition, Choon-ha. Bipolar disorder is tricky. You're fine right now, but something could happen tomorrow, so please keep taking your medicine." Kyun-ho's tone sounds almost scared, poor fellow, his eyes looking a bit watery as he watches a group of high schoolers laughing while whispering about them. "You and Yoon-ha both need to take your medicine. It-it's not safe to try to fix yourself ever. Let's just listen to the doctors and do what they tell us to, okay?"

"I said hypothetically! Also, I haven't even been depressed or wild in like ten months, so if it wasn't…!"

"It-it's been seven months, Choon-ha. Please keep taking your medicine."

"I never said I wasn't, mister dummy."

"Choon-ha, you can't— you're not supposed to call your dad rude names."

"Uh, but it's already something that's happened, so…"

Yoon-ha is a boy with very *few* words when it comes to interacting with others, so he stays silent during this argument. Too much speech only frustrates and confuses him in the moments when his mind seems blank, and all his dialogue washes away. Too little speech makes him too aware of the emptiness that will come so suddenly upon his mind, and although he always tries to stay balanced in between, sometimes he'll find he's said nothing at all for several days.

Other times, he'll use up all his words for one day in just *half* a day, so he's quiet throughout the rest, and his brain can no longer think of anything more to say. Perhaps he's just not good at such, or perhaps his brain just gets tired of speech when it's mostly used for himself.

"Choon-ha, please stop. I'm honestly begging you. People have already been staring, and I'm tired of being looked at. We can talk about this later, once you're not acting rude, but for now, let's just…"

"But don't you believe that we can get better without medicine? I don't like my medicine, when I take it for too long, it's hard to think, and I'm always tired, and I pee all the time, mister, I don't!"

"Choon-ha, the medicine is helping, believe it or not. You've gone through a dozen changes in your medication. We're not changing it, and you're not going to stop taking it." Kyun-ho says in response to Choon-ha's words, pulling Tae-kyun along as Choon-ha, determined to make his father upset just because he's mad now, continues to bother him.

"But that's not fair! I *hate* being your son! I'd rather live in a *hospital all day!*"

What Kyun-ho wants to say to Choon-ha and what he does are so different it's almost comical.

He wants to tell Choon-ha not to worry about that because he'll end up in the psychiatric hospital again sooner or later if he starts refusing his medicine, so he'll just forget to bring him

61

home. But he knows that's harsh, knows that's something his father would say. So he swallows his anger and says instead, "Choon-ha, I'm going to stop talking about it because you're making me feel really negative about that, and-and I'm already struggling to finish the day."

Choon-ha furrows his brows and bows his pink lips indignantly, crossing his arms as the wind weaves through the trees to scatter leaves this way and that.

He doesn't seem too concerned about upsetting Kyun-ho, which only makes Kyun-ho worry he's about to become like Hae-sol in some way or another because of his dislike of medicine and wanting to fix himself.

But Choon-ha does leave his father alone after realizing Yoon-ha hasn't stopped picking up the leaves that cascade around them, going to take his hand and pulling him along while a heavy silence falls between them.

"Sorry, Kyunie! Sorry~" Tae-kyun mumbles after rubbing his toy against his head, eyeing his brother with that strange gaze of his as Kyun-ho sighs and tells him it's okay, even though it isn't.

I guess Tae-kyun thinks this apology solves every reason his brother is upset with him because now he's rather happy, growing increasingly hyper and trying to run away from Kyun-ho while shouting, *"Let's go! Let's go!"*

"No, Tae-kyun, no running."

"Aahahaha~ Running ~ nai shin laay, ah heeme——"

Kyun-ho takes Tae-kyun by his shoulders, staring deeply into his dancing pale brown eyes as he says seriously, "Tae-kyun, there are bad people in this world who would love to hurt you if you ran away from me and got lost somewhere. Running isn't safe right now, so we're going to walk to get Min-ho, okay?"

Tae-kyun smiles that strange crooked smile of his, thick brows furrowing as he nods his head and chimes in English, "Yes~ Yes~"

"Then no running, all right?"

"Okay, Kyunie, no running, nai fwo nyow~" Tae-kyun quips, teetering in Kyun-ho's grasp as Yoon-ha falls behind them again to pick up more leaves, causing Choon-ha to falter with him.

Kyun-ho looks away from Tae-kyun for less than a second to tell his children not to take any more leaves, and Tae-kyun is gone. He's darted out of his hold and is running in a disoriented direction away from his brother.

Kyun-ho feels bad for doing this, as Tae-kyun is, most likely, running towards the street, but when he breaks away from him, his first response isn't to go chase after him.

It's to stare in utter disbelief and disappointment at him.

That worries Kyun-ho because he used to be so quick to react when Tae-kyun would do things like this, but as the years go by and his spool of compassion spins on, he finds the thread growing weaker and weaker because he doesn't feel the way he thought he'd feel towards people after saving Tae-kyun from Haven.

He actually feels as though he's afraid to care for people because he feels as though he hasn't accomplished anything by caring.

He lets Hae-sol make him his puppet to save Tae-kyun, yet Haven still follows Kyun-ho and his family as though it wasn't enough, as though he hasn't suffered enough.

He saved the children he never initially wanted, and they turned out to be just as complicated as Tae-kyun.

He tried to help all those children Haven stole, and they all ended up dead. Some of which, even by his own hands.

He tried praying for all the terrible memories to stop waking him from his sleep in the form of a nightmare, yet they still revisit him every time he closes his eyes.

He tried to tell his pastor a handful of times about the utter dysphoria coloring his life over the phone, too scared to actually bring himself through the doors of another church after his father's, but he's always been either too busy to listen or too '*emotionally moved*' by Kyun-ho's laments to actually help him fix the broken pieces of his life, which only makes it harder to believe God is even with him at all.

He always treats Tae-kyun and his children as kindly as possible even when they do things to upset him on purpose, but he feels as though the Lord has only reworded his kindness with more reasons to dislike his life instead of just taking away what makes Tae-kyun and children so frustrating or making at least *one* of the many prescriptions the three of them take a little less expensive or a little more effective.

Kyun-ho feels a little piece of his faith die each time he strives for happiness and is met with the reality that happiness, at least for him, would be erasing his past so it could stop eating him in the future.

Happiness, for Kyun-ho, would be going to sleep at night before it's nearly morning, without any nightmares to wake him.

Walking out of his house without anxiety.

Trusting he's safe.

Trusting they're safe.

Trusting that eventually, he won't feel like joining the ones he was forced to kill, whether that's in heaven or hell.

The bitter repetition of his life only ignites the tempting urge to succumb to the dark pleasures of the world like he did when he was younger, with someone who no longer exists now, someone he wishes he could have truly loved and appreciated before death vaporized her.

Before Hae-sol…

Shaking his head, Kyun-ho breaks out of his thoughts right as he hears the odd sound of Tae-kyun laughing, picking himself up off the street as the car in front of him screams at him to move, which he does, but only to retrieve his toy to rub against his head, expression failing to show his inner confusion as Kyun-ho yanks him out of the road and onto the sidewalk.

"Tae-kyun, I said no running!" Kyun-ho yells, wanting to smack Tae-kyun as he smiles and rubs his white alpaca toy under his long bangs, the danger of his abrupt escape holding little to no importance in his wandering mind as Kyun-ho pulls him back angrily to where his children sit, sorting leaves, under one of the fatter Maple trees.

"Tae-kyun's in trouble!" Choon-ha choruses, happy to not be the only one on his father's bad side, as Kyun-ho, still very agitated with Tae-kyun, forces him to sit beside his children under the tree before dropping to his knees in front of him.

"You do not run in the street or disobey your brother!" Now, he's fighting tears, upset at Tae-kyun for making him feel so frustrated with him and scared of the amount of people watching them.

But Tae-kyun is only smiling, cheeks flushed with the excitement of running as he smiles even wider before averting his attention to the trail of ants marching silently beside him.

"Tae-kyun."

Tae-kyun rubs his toy in small circles under his bangs as his eyes continue to stare intently down at the ants, humming a rather random and broken melody to himself and swaying happily to the tune of it.

"You have to start listening, Tae-kyun. You could have been hurt, w-why do you do things like that?"

"Mmhm..." Tae-kyun's eyes flit away from the ants to stare intently into his brother's, lowering his hand to show Kyun-ho the red marking on his skin as he says, "Naifwo..."

"You got hurt because you shouldn't have been running...!" Kyun-ho scolds, his own hands trembling from the amount of frustration coloring him as he continues, "Tae-kyun, that car could have hit you. You could have been *killed!*"

Tae-kyun bobs his head in agreement, still smiling that strange smile of his as his hand returns to his forehead.

He's not understanding me... of course he's not.

"Is Tae-kyun older brother still in trouble?" Choon-ha asks, wide eyes blinking innocently over to his father, who swallows the emotions paining him before forcing out, "No, let's just pick up Min-ho from school."

"P-perhapes we should t-take-take the bus, today..."

Yoon-ha is always apprehensive about going to get Min-ho, as they have to cross a busy road to his middle school, and he's paranoid about the cars hitting him, so Kyun-ho has always held his hand to ease his anxiety.

This time, however, Kyun-ho must swiftly wipe his eyes to ensure no tears have escaped before offering his hand, voice wavering a bit as he says, "I–It's okay, Yoon-ha, it will be quick."

"E-everyday s-someone dies of a hit-and-run… I–I know, that's why I told him I'm n–not going… y–you understand, don't you…?" He's conversing with himself again, glaring at the street from beneath his long bangs as Kyun-ho quickly advances with Tae-kyun and takes Yoon-ha's hand, walking them briskly across the road and frequently apologizing because he knows this only makes Yoon-ha's trust in him dwindle.

"D–daddy, I have to go-g–go to the h-hospital… they're saying I've been p-poisoned…" Yoon-ha murmurs, not noticing the way his father keeps his head bowed as though afraid of making eye contact with the people passing by, because he's too busy shaking out his wrists while several shrieks escape him.

There's not as much interaction between the Choi family and those who live around them. No, people are too judgmental to carry on a normal conversation, too focused on whispering about Haven and every child they believe Kyun-ho's father's killed to look at the Choi family normally.

Still, there's enough interaction to scare Kyun-ho.

That's why he's always so anxious when he picks his children up from school, acting as though the mere sunlight repulses him.

He shouldn't have to act like this, though.

No one knows *he* was a part of Haven.

No one even knows the reality behind his mother's *'mysterious disappearance.'*

No one would even imagine what Hae-sol forced Kyun-ho to do to those poor children, yet there are still people who act as though he's done everything he framed his father for, as though they know he's lying... still things that make him feel as though he's going to be arrested while getting his kids from school because someone found out he framed his father.

He lives in constant fear, this one, always looking behind him because of the past he's buried there.

"Yoon-ha thinks the water in the well poisoned him. I hate it when he talks to himself." Choon-ha states, breaking Kyun-ho out of his thoughts and skipping a little beside Yoon-ha, who is, indeed, conversing with himself.

"Are you still mad, mister daddy? Are you stuck in your PTSD or something?" Choon-ha asks after a moment of listening to the silence, frowning when his dad murmurs,

"I'm not sure..."

"Would you visit me if I lived in a hospital? Because what if I have to live in a hospital soon because my medicine turns me into a monster, like a zombie monster that eats people at night!"

"Of course, I would visit you. I'd visit you every day, but, uhm, you haven't been treating me and the people around us nicely, so maybe not every day, actually... unless you stopped getting into trouble."

Choon-ha pouts at this, slowing his jovial walk to utter, "I have *bipolar disorder!* I never *meant* to make people hate me! My mood, my mind, it's all so tricky...!"

Kyun-ho's heard this and so many other similar lies so often, he doesn't even respond or say much of anything until he gets to Min-ho's school, watching the lines of the sidewalk disappear beneath his feet as Yoon-ha grips his hand a little tighter while an empty chortle falls unconsciously from his lips.

Why is it still so hard to exist in this neighborhood?
Why is it still so hard to exist at all?
When should things be better?

- Three -

We are Not Yet Close Enough

"Uncle, you forgot about me again," Min-ho complains upon seeing them near his school, his lazy, hooded lids blinking in the brightening of the sun as he steps out of the white metal fence surrounding the building to further state his mistreatment.

"All the other children went home. I was the last one left, and the sun was so bright... I was miserable." The thick layers of Min-ho's wavy, chin-length, chestnut-colored hair grow messy in the wind as he struggles to adjust the strap of his large Tai Chi Chasers backpack, making Choon-ha snicker because Min-ho, with his prominent cheekbones, high nose bridge, and wide, pink lips, does not have the appearance of a small child, yet his whiny behavior and oversized backpack make him look that way.

"I didn't want anyone to take me, so I waited inside the gate. I knew you'd get paranoid if I walked home by myself, but that was so awkward, uncle, and embarrassing...!"

"I-I'm sorry, Min-ho... I keep forgetting things lately." Kyun-ho apologizes, letting go of both Yoon-ha and Tae-kyun's hands to try to loosen Min-ho's backpack straps as he laments, "I don't even have a real dad to pick me up, so everyone already thinks I'm weird because of you… not that you're weird, but… your life… well, I'm sorry."

Kyun-ho forces a small smile as a rather visible amount of hurt glints in his eyes, his hands finding Tae-kyun's and Yoon-ha's again as he softly says, "It's okay, Min-ho, I shouldn't have been late. Tae-ho's picked you up before though, he's, uhm, still your dad."

"He is, isn't he?" Min-ho says bitterly, a gale of wind sweeping a long strand of chestnut hair across the high bridge of his nose as he tilts his small face up at Kyun-ho, his lazy eyes of mocha seeming to sigh as sadness breathes into him.

Min-ho is one of those accidental children who merely happened because the adults were fooling around with no concept or intention of lasting love.

Tae-ho met his mother, or rather his *girlfriend,* as they're still not married, fifteen years ago in the saloon he calls his 'castle'. Her name is Everett, and she was a German foreigner who visited Korea purely for the fun of it, with intentions that were quite perverse.

She went back to live with her parents in Brazil after a year of lying to her family about her pregnancy and rarely visits, though she does try to keep in contact with Min-ho (not so much his father, though, she's upset with him for not letting her take Min-ho to live with her).

Kyun-ho's always wondered if Tae-ho feels guilty about this, as he's never once been violent to the fourteen-year-old like he has been sporadically with everyone else in their household.

"I wish he wasn't my dad at all. Why couldn't God give me a better option?" Min-ho laments, the color blue itself seeming to radiate from him as Choon-ha, always bothered by Min-ho's complaints, heaves a sigh before admitting, "You know it wouldn't even matter if Tae-ho actually cared about you because no one likes us still. That's why so many people have don't like our stupid neighborhood, dummy."

"That's a really crude thing to say!" Min-ho cries, looking to Kyun-ho for consultation and emitting an exasperated sigh because Kyun-ho's looking rather flustered with this situation.

He's terrible at this parenting job, utterly and miserably terrible.

He thought he would get better as the years went by and his children got older, but he still feels just as unprepared and timid about parenthood as he did when they first entered his life, perhaps because they were never supposed to be born the way they were, and the reality of that refuses to leave him.

"Choon-ha, that's not nice. N-not everyone dislikes us. You know we have… we have Yong-rae, Chae-won… Hyeong-cheol, and his caretakers, and also probably some kids at your school who want to be your friends."

"No one wants to be our friend because they all think we're connected to the stupid murders of that stupid Haven group because of your stupid dad. Your family ruins everything for us. We're permanently on people's naughty lists, even when it's not Christmas."

"Well… I think for you and Yoon-ha, it's because of your mental state, too…" Min-ho adds, uncomfortably shifting because he knows this conversation is saddening Kyun-ho.

"Also, you can't count Hyeong-cheol and Chae-won because they're weird too. Chae-won's better at pretending not to be weird, though, I guess. But I don't want weird friends sometimes."

"They're not… weird. Hyeong-cheol has autism, and Chae-won's got OCD, but none of you guys are weird. People can just be mean about the way you all are, but you're not weird. People can just be mean…"

Tae-kyun is growing restless again and begins to pull on Kyun-ho's arm as they near their home, the same house Kyun-ho's lived in since he was little… the same house his mother died in, and the same house that hid so much of the abuse he and his brothers suffered through.

"I think people hate us because we're weird. Even you hate us sometimes because we're weird, mister daddy. It's an unavoidable truth."

"Choon-ha, why? Why have you been wanting me to say such cruel things these days?"

"I dunno. Maybe it's funny."

"It's not funny to say I hate you because of your differences. I don't really hate anyone." He wants to conclude with, *except for myself,* but he opens the door to their home instead, letting go of the anxiety that always grasps him upon stepping out of this place as Yoon-ha, after murmuring several intangible sentences to himself, releases his father's hand and starts emptying his pockets of the gathered leaves to the ground, causing them to disperse in multiple directions as they dance onto the wooden floor.

"Yoon-ha, can you put your leaves outside? I don't…"

Yoon-ha shakes his head and furrows his brows, wringing out his wrist as he whispers through his shrieking, "H-has to be in-inside, they can't...They can't use the door anymore...! S-Sash-aro can't-can't help them all get inside!"

He truly does believe he wields the power to turn the leaves into tiny creatures as their creator, and he's overly obsessed with hoarding as many leaves as he can in order to stop his failed creations (the villains of his delusions) from growing too powerful and destroying their brethren and his family, for he's always worried someone wants to harm them.

It's a very complicated thing, creating leaf creatures and finding places for them to go, and after last year's gathering, the space under his window is too full, and he has nowhere else to put his leaves... So he puts them inside, leaving them around the house and growing upset when someone steps on them.

His relationship with the trees, however, is not as complicated, as they only exchange whispered conversations and secrets only trees know.

Yoon-ha thinks himself very special because of his talents, but this, unfortunately, is often referred to as grandiose delusion by his doctors, and they're often trying to get rid of his powers when he visits them.

"Yoon-ha, you can't put the leaves inside."

"I've-I've already given t-them orders," He says, head starting to shake more violently than before as Min-ho tugs on Kyun-ho's sleeve to feign the incapability of taking off his backpack, desperately wanting his attention.

"Uncle, I need help."

Choon-ha, still focused on upsetting his father, looks over at Min-ho with wide and unsuspecting eyes, contemplating his next course of action before deciding it would be most beneficial to dart up to Min-ho and push him, which does make the boy knock his head against the door.

"Choon-ha! Why would you do that? That hurt Min-ho!" Kyun-ho looks so helpless as he stands anxiously in the midst of this chaos, perspiration gathering beneath his bangs as Min-ho lifts a hand to soothe his head, and more leaves decorate the floor with red and golden colors because Choon-ha has run off to toss them in the air, despite Yoon-ha's protesting.

And Kyun-ho is unable to do anything at all.

He's afraid of attempting to change the atmosphere.

Too afraid of Choon-ha telling him something cruel because he knows right now that would truly make him cry.

He wants his children to love him.

He's wanted that ever since they were born, ever since he decided to love them first despite their circumstance.

Correcting their behavior, no matter how he does it, has always made him question whether or not the line between parenting and child abuse has blurred, partly because Choon-ha has accused him of abuse countless times throughout his life and partly because he's always been afraid of becoming like his own parents, so much so, I'm afraid he may just be a doormat to those he takes care of.

"Uncle, I need help. More so than before because Choon-ha may have concussed me." Min-ho says, standing to brush off his pants before reaching to tug on his uncle's sleeve, those lazy hooded lids of his blinking up at Kyun-ho as he frowns.

"Help, uncle. My head really hurts now."

Kyun-ho is trying to conjure up some sort of response, trying not to look as distressed as he is the more he takes in what's happening around him, but he's failing immensely, and within seconds, he's fighting tears, fingers trembling as they fiddle with the long sleeve of the white collared shirt beneath his blue and black argyle patterned sweater vest, his eyes flickering from person to person as memories from his past begin to crawl into his mind.

"Dad, he needs help...! Please, stop hurting him! The rituals don't make him better. Stop it, please!"

"Tae-kyun is getting better. He hasn't killed anyone else after your mother! He's obedient and compliant because the devil is nearly out of him!"

"Tae-kyun never did that. Why can you not just believe it was—!"

"Uncle...? You're acting funny. Would you like to sit down?"

Blinking rapidly, Kyun-ho pales as he averts his gaze to Min-ho, finding it difficult to focus on the boy because that memory is still playing in his mind, his voice so clearly arguing with his father as the cries of Tae-kyun begin to sound with the yelling of his father.

"Mister daddy, look, I threw leaves every..." Choon-ha pauses upon seeing his father's face, and he frowns quite sorrowfully as he says, "Darn...your mind is breaking again. It wasn't me who triggered you, right, mister daddy? I only wanted to bother you...!"

"You could have video evidence of Tae-ho, and I would still believe it was you before I even thought about it being him!"

"Dad, stop! He's bleeding!"

"You're ruining the candle placement. Get out!"

"No, it's not fair!"

"Life's not fair, is it? My wife's dead, your friend and his family are dead, and Tae-kyun is the cause of it all. Death has no boundaries when it's cast by demons."

Staggering while grasping his head, Kyun-ho moves with haste towards the kitchen with the intention of calming himself with the taste of tea. Dizziness forces him to lean against the sink while closing his eyes as he struggles to will his past to leave him.

"Kyun-ho, you have to come back, come back to Haven...! I'm so lonely...! I can barely breathe! I-I can make Tae-kyun better. I can make him work, so your dad doesn't abuse him anymore...! Please be my friend again, Kyun-ho, please stop ignoring me because I haven't done anything wrong...!"

"You're killing people for no reason! Haven helps people, why are you so obsessed with surgeries and death when——?"

"I'M GOING TO BLOW UP EVERYONE IN THIS STUPID NEIGHBORHOOD IF YOU KEEP IGNORING HAVEN!"

Gasping, Kyun-ho gropes for the faucet to turn on the water before leaning his face in, the abrupt cool of the liquid shocking him into a brief state of confusion before he realizes, quite suddenly, that Hae-sol's not here, just as his father and his younger self aren't, because he's not in the past, contrary to what his mind almost tricked him into believing.

"Mister daddy, are you okay...?" Choon-ha asks, the seriousness of his father's condition taking away the satisfaction his previous actions gave him and instead giving him a great load of unwanted concern and melancholy.

"D-d-do y-you want-want some-some tea…?" Yoon-ha whispers, pausing in his leaf-gathering to stare at his father, who merely blinks the dripping water from his wide eyes as a troubled silence falls over them.

The children will often fall silent when Kyun-ho is troubled by his past, so it's no surprise now that even the shifting of Min-ho's feet can be heard as a carousel of worried glances is exchanged around the room.

This is partly because they never know if Kyun-ho will successfully fall away from his trauma or remain in the thick of it, spacing out for long periods of time or mindlessly brewing and consuming tea for hours.

Presently, though, it seems Kyun-ho has pulled away from his mind, wiping the water from his eyes and vigorously shaking his head as though riding a terrible headache, his round cheeks flushed with the effort of regaining his place in reality as he stammers. "Wow, uhm, sorry, guys. I-I'm fine, it wasn't-it wasn't anything you did. I just…" he trails off then, small drops of water dripping from his bangs and onto the floor as he shakes his head again.

"Min-ho… you… you wanted to say something earlier. What-what was it? I'm sorry, was it about your day?"

Min-ho starts looking uncomfortable, his thin lips forming an odd sort of 'point' as they often do when he's uneasy, as he glances at his cousins before quietly admitting.

"Um… well, the other kids did keep bothering me about our family, but, well, I-I know not everything they say about us is true. But, well, they said some things that kind of…" Min-ho trails off, suddenly seeming guarded about the story, as if he's remembering things he's not sure if he should tell.

78

"Never mind, uncle. I don't want to stress you out again. Should I help Yoon-ha clean up the leaves?"

"No, what-what'd the other kids do? Was it about—?"

"The leaves—Yoon-ha's making a mess of things, isn't he?"

I will note, before the moment is gone, that although Kyun-ho tries his very hardest to be involved in Min-ho's life and care for him the way his father doesn't, his attempts are never good enough in Min-ho's mind because Min-ho will forever be jealous of the amount of attention those with mental peculiarities in his family get.

In his world, Kyun-ho will never truly love him the way he is because the way he is, is normal, and that has made him feel an odd mixture of bitterness and dysphoria throughout his entire life.

He wants to tell Kyun-ho what's happened today, he truly does, but he can't shake the silly thought that says, *'Perhaps you're not close enough for that one yet. Perhaps your words will push him into another one of his spells of despondency and distress. Perhaps you should pretend no one has said or done anything frightening to you at all today.'*

Choon-ha frowns…

He feels guilty for acting the way he did towards his father, not so much Min-ho, no, but Kyun-ho. Kyun-ho's been so stressed these days; why has he been so persistent in frustrating him when he knows his PTSD has been worsening because of the recent break his father had from prison and the crimes and riots taking over the news?

So he sighs, a small sigh, before admitting, "I shouldn't have been mean to you today. Sorry, mister daddy." He would normally add that it only happened because of his bipolar disorder (as he thinks it funny to blame all his wrongdoings on his condition, even though most of the things Choon-ha does have nothing to do with it), but these past few weeks he's been rather quiet about his condition, and besides the brief conversation he had with his father after school, he hasn't said anything new to him about his condition at all.

Perhaps it's because he knows talking about his bipolar disorder will only bring about the topic of medicine, and he knows Kyun-ho will not approve of what he's doing with those pills.

Min-ho looks up from his small handful of leaves, sounding hopeful as he says, "Uncle, can you stay with us at home today? You don't seem well, after all."

Kyun-ho seems significantly pale as he wipes more water from his face. He had forgotten about going to work, but he knows he can't call in again because he did that twice last week and the week before because his mind has been continuously torturing him with his past and present.

What if he's there again, complaining about the hospital and threatening to kill himself? What will I tell Yong-rae if he's there again, waiting until I get off work? What do I say if he does something that triggers me or makes the other workers uncomfortable? What will I do if people start asking about my dad again?

"Uncle...?"

"Oh, yes- I- I should probably work today because it's unfair to keep using your dad's money... He's got a lot of it, but he's always been bad at sharing."

Tae-kyun, who had gotten distracted by a bug that had flown off Yoon-ha's leaves, emitted a troubled sound at his brother's words before vigorously shaking his head and going to grab Kyun-ho's sleeve.

"No work, no work for Kyunie…!"

"I'm sorry, Tae-kyun, you know I have to work. I can't…"

"Tae-ho…! No Tae-ho, Kyunie, no…"

"Tae-ho won't be home until tomorrow, remember? He's staying with his friends, it's okay, Tae-kyun."

"As if. He's never home. I don't even know how that could be a worry of yours, Tae-kyun. He never even comes home, even when he promises…" Min-ho frowns, the resentment he has towards his father quite audible in his voice as he drops the leaves he's holding into the large bag Yoon-ha's filling.

It's true, though, what Min-ho had said.

Tae-ho's been avoiding their home even more than usual because of the recent and rather confrontational conversation he had with Kyun-ho involving the prison break of their father.

None of the children exactly know what was said, as they were talking outside in the garden right before bed, but they know it didn't end well, because they heard Tae-ho yelling at Kyun-ho and saw him get hit multiple times before being shoved into the flower bed and locked outside, where he stayed for several hours because Tae-ho wouldn't let anyone go near the back door.

"He can come in after… two hours. He's only crying because he got hit, Min-ho. You know how fights between brothers go. You win some and lose some. Staring at him won't make the time move any faster, though. Move away from that window, why don't you."

"I don't think you're well enough to go to work, uncle.

Yesterday, Yong-rae called because he thought my father, who of course wasn't even available, was going to have to take you home because you kept hiding in the bathroom and having panic attacks. He's worried about you. We're all worried about you, maybe—"

"I'll be fine, really! I'll take more medicine and-and…"

"Kyunie…home…" Tae-kyun sounds so sad as he wraps himself around his brother like one would a scarf, feeling Kyun-ho's heartbeat vigorously against his chest as he breathes, "No work for Kyunie, home time…!"

Kyun-ho trembles in his grasp as he returns the hug, struggling to withhold the urge to fall apart completely.

In an ideal world, Kyun-ho wouldn't have to work because of the high income of Tae-ho's saloon, but Tae-ho doesn't like sharing, so Kyun-ho must show up to work if he wants to provide for his family.

There are times when Tae-ho will give him money when he begs for it, but Kyun-ho hates begging, and so the money does not often come.

Kyun-ho checks the time on his phone, sighing as 4:55 PM turns to 4:56. He's usually already out the door at this point, as he clocks in at five thirty, and the walk to the bookstore is exactly twenty minutes, giving him time to gather his thoughts while organizing what books were left disturbed by careless customers.

"I'll be back soon. It's only till 10:45."

"So I'll have to suffer alone with these people."

Min-ho says this every time Kyun-ho leaves, no matter the mood he's in because he's bitter Kyun-ho has to have this job.

Mongsang-ga seojeom (Dreamer bookstore), the logo of which is *Nae chaeg-eul haneulgwa nanumyeonseo,* which means, *'While sharing my book with the sky',* is one of the later closing bookstores, shutting its doors at 10:30, which means Kyun-ho, who's one of three night shift workers, has to make sure everything is in place for the morning workers on the next day even after closing, which often makes him come home late.

"Tomorrow is Saturday, then I can be with you—not the full day, but mostly."

"What about Sunday? Will you be home all Sunday?"

Kyun-ho claims he has therapy on Sundays and goes every week to group sessions, though he always seems more anxious when he arrives home than when he left, frequently startling at the smallest sounds and emptying multiple pots of tea in a frantic attempt to calm himself, perhaps because those therapy sessions are not truly therapy at all.

"Can you at least look at the new home I made for the bugs outside?"

Min-ho views the little animals and bugs outside as homeless children with nowhere to go (despite having many homes outside), so he frequently makes little houses out of sticks and whatever else he can find and places them under the trees or in the garden of their backyard. He also tends to save a small portion of the food he eats during the day to set on the tables he's made inside the homes. The houses usually only attract ants and curly bugs, but that's okay because curly bugs are his favorite bug (he has several jars of them hidden secretly under his bed), and ants, he says, need a home and food too.

He once made a two-story home out of various Amazon boxes for a stray kitten after seeing it on the way to school when he was seven. It rained the following day, though, causing the home to collapse upon itself and leaving the kitten without shelter. Cardboard hasn't been his friend since.

Kyun-ho smiles, nodding in agreement, as Min-ho mirrors his expression and thanks him, only to abruptly ask, "Do you think Hyeong-cheol can come over while you're gone?"

"No, wait! Can Chae-won come over? Or both of them so they can fight and be on live television?" Choon-ha exclaims, toffee-colored eyes staring intently into his father's eyes as he says, after a moment of silence, "Well… Chae-won will already be here because it's Friday, but Hyeong-cheol can't come over unless one of his caretakers is with him. Plus, it's not a good thing to want your friends to fight for the sake of your own amusement, Choon-ha…" He swallows deeply and averts his gaze to the ceiling to avoid looking at his children, fearing they'll dislike his response.

Really, Kyun-ho would rather Hyeong-cheol *not* come over, even with his caretakers, as Tae-kyun has exhausted him enough, and Hyeong-cheol, who's a very troubled boy, invites a tricky atmosphere wherever he goes, simply because too many things can upset or depress him, and Kyun-ho does not wish to come home to his children and Min-ho complaining about it.

But of course, Kyun-ho doesn't voice those thoughts.

No, he only swallows deeply before turning to head to his room, thinking it's best to prepare for work instead.

Tae-kyun, upon noticing his brother's descent down the hall, runs to follow him, bounding into their room to disappear behind the small corner of bookshelves and chorusing, "Work with older brother."

"Yeah… older brother has to work," Kyun-ho sighs, going into their shared closet to change into his uniform, which consists of a pale blue vest with the store's logo on the front, and a long-sleeved white collared shirt over white slacks to fit the store's cloudy sky aesthetic.

He doesn't bother going inside the bathroom because Tae-kyun would only follow him inside anyway, and Kyun-ho's only been able to force him out when he needs to use the toilet (as he and Tae-ho both would make up stories about monsters jumping from the dirty water to scare him) because toileting is where they both draw the line for privacy, funnily enough.

"Kyunie, older brother, I love you. Work with you."

"Yeah, I love you too, Tae-kyun, but you have to remember I don't come home when you turn your sign over, okay?"

Tae-kyun lets out a gale of playful laughter, peeking over the top of the shelves to drop the cardboard sign he made that has Kyun-ho's bookstore name (although very misspelled) scribbled on it.

Tae-kyun's self-created bookstore was a pleasant idea when he first made it upon discovering he couldn't be with Kyun-ho at work, but as the days went by, it just became a tiring (and rather repetitive) reminder that when he got home, he would have to explain all over again his reasons for being 'late,' is Tae-kyun's concept of time is that of a very small child, and 'later' for him is either 'when I want it to happen' or 'when it feels right,' because that's how things were in his world back in 1976.

And yes, sometimes Kyun-ho is late, but Tae-kyun assumes when he's tired of sitting behind his bookshelves and leaves that

Kyun-ho is leaving too and will be waiting at the door to be let in. He can't seem to grasp the concept of his brother being away from him for more than an hour and grows frustrated and confused when the hour passes.

Kyun-ho explains to him his work hours and when he'll be home every day, but Tae-kyun never retains this information and instead replaces it with his own.

"I'm going to be home after 10:45, okay…?"

"Okay. Okay."

"I set the alarm on your tablet again, so when that timer goes off, I'll be home soon, okay?"

Tae-kyun merely smiles and says something in that odd language of his, rubbing a fist beneath his long bangs as Kyun-ho sighs and pulls his shirt over his pants, stepping out of the closet and walking towards Tae-kyun's bookstore to peer over while adjusting the name tag on his vest.

"That doesn't mean that if you close your store, older brother will come home, right?"

Tae-kyun sits cross-legged on the floor, slightly swaying as he pulls his electric piano into his lap, slowly nodding as he stares blankly up at him.

"I'll see you after your alarm goes off, okay?"

"Ehng…" Tae-kyun frowns before standing on his knees to place his piano on top of the wooden shelf, rubbing one of his many Ryan lions under his bangs as a crooked smile doodles across his face.

Kyun-ho returns his smile, but it's laced with a certain kind of sadness because he can't help but feel that no matter how many times he reminds Tae-kyun or sets alarms on his tablet, his concept of time will remain the same.

"Maefwew…" Tae-kyun murmurs, smile widening as he stands to offer Kyun-ho his kakao toy after saying, "Toy for hugs, hugs from Kyunie."

He's not sure why (because this exchange has happened so many times before), but taking the toy from Tae-kyun's hand before embracing him feels quite sad today, perhaps because he was already laced with melancholy.

"I'll be home really soon, okay…? And then we can read one of your books and play your piano. I-I'll be back, okay?" Kyun-ho feels as though too many negative emotions are attacking him at once.

The fear of leaving Tae-kyun when he has to do it every day.

The dysphoria that colors him when he realizes how unfair time is to those who can't comprehend it.

The intense sting of guilt that pales his face because he's remembering how often he left his brother alone when they were younger.

The confusion laced with anger because he's wondering why he's loved as much as he is in Tae-kyun's eyes when he broke so many promises.

"Kyunie's crying. Don't cry, Kyunie. The alarm goes off. Time for home, no more working."

Blinking rapidly, Kyun-ho pulls away from his brother to swiftly wipe his tears, unaware that he had been crying and blushing because of it.

"I-I was… Yeah, you're right, Tae-kyun. Sorry."

Tae-kyun blinks at him for a while before moving to retrieve a small black recorder from his desk, his gaze never leaving Kyun-ho as he teeters up and leans into him for a second hug before emitting a pleasant sigh and returning to his bookstore, turning the recorder on to say, in his breathy voice,

"Bye, Kyunie." before dropping into a sitting position on the floor.

Tae-kyun finds the strangest ways to entertain himself. He can stay in one place for hours just smiling and speaking his language into that tape recorder, swaying gently as though a leaf, ready to blow away.

Other times he'll just carry it around, the tape recorder, rubbing it against his head before settling down and playing back all the recordings he's gathered to a piano tuning app he'd downloaded on his tablet, as he then tries to match the pitch of the words to a note to create various melodies.

Kyun-ho says one last goodbye before forcing himself to leave the room, squeezing his eyes shut and inwardly scolding himself for such an abrupt display of emotions.

"I think we should look at my bug houses on a different day. Perhaps tomorrow, uncle." Min-ho says, peering over from his position on the couch in the living room as Kyun-ho, still bothered by his tears, bites his tongue while nodding slowly, his steps seeming as though there's no weight to them at all.

Yoon-ha, who had been underneath the kitchen window inspecting the leaves that were hurt upon their arrival, stands to quickly hug his father, wide eyes dark with paranoia as he stutters, "Y-you won't-won't let anyone-a-anyone bad come while-w-while you're gone, right...?" to which Choon-ha laughs and exclaims, throwing himself over the back of the couch to hang upside down, "He'll be all the way at his job, he can't do anything if he's not with us, Yoon-ha!" which only aids the boy's anxieties.

"Uhm...well, nothing bad should happen, Yoon-ha, and if it did, you could always call..." he stops himself then... unable to continue because after all these years, he's still scared to tell his children to go to the police for their troubles, because they never helped him with his... perhaps because they were too busy making things around him worse.

"You can just call me if something happens, okay? Then I'll come right home, and we can all be safe or... scared together."

"But why would you come home if Yoon-ha told you someone was trying to hack us to death?" Choon-ha inquires, tilting his head as Kyun-ho significantly pales while fidgeting with the cuff of his sleeve.

"Because I'd want to save you...?" He feels as though he chokes a bit on those words as his child grins a grin one can only describe as Cheshire, purposefully falling from the couch and onto the floor to exclaim, "Save us? Mister daddy, you're too scared to save anyone!"

Haven.   Murder.   Torture.
          Children.

                                        Bleeding.
          You have saved no one.

"That's not true. He saved Tae-kyun, right, uncle? You saved him from your father lots of times, even though you would get hurt too." Min-ho's lazy, hooded lids blink imploringly at his uncle, who looks, frighteningly enough, close to tears, scratching vigorously at his wrist even though the motion pains him.

"Y…yeah, I-I did."

He hates it, but he can't help but feel like a liar because he's never truly saved Tae-kyun in his mind because Hae-sol had already broken him, just like his father.

Just like Tae-ho.

And those children… those children that Haven hurt; One can never truly feel like a savior if there are so many fallen ones.

I haven't saved anyone. I've only been there to watch them all suffer. I wasn't helpful at all to those children, and Tae-kyun should honestly hate me.

He must have mentally dozed, Kyun-ho, for he only realizes he momentarily left the world when Yoon-ha moves to tug on his sleeve, wide eyes rapidly blinking as he whispers, "D-daddy, you're bleeding… Y-y-you should st-stop hurting yourself like that…"

Oh, yes, his wrist… isn't much, but I do suppose his nails have done a noticeable job of making themselves known across his reddened skin.

It's never truly intentional, harming himself, or rather, he never truly remembers to be conscious when his emotions cause him to bite a bit too hard on his tongue, scratch violently at his skin, or chew well beyond his fingernails, whether he's in the presence of others or not.

"Y-you need a band-aid…"

"No, I'm okay… I should start heading to work. Sorry, I got distracted." Swallowing hard, Kyun-ho moves past the children to go retrieve his shoes by the front door, several beads of perspiration gathering beneath his dark brown bangs as he kneels to slide his high tops on despite the tremors shaking his hands, as anxiety is making itself a rather present monster in his heart right now.

He knows Min-ho is trying to talk to him because he feels the child's hand on his shoulder, but he's unable to render any attention to the world outside his mind, for it's going down a rather continuous path of troubles... both imagined and painfully real.

What if I don't come home at the right time today, and my dad comes to hurt my family?

What if someone who saw what I did in Haven tries to hurt me?

What if Hae-sol gets mad at me for not talking to him yesterday and does something bad?

What if my manager fires me for missing so many days, and I have to get jobs from Tae-ho again?

What if I can't stop worrying and my medicines stop working?

Staggering up into a standing position, Kyun-ho lingers by the doorway for a moment while gently rubbing his head, feeling sickened by how damp perspiration has made him feel.

"Uncle, you weren't even listening..." The disappointment lacing Min-ho's voice causes Kyun-ho to blink rapidly before averting his attention to the one beside him, his tone a bit strained as he stammers, "I-I'm sorry, I'm... I think I should leave before this gets worse." He tugs a bit at his shirt collar as though it's uncomfortably tight, panic so clearly draining the color from his face. It's impossible for the children around him to pretend Kyun-ho's condition isn't getting worse, because it has been ever since his father escaped the prison his and Hae-sol's lies placed him in all those years ago.

He's in constant fear, constant fear of his father hurting him and those around him.

A constant fear of what his father may do to him because of all those crimes of Haven that were placed on him.

Constant fear of his best friend, Hae-sol, the one the world pronounced dead a long, long time ago.

- Four -

Causes of Dysphoria

"Oh, no…! Are you wanting to play in the kitchen instead?" Hyeong-cheol quietly exclaims, moving the paper cutouts of *The Little Prince* characters atop a pillow from where he crouches beneath his canopy of blankets, the audiobook of that favorite story playing beside him on his phone as the uncertainty of this day continues to sigh into his mind.

"Oh, yes…! I want to play in the kitchen instead because it is so very quiet in the kitchen, and it will make my rose so very happy to be away from so much yelling…" The boy trails off, then… those sad eyes of ghostly hazel staring down at the paper rose in his hands while a strange yet contemplative look replaces the usually somber expression on his oval-shaped face…

He's been trying to be happy all day, this boy.

But nothing seems to be working at all, perhaps because the day is just meant to stay sad and colorless because perhaps it was never supposed to be happy.

This boy who's failed to capture rapture is a friend of the Chois, just like Chae-won (who you'll soon find in between the pages of this book), and his name is Hyeong-cheol.

A boy easily overtaken by emotions, he's frequently crying and has the permanent evidence of this beneath his pale hazel eyes, which are often clouded with the unspoken desire to smother his past and present circumstances.

He's seventeen and a half, the oldest and most sorrowful amongst the friends, and is often thought to be much younger than he is due to his small stature and somber, toddler-like appearance.

He's in need of a haircut, according to his mother, because his tousled, sorrel waves are constantly trying to assault his eyes, but he's always hated those and feels an inconsolable amount of rage at the sound of the razor, so most likely, his hair will be left alone until it dares to go past his shoulders, just like last year and the years before.

Anyway, today Hyeong-cheol's mother, Song Shi-yoon, was released from rehab and back into society. She's been in and out of rehab ever since Hyeong-cheol can remember, and he cannot, for the life of him, convince his heart to withdraw any happiness for her.

She was away for twelve months this time, and he's been told she's finally able to live independently after that long year of treatment for the drug addiction that caused the divorce of her husband when Hyeong-cheol was three. Back then, they were having too many arguments, Shi-yoon and her husband, about the money she kept stealing to aid her addiction, about the many parties she would have with other addicts while her child was still present, and the promiscuity that often ensued with those not even she truly knew or remembered.

And despite the many times her husband pleaded with her and suggested she put herself back together, he never really *tried* to stop her because he knew if he reported such to the police, he would have no one to care for his son, for he worked disturbingly long hours just to avoid the boy.

And so the drug parties continued throughout Hyeong-cheol's life, and with it came the first veiling of his depression, his first cause of dysphoria that would lead to several others as he got older.

She claims she truly missed him and that this time, she won't have to go back to all those centers. This time, she said he won't need to be afraid of suffering an asthma attack late at night due to the heavy and foul-smelling smoke that would hurt his eyes and make it near impossible to breathe, because she says she's no longer going to smoke or take any drugs at all.

She also said she wants a celebration, to reconcile with Hyeong-cheol and pretend she's never done anything harmful to him at all because, *"We just need to be happy with each other, and remembering the past won't change anything at all."*

But those words have sounded strange to Hyeong-cheol ever since they settled in his ears, and he's been unable to conjure any sort of joy or happiness about this situation because they've tried and failed so many times before to do the same things with Shi-yoon when he was younger, and like most things that start off hopeful in his life, they failed miserably.

"Oh, let's build something glass to put over your rose... then it will be so very protected from all the yelling... with one more thing of glass over it." Hyeong-cheol moves to gather all the cray-ons scattered around him, his body tensing at the sound of yelling downstairs as his breath catches momentarily in his throat, and his heart begins to stutter.

His eyes, those of pale fawn with shades of muted green, stare at the door from beneath his tousled sorrel waves as an odd and foreboding sort of quiet enchants the apartment.

He waits for a while, wondering why it's grown so quiet all of a sudden and biting back a yawn to suppress the fatigue that's been tailing him all day, the red blush that's forever beneath his eyes because of so much crying making him look a bit sickly as he gazes blankly down at his paper before murmuring, "Let's color… let's color our glass" coloring it quite feverishly with his white crayon as the bright yellow scarf around his neck tickles his chin.

It's always scary visiting his mother, but thinking of living with her again after so many years of being with her friends has made his heart feel rather sick, because she's never better when she claims to be, and so many things frustrate her into hurting him, it feels almost constricting being around her.

So he's been hiding.

He's been here, in the room she claims is his own, coloring paper dolls from his favorite story and trying to erase his anxiety by pretending he's very happy his mother's out of rehab because he still loves her, but just needs time to strengthen that happiness before coming out of hiding to greet his mother, as he vanished from her sight the moment she slapped him when he first arrived.

He couldn't help it.

The slap… the forced hug that happened before the slap…

It all just felt too heavy on his already anxious heart, and so he had no choice but to run away to soothe it.

"Grownups aren't supposed to treat you like that, Hyeong-cheol. That's why Miss Song is bad. It's wrong to hurt your children like that. That's why you live with us now…"

Finished with his picture, Hyeong-cheol holds the paper to his ear and begins tearing it carefully into a crooked sort of oval, those small and enchanting shivers of happiness pulling the corners of his small lips up into a smile as he squeezes his eyes shut to further enjoy the sounds most of us wouldn't care to enjoy at all.

Before Hyeong-cheol's mother's addiction worsened, they used to live together, just as he used to have two parents instead of his mother's friends as caretakers, though Dae-sung wasn't his biological father, and as I said before, he didn't like being around the boy. Especially after receiving his diagnosis of autism and ADHD at three, cutting off contact with him and his mother entirely when his teachers reported he was most likely suffering from depression as well at the young age of five, far too despondent because there were too many things a five-year-old ought not to be troubled with crowding his mind…

Still, they were a family then, even if they were only held to that term by definition rather than living style, too much distance within the household when abuse was absent to ever feel like a family should.

He can't remember it all entirely because he was, as you know, quite little, but what he does remember is being afraid to come downstairs when the arguments got too loud and his mother hitting him for covering his ears.

He remembers being uncomfortable and hating the existence of his nose, not just because of the drugs she'd smoke, but because his mother rarely remembered to change his diapers, and this, in turn, would force the child to hold his excrement due to the fear of being trapped in them for days, which in turn would either make him very sick or cause his diaper to upset both himself and his mother by bursting, something that would guarantee presence of abuse.

Hyeong-cheol used to think it was a game to his mother, hitting him so often, because at times there would be no reason to hurt him at all.

She would hit him while he'd be playing, when he would try to converse with her, and especially when he dared to call her *'mommy'*, as she's always insisted he call her *'Miss Song'*.

She hit him for crying, too, and most frequently she'd hit him for stimming, as she's always hated the various things he does to regulate himself and could never once refrain from inflicting some form of pain upon him for doing such.

And the hatred of her child only grew worse once Hyeong-cheol's father left, unable to stand the frequent drug altercations and issues with finances, so of course, the number of cuts and bruises adorning Hyeong-cheol increased.

He's never fully understood his mother's addiction, only that whatever she's taking is making her sick and that despite its many forms, it's always labeled a drug, whether it looks like candy or not.

Hyeong-cheol remembers tasting some at one point when he was seven, and the drugs were so cleverly disguised as small pieces of star-shaped candy, which greatly intrigued him because they reminded him of the stars in his favorite story.

"Hyeong-cheol, what are you eating?" Eun-seok had asked him this while he sat on his knees in front of his mother's bed. He had been chewing rather slowly on what he assumed was a candy, while poking slender fingers into his mouth to feel the odd way the star had started to tingle on his tongue.

"Those are Miss Songs, they're not for children because they aren't candy." Eun-seok said, and he took the small dusty bag filled with so many yellow stars away from the boy before he gently removed his fingers from his mouth.

"You can't eat those like candy because they're not, and they'll make you really sick because your body's not old enough to understand how to digest them." He had to pry Hyeong-cheol's jaw open to scoop the remaining yellow substance from his mouth, and the boy had shivered as though struck by a very cold wind.

"Miss Song has so many stars… taste is so… so bad…" he forced out, the taste nothing like the candy he was used to eating because the yellow stuff Eun-seok had taken from his mouth tasted rather foul.

"They're not candy. They're drugs. But you're not old enough to take them, because you'll get sick. But maybe when you're older, you can have some if you still want them."

"'They're not candy… they're drugs…'" he reiterated, and placed a finger in his mouth to try to rid the uncomfortable tingles on his tongue while he blinked pale eyes over at Eun-seok.

"Eun-seok said, don't eat them, because you could get so very sick… Miss Song eats so many stars… does she want to go all the way to the hospital…?"

"Well, she takes them because it makes her feel nice, and sometimes bad things are okay if they make you feel nice because they're not actually *bad. People just label them as bad because they don't use self-control, and so it turns bad because they get too much at one time."*

"Drugs are very bad, even if they look like very happy stars."

"Well, if anyone asks you, you should always say yes, but honestly, drugs are only bad if you take too much at one time because then you're not using them responsibly. Miss Song is sick all the time because she isn't responsible, and so now she always wants more than she should have, which is what addiction is."

"Oh, but..."

"Hyeong-cheol, help Eun-seok set the table so we can celebrate! We're done arguing!"

Hyeong-cheol drops his rose to cover his ears, panic grasping him because she sounded so close, that terrible lady, yet he sees nothing at all when he peeks out of his fort, and so he uncovers his ears to hear the pleasant rush of his fingers rubbing together beside them instead, pale eyes sweeping across the silent paper ones staring up at him from the floor.

He doesn't want to listen to Shi-yoon, as it's never granted him any favor in the past, and he surely hasn't convinced himself of the happiness needed to see that lady, but she's calling for him, and what if she were to stomp up here to ruin his fort due to such disobedience or take away the paper friends he's made from his favorite story...?

"Hyeong-cheol, hurry, Eun-seok got ice cream!"

"'Hyeong-cheol, hurry, Eun-seok got ice cream...!'" he echoes, carefully gathering his paper friends and his phone after pulling the chairs around him closer and backing up against his bed, where the books holding down the thin and starry blanket slip and slide a little when his head brushes up against them.

"The fifth planet was very strange. It was the smallest of all. There was just enough room on it for a streetlamp and a lamplighter..." The story quiets as Hyeong-cheol lowers the volume into silence, raising his hands to gently pat his ears while pulling his knees to his chest to try to make himself seem very small, as he's decided quite abruptly that perhaps no one will bother him if he pretends he had left this room a long time ago, as his mother's never been good at hide and seek because she never participates, and Eun-seok is always looking in the wrong places.

And he thinks it may be working, but oh no, that's the sound of the door opening, the sound of someone stepping inside.

"Hyeong-cheol, we need to use the chairs you took for your fort, otherwise, we can't sit at the table... Miss Song is already getting frustrated with you."

Holding his breath at the sincerity of Eun-seok's voice, Hyeong-cheol pats his ears a little faster while an odd mixture of worry and excitement torments his belly, because yes, of course, he's afraid of his mother growing upset with his disobedience, but it's also near impossible for him to withhold the urge to burst out of his fort to invite his caretaker to play with him, even with the recent and rather frightening calamitous event that occurred inside the fort they made yesterday, because Hyeong-cheol often forgets the bad things when a good thought catches him, just as he often forgets something good after something bad has happened.

"Hyeong-cheol, we can't play in here right now. Miss Song is getting impatient." Eun-seok's plump, cat-like lips form a frown as though the boy's thoughts were already voiced, combing a hand through layers of wispy brown hair as he continues, "We have to celebrate with Miss Song first. I know you don't want to, but if you really are living with her again, you'll have to get along regardless. At least to some degree."

Frowning, Hyeong-cheol lowers a hand from his ear and into his mouth, staring at Eun-seok's charcoal-colored jeans from the gaps in the chairs his blanket failed to cover, as all the excitement he felt upon thinking they would play has vanished, and he's back to being rather gloomy again.

"You can either come out yourself, or I can take your fort down and—"

Frustrated with the man for coming in just to ruin things, Hyeong-cheol moves to kick the chair nearest to Eun-seok into him, ripping down his blanket and throwing it at his caretaker in one swift motion before retreating to his bed with a shriek and erupting into tears.

"Hyeong-cheol, that wasn't very nice. I understand you don't feel like celebrating, and you're probably still upset with me, but you don't really have a choice today." He pulls the blanket off his head, placing it on the floor and suppressing a sigh of disappointment upon feeling the impact of a book hit the side of his neck, those bright caramel-colored eyes of his looking so tired as he says, "Hyeong-cheol, buddy, throwing books isn't nice, either. Let's take the chairs back into the kitchen first, and then…"

"Hyeong-cheol does not want to celebrate with Miss Song!"

"I know, Hyeong-cheol, but you've been up here hiding for more than three hours. I don't like this either, but it's time to—"

Hyeong-cheol covers his ears and emits such a loud and shrill scream that the effort of such has flushed his cheeks, his body shaking as though struck by cold water.

"She's in a happy mood, Hyeong-cheol, that's why she wants to see you," Eun-seok insists, sitting beside Hyeong-cheol on his bed only to have the boy slide off and onto the floor, his paper friends scattering around him as his hands begin to violently pat his ears.

"'She's in a... sh-she's in a very happy mood, Hyeong-cheol, that's why she wants t-to see you!'"

"She is. I promise I'm not trying to trick you, Hyeong-cheol. Do you want a hug? I know this situation—"

"G-go away, Eun-seok! He's s-so mad at seeing you!" Hyeong-cheol raises a finger to gesture wildly at the door before allowing his teeth to adopt it, wrenching away from Eun-seok when he tries to pull his hand down and shouting,

"Eun-seok has already tricked Hyeong-cheol with s-so much blood! E-Eun-seok is-is s-so bad!"

"I already apologized for that, though, Hyeong-cheol. I shouldn't have tricked you yesterday. I know I scared you, and that wasn't nice."

"'I-I know I scared you...!'" Hyeong-cheol echoes, both hands now patting his ears again as his pale eyes travel slowly up to stare at Eun-seok's piercing caramel ones, an odd silence settling around them before the boy says slowly, in that odd indolent lilt of his, "Eun-seok was s-so very sorry for causing so much blood, and he read Hyeong-cheol's book to make it better... and gave him so much... so much medicine... s-so it is not very bad anymore, because 'it was a-a... thoughtless mistake...'"

"Yeah, it was... you already told me you didn't like that game, but I kept playing it because I wasn't thinking. After all, I was only focused on how I felt, but it's okay though, because I apologized and did something good to correct what was bad, and gave you lots and lots of medicine.

"The game isn't bad. You just didn't feel like playing it at the time, and my persistence made it bad. I wish we could stay up here and make you feel better with your favorite story, but unfortunately, it's time to be with Miss Song. Do you want to hold my hand?"

Hyeong-cheol is quiet for a moment as he averts his gaze down to Eun-seok's outstretched hand, eyebrows furrowing beneath his tousled sorrel bangs as a feeling of unease drains the color from his cheeks because there are too many memories trying to stutter his breathing and disorient his mind, and he's unsure of what to do about it.

"You can say 'no, thank you,' Hyeong-cheol. I'm not forcing you."

"Oh, no, thank you. He is… he wants to show Miss Song all his Little Prince toys he made from so much paper. Can E-Eun-seok help him find them?" Hyeong-cheol asks quietly, tensing when Eun-seok moves to pry his fingers from his teeth and looking rather troubled as he scoots a bit away from the man before grasping his phone, unmuting the volume of his story before he presses the speaker against his ear.

"*When one wishes to play the wit, he sometimes wanders a little from the truth…*"

Eun-seok smiles at Hyeong-cheol as he begins to gather the paper characters from the floor, moving to sit beside him after he's finished to say, "Okay, Hyeong-cheol, I have your paper dolls. Let's stand up so we can take the chairs to the kitchen."

"'Let's stand up so we can take the chairs to the kitchen.'

Oh, can he have his paper toys?" Hyeong-cheol inquires, taking them before Eun-seok can even answer (as he's always forgetting to wait for a response once his question is voiced) and placing them atop his Little Prince book after turning away from Eun-seok.

"Hyeong-cheol, you have to wait before you take. Otherwise, it's called stealing, and that could make somebody angry." Eun-seok warns, leaning over to run his fingers through Hyeong-cheol's thick hair and withholding a sigh when he ducks away before moving to sit in the chair farthest away from him, drawing his knees to his chest and heightening the volume of his audiobook while exclaiming very seriously,

"Eun-seok cannot sit with Hyeong-cheol right now while he's having so many bad thoughts! He can only pull his chair and make them go so very fast…!"

"That's okay. I understand you're feeling confused again about our relationship. It's my fault. I'm sorry, Hyeong-cheol. We can fix it later." His tone is so light and full of sincerity, but it feels so heavy and laced with perversion when it enters Hyeong-cheol's ears that it makes him want to rid himself of it.

"Don't use that voice, he does not like it."

"Oh, I'm sorry, Hyeong-cheol. I'm not sure what you want me to change about my voice, but I'll try to make it better for you. Okay?"

Unsure of the man's words, Hyeong-cheol raises a hand to cover the ear his phone isn't pressed against, brows still furrowed as though terribly troubled as that somber expression of his darkens a bit with the color of disturbance.

"Do you want me to push your chair?"

Startled by the sudden proximity of the man's voice, Hyeong-cheol shakes his head and quickly leaves the chair, causing both his book and his paper dolls to scatter onto the floor, for he'd forgotten they wouldn't stay with him if his hands were unable to hold them.

"Oh no, you look like you need help. It's not loud, Hyeong-cheol, you don't have to cover your ears. The only loud thing here is your audiobook, and you know you're not supposed to turn it up like that. If you want to feel the vibrations, you can use one of your sensory toys that vibrates."

Hyeong-cheol's heart begins to stutter as Eun-seok pries his hands down from his ears, his phone dropping from his fingers as fear starts to shake him.

"See? It's not loud in here. You're okay. Miss Song is waiting for us, so let's go visit her first before I move the chairs."

The audiobook's volume decreases once the phone is in Eun-seok's grasp, and Hyeong-cheol no longer wants to hold those paper friends of his when they're offered to him because the per-spiration from the man's hands has visibly affected the paper, and he feels almost paralyzed staring down at them.

"Here, Hyeong-cheol, hold your paper dolls before I give you your phone and book. You still want to show them to your mother, right?"

The lamplighter has an odd smudge on his face, and the pilot looks as though the imprint of Eun-seok's thumb will surely rip right through him.

"Let's hurry before we make Miss Song upset. We've been gone long enough."

Unsure of what to do, Hyeong-cheol blinks a few more times down at his paper friends before deciding they would only suffer if he left them in his caretaker's hands, placing them carefully inside his book to try to make them new again, for perhaps being so near to the place of their birth will take away everything Eun-seok's hands put on them.

"Okay. I'll walk you out to your mother first. Then, I'm coming back in here to get all the chairs, okay?"

Hyeong-cheol merely blinks as he slowly closes his book, still looking quite troubled as he takes his phone and holds it to his ear again before turning to walk out of his room, trying to gain some sort of solace from the audiobook because right now, this day is offering very little.

"I'll just walk beside you, okay? I know you're not wanting to hold my hand right now."

This apartment looks so new compared to all the other ones Eun-seok's given her in the past, because this time, he said, she's finally going to stay…

"She's supposed to be better now, so she shouldn't try to hurt you anymore… But if she does, don't panic because you can just continue living with me and Sung-hee, okay…? Adults aren't supposed to treat children like that."

He feels his stomach churn at the thought of living with his mother again, and for the seventh time today, he wishes to remain hidden inside his fort, tucked away from monsters in his life that are colored and perfumed with dysphoria.

And this is when he decides to return to his room.

I suppose he forgot Eun-seok was behind him, though, for he knocks into him rather hard, perhaps because he was too hasty in his escape.

"Hyeong-cheol, buddy, if you feel too scared, you can ask for a hug. We won't stay with her if she starts hurting you. You know I wouldn't let that happen."

"Oh no, h–he's so scared. Let's try again later." His voice is tremulous, Hyeong-cheol's, pale eyes blinking rapidly down at the floor in a failed attempt to keep his tears from escaping as his fingers find residency between his teeth.

"It's okay to be afraid. I'm afraid too because I don't know how she's going to act with you... but we have to try being with her, just like we have to try being brave. Do you want a hug?"

He's visibly shaking now, large and stinging tears slipping down his cheeks as he hugs his book and phone closer to his chest while he bites harder at his fingers, the world around him appearing quite blurry as Eun-seok's *Careless mistake'* plays over and over again in his mind, his cries so much louder than his heartbeat as another side of him says hugs, especially tight ones, will provide an escape from the growing panic eating him because they always have before.

"I really messed up yesterday, huh...? I'm really, really sorry, Hyeong-cheol. You don't have to be afraid to come to me for hugs, though. Mistakes are like sandcastles, remember...?"

"The bad things we do in life are just like sandcastles, Hyeong-cheol... They can be washed away just like they can be built up. We can be happy the bad castles got washed away through apologies and kind favors,

or we can cry about how sad it was that it happened at all. We can't forget that everyone makes mistakes, and mistakes are what make us human…"

"You don't have to forgive me yet, Hyeong-cheol. I under-stand I scared you. You can still ask for a hug, though. I'm really sorry I scared you…"

He's holding out his arms.

He looks and sounds genuinely sincere, and there's not a sin-gle hint of malintent colored on his face.

It's okay, Hyeong-cheol. Eun-seok is so very sorry about his thought-less mistake, and he wants to make him feel safe with hugs. He's so, so sorry. It's okay, Hyeong-cheol. It's okay…

It's those thoughts that finally sway the boy to accept his caretaker's hug despite his overflow of tears, because those same thoughts have always grasped him when calamitous events occur between them, and the hugs that follow have never failed to return the trust that was so abruptly stolen.

"We can't forget that everyone makes mistakes, and mistakes are what make us human…"

"Hyeong-cheol, what took you so long? I've been waiting to see you ever since I got here!" She sounds more happy than she does impatient, but that's how it was before he refused to hug her upon arriving here… before she got mad and slapped him.

"Come here, Weeping Willow, I want to hug you!" She announces this as though she didn't already try and fail to initiate such, holding out her arms and looking at him with eyes that say, *'I have never tried to hurt you,'* even though she has, each time they see each other.

"'I want to hug you…' 'Hyeong-cheol, you can say no.'"

Hyeong-cheol doesn't want to hug his mother. He's always hated being that near to her, so he simply presses his phone close to his ear and hugs his book instead before trying to escape this kitchen entirely, tensing upon being hindered by Eun-seok, who gently reminds him they're here to celebrate with Miss Song.

"You don't have to hug her if you don't want to, but please be nice and talk to her. And let me see your phone. You know she doesn't like you listening to stories when you're supposed to be talking."

Hyeong-cheol's brows furrow once more beneath his bangs as he turns to glare at Eun-seok, who smiles a tired smile before taking away his phone and walking him back to that wretched table with the scowling woman and her unpleasant-smelling coffee.

"Oh, boy. That wasn't a very nice welcome, Hyeong-cheol. And this was your makeup round. I would have to be crazy to assume you wanted me to get out of that prison."

"Rehab facility. It wasn't a prison." Eun-seok softly corrects those piercing caramel eyes of his staring down at the lady, who withholds a curse and says instead, "It was a prison to me, Eun-seok. It was torture. You understand, don't you, Weeping Willow?" She reaches to pull her child closer, noting the way he tenses and forcing a hug because of it.

"You always act so rudely around me. No hugs, no eye contact beneath all that messy hair, not even a simple hello. It's not as though you lack those skills, though. Don't you think treating me like a witch could make me hate you?"

"Shi-yoon…"

"Oh, I'm just being silly. Of course, I love you, Weeping Willow, even though you probably don't love me."

It confuses Hyeong-cheol how often she'll use that nickname and baby him… because she's told him time and time again she hates infantile behavior and wants to physically abuse him every time she hears him crying or sees his hand trapped between his teeth.

Yet here she is, calling him Weeping Willow and telling him to sit on her lap, as though he won't be turning eighteen in the middle of December, which is less than a month away.

What should he think of Miss Song…?
What should he think when she's so very confusing…?

Resisting the urge to run when she pulls him onto her lap, Hyeong-cheol impulsively begins to chew on his fingers, his heart stuttering in his chest as anxiety sits closer to panic, and a voice inside his head cries, *"She's going to bite you! Just like the snake in The Little Prince, and then you'll be dead, forever…!"*

"I guess I need to be more aware of how fortunate I am!

You can talk, read, and, well, I can't exactly say you're potty-trained because you won't step foot inside a bathroom, but I'm sure there are lots of other things I could list about you that just aren't coming to mind!" She exclaims, her tone making him want to cover his ears and get away from her as her arms hug him tighter, and his stomach churns as though it wants to empty itself onto the floor.

"Hyeong-cheol, I'm so happy to see you! Are you happy to see me? I would really appreciate a response, not a reiteration."

He tries to speak; he really does, but there's something in his throat, perhaps a collision of words that have tangled into one another, and trying to untangle them is bringing about the urge to cry, especially because his mother has gone and pulled his hand away from his mouth.

And so he says nothing at all, struggling to calm himself with the hurried sound of his fingers beside his ears while perspiration gathers beneath his tousled waves.

"Hyeong-cheol, your m— Miss Song is talking to you. You can answer her..." Eun-seok's voice sounds a bit odd to Hyeong-cheol, and he remembers that he feels scared, too.

Again, he tries to speak, and again, his absence of words upsets his mother.

"The least you can do is look at me. You're actually making me want to cry."

"M-miss Song is holding Hyeong-cheol," Hyeong-cheol stammers, shakily inhaling as he forces himself to look at her, finding that he can only hold her gaze for a minimum of three seconds because he keeps thinking she's going to hit him, so he keeps turning and flinching as if she has because he isn't feeling very safe at all... and this insecurity is making him forget how to converse entirely.

"Miss Song is... 'Oh... it's Miss Song. Say hi, Hyeong-cheol.' Hi Hyeong..." He can't shake the clouds crowding his mind right now, nor the fear pounding his heart. He tries to swallow his feelings and pretend she's much nicer than she actually is, but it's just as impossible as holding her gaze.

And before he knows it, he's gone and said, "'She's going to bite you! Just like the snake in *The Little Prince,* and then you'll be dead, forever!'" but he didn't mean to say that; that was supposed to stay between himself and his mind, so now he must say, in hopes they both forget his outburst, "Hi, Miss Song!" and turn to look at her, waving his hand rather hastily in an up-and-down fashion rather than the usual side-to-side as he continues, dropping his gaze, "She's home after a very long time today, but her visits are always so very short."

"Did you call me a snake, Hyeong-cheol? Do you think I'm going to poison you, like the snake in your silly story?"

"'Sometimes, Miss Song stays for a day, and sometimes it's only an hour. But no matter what, Hyeong-cheol—'" She grabs his chin, disabling him from turning away from her as she says, "It's not like I'm going to hit you. Stop acting like I am. Are you really that afraid of me? Calling me a poisonous snake and trying to ignore me?"

"Oh no, he-he doesn't like that. Miss Song h-has to stop."

"Shi-yoon, we're all supposed to get along today." Eun-seok reminds her, a slight smile on his lips as he steps closer to gently pry her fingers off her child.

"Hyeong-cheol says things like that all the time, he doesn't really mean you're a…" Hyeong-cheol hears him stifle a laugh, and feels his mother tense as he continues, "He doesn't *really* mean you're a snake, he just…"

"Oh, yes. I almost forgot. You know *everything* about Hyeong-cheol and what he did and didn't mean."

"Well, I have spent more time with him than you, that's just the honest truth."

Shi-yoon ignores Eun-seok and looks down at Hyeong-cheol, her voice clipped as she says, "Hyeong-cheol, I'm so sorry you had to live with to live with him for so long. He's making this moment annoying, isn't he...? What should we do to make things fun? Do you want to go to the store to pick some toys for your room?"

Somewhere between wanting to leave his mother and wishing to go to the park, Hyeong-cheol finds himself detaching from the world around him as thoughts of *The Little Prince* and his sheep dance in his mind.

He isn't purposefully trying to ignore her; no, it's just that his mind will often take him on adventures he hasn't the time to consent to.

But this, unfortunately, is something else that Shi-yoon has no desire to understand, nor care for.

"This is pointless... There's literally nothing normal about him, and he hates me... That's why he won't respond. How am I supposed to keep him here...?" Shi-yoon almost whispers, staring at the boy who's yet to return to the present while Eun-seok muses, "He never said he hated you, and most likely he's not answering because the new medication he's on for his ADHD makes him space out at times, and he's still adjusting to it. I'm sure if you truly are ready to live with him again, it will work out." to which Shi-yoon laughs and says, "Oh, I bet. It's always something with you, isn't it, Hyeong–cheol...? Oh well, I still love you... I just might not miss you when the government takes you away."

At that, Eun-seok pales, and Shi-yoon swears she hears him panic as he says, "Shi-yoon, what are you talking about? Those are just rumors. Rumors." to which she only laughs, brushing away the hair that shields Hyeong-cheol's eyes as she murmurs, "Hyeong-cheol… I know I say I hate you sometimes, but I do have days I love you. Do you have those days?"

"'Do you have those days…?'" He's just returned from his adventure, Hyeong-cheol, and trying to think of a response, trying to process her question after being away in his mind is proving rather difficult.

"I asked if you have days you love me, Hyeong-cheol."

He does want to answer his mother, but love is such a complicated emotion for Hyeong-cheol that he's often not sure what to think or do about it at all.

Eun-seok says it's one thing, and his mother says it's another; even the prince in his favorite story seemed baffled by it.

Does he love his mother…?

She's such a tiring cycle, this woman, yet he's unable to fully agree with the feeling of hatred on the days she frustrates him into tears, completely fails to notice him, or even the days she's hurt him so terribly he's unable to feel anything else but the pain she afflicted, and the horrible case of despondency that always follows after.

He's tried to hate her… He really has, but something always stops him.

The same thing will happen to his caretakers, and they're constantly insisting he loves them, so he supposes he must love them all.

But that doesn't feel right either…

Oh, no… How very strange this is… He thinks to himself, his brows still furrowed beneath his tousled bangs as he turns to study his mother carefully while chewing his fingers.

"Hyeong-cheol is… Hyeong-cheol is thinking he does not know. He's so very puzzled. Do you want a hug?" He says this because he remembers she wanted one earlier and feels she won't be as sad about his answer if he gives her one, even though he's still rather opposed to it.

But she's not responding.

She's merely staring at him as though he shouldn't have offered such at all.

But why does she look like that, though?

Eun-seok clears his throat.

The clock above the stove chimes.

And this is all that happens before Hyeong-cheol finds himself harshly shoved off his mother's lap and onto the floor.

- Five -

No Longer any Difference

Hyeong-cheol's book falls from his hand the moment his knees hit the floor, his paper friends flying from between the pages and scattering around him as the warm sensation of urine confirms his mother has truly frightened him.

"Okay, Hyeong-cheol, we're leaving. Miss Song isn't treating you right. Maybe tomorrow we can try again." Eun-seok bends to lift Hyeong-cheol up from the floor, but Shi-yoon is not done releasing her rage, and Eun-seok does not expect her to take her coffee and throw it.

"THIS IS THE THANKS I GET FOR TRYING TO GET BETTER FOR YOU! THIS IS THE THANKS I GET FOR TRYING TO BE A FRICKEN MOTHER!"

The cup shatters on the floor after hitting the side of Hyeong-cheol's head, the liquid splashing against his clothes and causing the air around him to dwindle.

And yet, despite the red blossoming from his scalp, it's the coffee that pains him.

Yes, it's cold, but Hyeong-cheol has always hated the feeling of liquids assaulting him.

It's frightfully discomforting, and it's never failed to bring about the desire to detach his soul from his body, and this is why he can't escape when she starts hitting him, smacking the back of his head and screaming obscenities that have forced his hands to press against his ears so hard they're shaking, his breath hitching in his throat as panic alerts his asthma they're very close to fighting each other.

He's so wet, he has to change his clothes!
He's so wet, he has to change his clothes!

They're stepping on them.

Miss Song and Eun-seok are stepping all over his paper friends as Eun-seok struggles to pull his mother out of the kitchen, the head of the prince himself torn by the heel of his mother's worn purple sneakers as a terrible case of vertigo worsens this boy's panic.

"Shi-yoon, you're making this worse. Stop it!"

"I don't want to see that ungrateful fool ever again!"

"You don't have to! Hyeong-cheol can continue living with Sung-hee and me, as I've been telling you. We're not going to court for shared custody if you're still—!"

"I SHOULD HAVE LEFT YOU JUST LIKE THAT STUPID EXCUSE OF A MAN WHO CALLED HIMSELF MY HUSBAND! IF I'M SUCH A WITCH, MAYBE YOU SHOULD…!"

She tries to pull away and hit him, but Eun-seok swiftly pushes her against the wall while tightening his grip on her wrists, his tone so much softer now as he says,

"Shi-yoon, stop. You can't hurt him like that and expect him to love you when all you do every time you see him is verbally and physically abuse him.

You and Hyeong-cheol are both upsetting each other because you're still resenting him. I can take him home, but you have to stop antagonizing him. You know how he is already. It doesn't matter how long it's been since you last saw him.

He's still autistic, he's still afraid to be around you, and biologically, he's still your child, whether you like it or not."

Shi-yoon's hands shake in Eun-seok's grasp as she stares up at him, thinning cinnamon-colored hair falling into her wide hazel eyes as she chokes, *"I don't even want him, though! I've never wanted him, you know that! And you always pretend I'm the only one hurting him...! But your touch is bad too, yet I'm the only one who—!"* Shi-yoon pales when Eun-seok grips her harder, blocking Hyeong-cheol's view by stepping in front of him as he says, sounding heavily offended, "Shi-yoon, my touch is anything but wrong. It's pure and uncorrupted because of the work we put into our relationship and the consensual feelings we have towards each other. Your touch lacks consent and leaves bruises because you have no relationship whatsoever with Hyeong-cheol. It's formed from pent-up anger and aggression towards a child you've hated since he was born, and that's why he's afraid of you."

"Eun-seok, you *know* why I hate him! And you justify yourself in the same *stupid* way every time when we talk about this! You're a *pedophile, and I know it!"*

"I am not a pedophile!"

"Then what the heck are you? You're a grown man who sexually abuses a cognitively impaired child! With his girlfriend, at that! Who knows what else you're doing? Maybe you're a part of that sick cult of Haven! Maybe you're—!"

"I am not affiliated with that organization, and I don't abuse children." His tone is so stiff, those bright caramel-colored eyes of his glaring down at her as he continues, "I have never abused any child. Hyeong-cheol knows I'm not abusing him. He consents to our games because he likes them, and he knows that's how we express our love for each other. He's not afraid of me like he is of you because I'm not abusing him. I make him feel safe and loved, just like Sung-hee. Pedophiles hurt and destroy children's lives. Hyeong-cheol has a great life, he gets anything he wants, and he's loved unconditionally."

"You're completely *delusional!* Do you even hear what you're saying? Why can no one else but me see it? It-it's like you're the one who never stopped doing drugs! You said we would change together, and yet you're still a *complete monster!*"

"If I'm a monster, then what was your mother? What was mine? Do you really think I act like them?"

"I think you've been brainwashed to cope with your childhood through—!"

Hyeong-cheol edges further away from the grown-ups until he's beneath the little round table and surrounded by the wooden legs of the chairs, which act as though the bars of a prison cell he's peeking through.

His ears are ringing from the volume of his mother's shouts, and dizziness is starting to distort his senses, but there is nothing he can do but continue covering his ears while hiding beneath this table.

Perspiration is gathering beneath his bangs as he struggles to inhale, and his chest aches from the effort of breathing while tears haze his vision, giving the illusion that perhaps he is dying, perhaps the snake did bite him, and maybe that's why he's unable to release his ears and retrieve his inhaler, which has always hung conveniently from his neck, right beneath his yellow scarf.

"If I were the monster, I think Hyeong-cheol would be treating me more like you, Shi-yoon. Look at what you're doing to him." Eun-seok turns Shi-yoon in the direction of her child, his small and shaking form barely visible from beneath the table.

"I would hate to be the cause of that reaction." He lets her go then, making his way over to the boy who's struggling to breathe and pushing back the chairs to join him beneath the table.

"Hyeong-cheol, you need to take your medicine. I understand you're scared, so I'm going to help you, okay?" Eun-seok's tone is so gentle, so much sincerity lacing it as he begins administering the boy's medicine, reiterating hushed words of reassurance as Hyeong-cheol's eyes lock with his own, the scattered shards of green within the pale fawn shimmering with the bubbling of tears as his hands shake against his ears.

He's calming down with me. He always calms down with me because he trusts that I can make him better.

He's not afraid of me because he knows I will never treat him harshly like the pedophiles Shi-yoon associates me with because our relationship has everything theirs doesn't.

Gentleness...

Consent…

Eternal love and a mutual agreement that we have in our relationship is because of devotion, not age.

That's what makes our relationship so special.

Shi-yoon is watching them; Eun-seok knows this and hears the cries she fails to hide behind her hand as he continues to calm her son.

But Eun-seok exhibits no sympathy as he murmurs, frowning down at the boy, "Miss Song scared you, didn't she? Now you're all wet and uncomfortable because of it, and your head is bleeding. But it's okay because we can go upstairs and change you and help your head. I know how unhappy you feel right now…" He can feel Shi-yoon's eyes casting her anger upon him, but it only makes him start to smile as he runs a hand through Hyeong-cheol's tousled head of sorrel, carefully avoiding his injury while continuing, in a tone so soft and therapeutic, "Let's go upstairs so we can get better together. Should I carry you so we can run and pretend she's the snake in *The Little Prince* book?"

Though he's forever confused and unsure of his feelings towards Eun-seok, *The Little Prince* has always been something he's sure of. And despite the many ways it's been used to manipulate him most of his life, Hyeong-cheol is still unable to reject anyone that mentions his favorite story, because once they've mentioned it, all the negativity associated with them will cease to exist, no matter the situation, because it's very difficult for this boy to differentiate between good and bad when both are happening at once. It seems to him you can't be bad if you're doing something good, and you surely can't be good if you're doing something bad.

So Hyeong-cheol can't help but display a faint smile after his inhaler leaves his lips, and images of his favorite story haze his mind as though a bombing of drugs.

A laugh escapes him once gravity shifts beneath him after leaving the tables of security, and veils of delight have made that faint smile brighter as Eun-seok rushes past his mother and swiftly ascends the steps, too familiar with the boy's accidents to reconsider carrying him.

"We made it, Hyeong-cheol! Now we have to close the door so the snake can't get in," Eun-seok says after setting the boy down, pushing the door shut as Hyeong-cheol utters over his fingers, "O-Oh no-! This is not… this is not the room for…!"

"Yeah, I know this isn't your room. We're hiding from Miss Song, though, remember? She's the snake now, so, of course, she won't think to check her room first."

"Oh, but he does not enjoy the room of the snake…!"

"It's okay, Hyeong-cheol. We'll have fun." Eun-seok tells him, a strange and impatient sort of look in those caramel eyes as his hand finds the doorknob again to crack it open just a bit, because now he wants to prove a point to Shi-yoon. Now he wants to remind her that no matter what she says about him and the way he treats Hyeong-cheol, he will never be abusive like she is because it's what he believes that makes him think he's not.

"Hyeong-cheol, quick! We have to go into the bathroom before she sees us. She's coming up the stairs— let's go…!"

Hyeong-cheol tilts his head as he bites harder at his fingers, anxiety tormenting his belly as he reaches to push the door closed, only to be lifted and swiftly carried away into the bathroom the moment his fingers brush against it.

"She almost got you, Hyeong-cheol! It's a good thing my the airplane was working, wasn't it?" Eun-seok can tell the boy is getting anxious upon being in the bathroom, patting his ears and furrowing his brows beneath his sorrel hair as he presses himself into the corner right between the toilet and the sink, slowly sliding down the wall and into a crouch as he says, as if that one sentence from his caretaker has exposed his intentions, "Oh no, Eun-seok is not the pilot! Min-ho is the pilot because Eun-seok has always been the snake!"

"Hyeong-cheol, the roles of the game don't have to be the same every time, and I can't be the snake because Miss Song is the snake." Eun-seok gently reminds him, feeling slightly agitated at his words as he lowers himself to his knees in front of Hyeong-cheol, fighting the urge to cover his mouth when he cries, erupting into tears, "*E-Eun-seok wants to make Hyeong-cheol bleed again! It was s-so very—!*"

"Hyeong-cheol, that was just an accident because you weren't ready, and I didn't prepare you the way I should have. I'm sorry I hurt you. It was wrong of me to rush you, but we aren't playing that game today. We're just going to play our feelings game while I change your clothes and clean your wound, because I know being in here scares you and—"

"*N-no bathroom, no game! He does not like to be here!*"

"Hyeong-cheol, do you want to wear your Little Prince clothes and read me your story after? Because I don't remember it as well as you do, and you haven't gotten to wear those clothes today."

Confused yet intrigued by the preposition, Hyeong-cheol lowers a hand into his mouth while hitting the other quite hard against his ear, echoing over his fingers while staring into Eun-seok's eyes, "'Do you... do you want to wear your Little Prince clothes and read me your st-st-story?'"

"Yeah, we can read your story after we play our game because I feel bad for scaring you last time, and I know playing this game will make us both happy. Then we'll be all done, and you can visit your friends while I stay and help Miss Song. I won't even turn the camera on."

"'Then we'll be done, and we and you can visit... y-your friends...'"

Disorientation colors Hyeong-cheol's mind as Eun-seok vigorously nods while pulling him out of the bathroom's corner, softly reminding him how much he loves him, for he always voices such before he paralyzes him with his touch, and it's always confusing, every single time.

Hyeong-cheol seems to slip into a spell of vacancy, staring at the ground to avert his gaze from the growing pile of clothes before him and resuming the vigorous patting of his ears, momentarily leaving this world entirely.

"Hyeong-cheol? I said if you need your inhaler, we can take a break, okay...? Anytime you're feeling uncomfortable, just..."

"*Oh, he's feeling s-so very uncomfortable, t-time for a break!*" Hyeong-cheol forces out through his tears, clapping his hands harder against his ears as Eun-seok, growing frustrated with Hyeong-cheol's attempts at escaping this game, pulls him closer and says, leaning forward to capture eyes that swiftly avert themselves to the floor,

"I know it's hard for you to be in here because of what happened with Miss Song's bad friend, but he's not here anymore, and being inside the bathroom won't bring him back, and it won't make me hurt you like he did, okay…? That was a long time ago. You were barely three, and I didn't know that man wanted to hurt you, no one did. He was terrible, and that's why he got sent away. That's why it was so scary. I'm really sorry that happened, though. I was irresponsible and assumed things I shouldn't have because me and Miss Song were taking things we shouldn't have…" He pauses then, studying Hyeong-cheol's tear-streaked face before continuing, a bit softer now, "That's why I stopped making myself sick with those drugs after that. Because I love you, and I don't want anyone else to treat you that way. Do you still love me…?"

"'*Do you still… do you still love me?' Oh, no, thank you, let's be all done, a-all DONE!*'"

"Hey, Hyeong-cheol, we're not yelling. And you can't be all done because we haven't even started yet. We can't read your book or get your Little Prince clothes unless we play our game, remember? And you like playing this game, it makes us both really happy. It's okay to…"

Hyeong-cheol tries repeatedly to cover his ears and get rid of the uncomfortable feeling Eun–seok's voice is bringing him, but he keeps removing his hands, his tone remaining the same as he reassures, "It's okay, Hyeong-cheol, I know you're scared, but it's not a bad game we're playing… It's a special game because of how we feel towards each other, remember…? You don't have to be scared, you can tell me you want to play, and then when we're all done, we get your reward."

"*Bye, E-Eun-s-seok! Bye!*"

"Oh, Hyeong-cheol, I'm not leaving. I know it's a lot, but you don't have to get frustrated. Would you like to play it in your mother's bed instead? So then the snake won't have a place to sleep? I know the bathroom scares you. I just wanted to try to clean you up, but we can wait until we finish our game. You could have told me you had to use the bathroom earlier, Hyeong-cheol, why did you wait?"

Hyeong-cheol dismisses the question and claps his hands repeatedly over his ears, sorrowfully reiterating as he stands once Eun-seok releases him, "'*Would you like to play it in your mother's bed instead? So then the snake won't have a place to-t-to sleep?*'" while going over to sit on his mother's bed, bringing his hand to his teeth to try to feel something other than what he's feeling right now, because right now, anxiety is wrapping too tightly around his throat. It seems as though the same elephant that made his asthma attack him earlier will sit again, very soon, on his chest.

Oh, it's not the scary game! Eun-seok says it's the feelings game, so there will be no more 'thoughtless mistakes' and no more blood...! Hyeong-cheol should be very happy, but he is still feeling very afraid and so very unwell. What should he do about all these bad feelings? What should he do?

He's bleeding now; his teeth have bitten his fingers too hard, and the sight of such has sent him into panic.

He wipes his fingers frantically onto the blanket beneath him, but it's worse that way, and now he's crying too hard to catch his breath.

Eun-seok reiterates his love for him, and a veil of discomforting emotions wraps around this boy as his hands are captured and the world around him seems to flicker between monochrome and carmine, too many memories assaulting him along with this game as the terrible urge to vomit clenches his stomach and claws at his throat.

"It's okay, Hyeong-cheol, you like this game... It's fun, and fun is good, remember...? You're just feeling shy, but that's okay because we can still love each other, and that makes me feel really happy."

They didn't play the game they played yesterday, yet he still sees red after it's over, after Eun-seok makes him take a bath before changing him into his Little Prince attire.

Still sees red after they read his favorite story right inside the fort Eun-seok made on his mother's bed after discarding the blankets.

He sees it on his hands, even with the new band-aids.

He sees it on the floor, on Eun-seok's face.

There seems to be no difference anymore, no difference to these games, because his feelings towards them keep being the same in his mind.

Eun-seok is making 'thoughtless mistakes' even when it's the feelings game... and he still does not like it... It's still so very scary to play those games, but Eun-seok is reading his book, so everything's okay now?

He draws his knees to his chest to try and quiet the trouble-some thumping of his heart, but everything sounds so loud he's forced to cover his ears because everything feels as though it's talking to him at once.

Eun-seok is too loud, and it's merging with the sound of his heartbeat.

The wind outside is jarring.

The clock above the door is paining him.

The sound of his own breathing is agonizing to him, and now he's crying, which doesn't help at all, especially when the world around him has yet to awaken from its odd coloring.

"Hyeong-cheol, what's wrong…? We're reading your favorite story and cuddling. Why are you crying?"

Eun-seok's words sting his ears despite how hard he's pressing down on them, perhaps because he's too close because he insisted on holding him.

He refused to let him go, despite his pleas to sit by himself.

Everything is still red, even with the tears that blur his vision, and the cacophony of sounds continues even after the story is finished.

– Six –

Life Is Often Uncomfortable

Chae-won is in the garden again, sitting amongst the various flowers surrounding him in this circle as he draws his knees to his chest and folds his arms over them, tilting his head to view the sun descending into the gradually darkening sky.

He's out here again because his aunt isn't, and he and San-ah don't have a very good relationship because he and San-ah disagree too much to ever truly have the relationship Chae-won's grandmother thinks they have...

This front garden, the one Chae-won's maintained from the time he was very young, has been his safe place away from all those troublesome thoughts that occur when he sees those videos that should very well be illegal on his aunt's computer, the only place he can go to pretend she's not as disgusting as she is because he doesn't have to be reminded of what she watches in her room when he avoids his home.

But even though Chae-won's here and not there, his mind won't stop repeating those images as though he is, indeed, in that house behind him, and those thoughts bring anxiety, and Chae-won hates anxiety almost as much as silence, because anxiety so often threatens and compels him to do things that he has no desire to do, and when he ignores those urges, however meaningless they may be, his mind offers terrible consequences.

And even though he knows his house won't burn down if he fails to count every blade of grass in his vicinity, he also knows it *could*, so he's forced by such paranoia to do whatever the little voice he inwardly calls Despondency commands him to, because what if the voice is right, finally telling the truth? What if he really does get sick if he doesn't mirror the movements of those around him at school?

What if the world really does end because he ignores the voice that warns him? If he fails to count to ten approximately forty times after a small child sneezes on him, his life, and every-one else's, could truly be over.

Such things are very troublesome for Chae-won, but he knows there must be some truth to the voice because of how sick he feels when he tries to ignore it.

And being sick means your body is unhealthy, and an unhealthy body can often lead to death.

Chae-won swears he nearly loses his life ten times each day, and others (because he's so often threatened with the lives of those he loves or doesn't even know) about six or seven.

Even with the medication he takes for his Obsessive Compulsive Disorder, he still finds his life very, very mentally exhausting at times...

Anyways, it's almost seven o'clock now, and he's supposed to have already started walking to go and sleep over at the Choi's house moments ago, but then again, that was before his aunt decided to come home and watch those horrid videos, before he was deeply troubled, and before he started wondering if sleeping over at his friend's house would be worth enduring so many hours of Choon-ha's antics when he could just stay and take more notes on the world around him, something he particularly likes to do with Eun-seok, for he's never liked that man, and strongly feels as if he's some sort of criminal the more he watches him and his *family* from the living room window, as they have a habit of leaving their window open…

He sighs a heavy sigh, a faint wind whispering through his flowers and causing his dyed, mellow blonde hair to fall over the wide-rimmed glasses his small, nutmeg-colored eyes hide behind.

"Why do I always agree to be social when it literally kills me…?" Chae-won mutters, pushing up his glasses as he stands to pull his oversized blue hoodie over his jeans, which match his hoodie's color perfectly, for he's never able to leave his home without matching colors, as not matching brings about the anxiety that *something* isn't right, while matching gives him an odd sort of peace, a comforting feeling of reassurance that says, *'Ah yes, whatever wasn't right before is certainly right, now.'*

And though he can't truly dress in such a way at school, he does try his hardest, matching the color of his socks with his shoes and jackets and writing the day's color across his forefinger with marker, something he has to be quite consistent with as it fades with the washing of his hands.

But enough about that.

It's time to return to the present, where Chae-won is sighing and deciding begrudgingly to go back into the house he ran from to gather what he needs for his routine weekend escape.

The sky above him darkens as he shifts uncomfortably while drumming his fingers nervously against his thighs, trudging up the walkway as his glasses slip a bit down his slender nose.

I suppose I should tell you a bit more about this friend before we continue his story, as it's hard for one to fully comprehend another's life without any telling, and he's walking slowly on purpose, you see because he has no desire to open that door.

Chae-won's seventeen, like Hyeong-cheol (although that boy is older than him by a few months), is often wearing a look that says, *'The world is ending, and I'm not sure what to do about it,'* and has a bad habit of dying his brown hair blond because he believes lighter colors ward off anxiety (despite practically being made of such).

He's been told his eyes are small like his face (though he's never cared too much to confirm it), with a slender nose and a thin frame, which comes from eating inconsistently throughout his life.

"Please don't be awake…" Chae-won mutters as he carefully opens the door, cringing at the shrill squeak of it as his eyes dart around the unlit room while sending several prayers up to be left alone.

As he gets closer to his room, he sees the pale glow of the TV spilling out into the dark hallway and realizes his grandma, at least, has fallen asleep. The remote falls from her slender hand as Chae-won enters the room to silence the TV, pausing because there's a crime scene being documented on the news, and crime scenes have always been a bit of an obsession for him, for better or worse.

"*It's not just our district that has faced these kinds of assaults and-and attempts at murder.*

133

The police, as a whole, are being targeted by mentally disabled and psychotic individuals who are in alignment with…"

A soft groan causes Chae-won to jump, his finger automatically powering off the television as though he was caught watching something he wasn't supposed to be watching at all, which, I suppose he was, as both his aunt and his grandma have told him countless times the news and anything else involving real people and crimes is to be shut off immediately due to his paranoia.

Though Chae-won would argue, he actually feels more paranoid without knowing what's happening in the world, as being aware of a murderer and their tactics only makes you more prepared in case the murderer were to target you.

"Sorry for waking you, Grandma. I'll be going now." Chae-won says, hurrying towards the door and tripping over the remote in the process, which was bound to happen because this room, like the entire house, is practically shrouded in darkness.

"Goodness, turn on a light for once around here. You and your aunt are obsessed with darkness."

"Auntie keeps the lights off because she's weird. Disgusting, some might even say. I keep them off at night because no one can see whose home it is if there's no light. Most people would agree it's safer that way."

His grandmother laughs, the loud creak of her bed indicating she's sat up as she reaches to turn on the small lamp atop the table beside her, her smiling face illuminated as she squints at Chae-won through square lenses and says, "Aren't you supposed to be a sweet boy?" to which Chae-won, who hasn't once referred to himself or anyone else for that matter as a *'sweet boy,'* cringes inwardly before deciding to lift his shoulders in an awkward shrug.

What else is one to do?

Chae-won's grandmother is sixty-seven, though she looks like she's only forty, with twinkling, upturned mocha eyes, a nose she's paid quite a bit for, and skin that's smooth and radiant after several Botox treatments.

She hides her thinning silver hair beneath many different wigs, some colorful and eye-catching, others simply black or brown, with subtle waves.

She wears a pink bonnet now, as she's supposed to be sleeping, and Chae-won wonders briefly what wig she wore today because he hadn't had the time to say goodbye to her, as his daily routine of ensuring everything was unplugged and turned off before school caused him to be a whole dreadful hour late, simply because nothing felt as though it was truly unplugged or turned off, and his mind refused to stop obsessing over whether the house would explode because of it.

"Chae-won, be honest. Has your auntie really been as disgusting as you say she is?"

"Oh, grandma, we have this conversation every time she's not around. Of course, she's disgusting." He shifts uncomfortably, suddenly wanting nothing more than to delve into the news story he was forced to shut off. "You should try setting her up with someone her own age. Anyway, I'm off to have a sleepover."

"But she's never given me any indication—"

"Uhm, I've said goodbye already. I'm afraid that's because I'm leaving."

He hates sounding so cruel, but it's frustrating, these frequent conversations about his aunt, because his grandma never seems to understand or remember them.

135

And so he's walking out of her room and off to venture into his own.

While Chae-won's venturing to retrieve his sleeping bag and such, I will mention, because this is very important, that he lives four houses down from Eun-seok Sung-hee, and that Kyun-ho and his family live six houses down, the last house on the block nestled in the more wooded area of dalkomhan.

This neighborhood is supposed to be home to the more wealthy families, despite not having very many amenities.

Chae-won's aunt is a lawyer, Kyun-ho's brother owns a bar (plus they inherited their parent's house), and Sung-hee owns a very successful independent fashion line, while Eun-seok, a retired therapist, works from home to help her care for Hyeong-cheol. He also claims he owns some sort of company involving finance, and often shows off his wealth through the arrival of different cars.

Eun-seok has so much money, he owns *another* house in *another* neighborhood that he and his family will often take vacations to, the much larger house in the much wealthier neighborhood, with the fancy TVs, the pool, and the large indoor playground containing a ball pit (which is often where you'll find Hyeong-cheol if he's not hiding beneath the slide).

Undeniably, it's quite a lovely home, and although Chae-won's been there with his friends multiple times before, he can never truly enjoy all it contains because he can never feel comfortable in that house, because to him, it always feels as though someone is watching.

Anyway, Chae-won has finished packing his sleepover necessities, but he hasn't left his room yet because the lock on his window is bothering him.

He's shut and locked it five times already, yet it doesn't *feel* as though he's done those things at all.

And so he does it again, this time turning the lock rapidly back and forth while counting down from forty because forty usually feels right, and not counting at all feels quite foreboding.

Eventually, after five minutes of repeating his counting and locking, the window seems to smile, and he's able to step back and say, "There, now no one can open you unless they're inside."

And so, satisfied, Chae-won puts on his backpack and leaves his home, his thoughts returning to the news and what all they were going to say before it was shut off.

Halfway down the driveway and knee-deep into his thoughts, though, he has to pause and turn back to his house because he worries the door isn't *truly* locked as it should be and that someone, maybe even someone psychotic as they said on the news, could easily slip inside and murder both his grandmother and aunt.

And so he has to go and fumble with the handle a couple of times to ease the rising anxiety in his stomach, drumming his fingers vigorously against his thigh to mentally track the number of times he's turned this handle as perspiration begins to gather beneath his bangs.

He's so engrossed in this compulsion that he doesn't notice the bright headlights from the red Mercedes that pulls up into his driveway, closing his eyes to inwardly curse himself because he's forgotten what number he'd been on and now must start again.

"Chae-won…? Do you need a ride…?"

The strange and familiar sincerity of Eun-seok's voice causes Chae-won to jump and fall on his bottom to the cement, more than startled by the man because he hadn't expected to see him walking up his driveway.

"No, I-I can walk...!" He stammers, forcing himself to stand and gather what little composure he has as he looks up at Eun-seok.

"Chae-won, why do you always get so scared when I talk to you? We've known each other for so long— have I ever done anything to harm you or someone you know? If so, you need to tell me because it makes me feel bad."

A soft breeze whispers through the trees and ruffles Chae-won's hair as he lifts his shoulders in a rather weak shrug, always feeling uncomfortable in the man's presence and never truly knowing why...

Well, no, maybe he does know why.

He'd written about it time and time again in so many note-books, it'd be impossible to say he didn't know why he felt so uneasy in Eun-seok's presence.

He's paranoid the man's like his aunt, but worse because he feels Eun-seok does not keep his addiction inside a computer screen but acts upon it because he has the resource.

Chae-won strongly feels this man is a pedophile.

"I... no, I-I don't believe I've caught you harming anyone yet. I mean..." Chae-won flushes and runs a hand through his bangs. "I guess I'm just a person who gets easily intimidated because anxiety puts me on edge." He laughs then, instantly cringing at such because Eun-seok does not look amused; he looks, for what-ever reason, greatly offended.

"Well, I'm sorry I intimidate you... Is it... is it because of my height?" Eun-seok frowns, seeming genuinely concerned about this matter as he stares down at Chae-won, the wind blowing a loose strand of chocolate-colored hair in his eye.

"N-no-no, Kyun-ho's actually taller than you by-by like an inch. It's not the height that intimidates me. No, no, it's-it's just my imagination. It runs rampant and distorts my perception of most people." Chae-won reassures him, drumming his fingers nervously against his thighs as he forces himself to hold Eun-seok's gaze, unable to rid the feeling that there's something terribly wrong with this man even though there's no evidence big enough to currently support such thoughts, for Eun-seok is such a kind and considerate fellow, it makes Chae-won's friends and those around him furrow their brows whenever he says something negative about him because no one else seems to be unsettled by the man's presence, no one else but Hyeong-cheol on the days he's unhappy with his caretaker, and Kyun-ho on the days his paranoia gets the best of him, though he's always struggled to fully trust those who claim to be his friend.

I know he's a pedophile, though, I just know it.

There's so much more to Eun-seok than his perfect smile, bright caramel eyes, and sincere voice...

His actual body and all its organs, yes, but... more in the sense that he's hiding something.

"Well, I'm sorry anyway. Maybe if we knew each other a bit more, you wouldn't have to feel that way. I would say we could do something tonight, but I won't be able to stay after I drop Hyeong-cheol off because his mother's not having a good day."

"Oh, uh, Kyun-ho is actually at work right now. He's only off on Sundays still." Chae-won stammers, trying to politely tell Eun-seok *not* to bring Hyeong-cheol over because he's never been able to visit when Kyun-ho or his caretakers aren't around, mostly because violence can be rather abrupt in that boy, and partly because he refuses to use or go into a bathroom, resulting in 'training pants' (that simply look like toddler pull-ups to Chae-won) that are to be changed strictly at his own home, which gives Kyun-ho the unpleasant task of walking the boy over to his house every time he says he needs to change, which is rare because Hyeong-cheol has mastered the art of holding his bladder and burdening his caretakers with numerous trips to the hospital.

"Also," Chase-won adds, "if Kyun-ho were home, he'd most likely be suffering from a lack of sleep, making him very unreliable for babysitting."

Eun-seok merely smiles, those bright caramel eyes of his emitting such a warm sense of security that Chae-won momentarily forgets to dislike him.

"Luckily, I asked Min-ho about it before I told Hyeong-cheol we were going. He said he's getting off early today and would love to have him, which is really something because I just wouldn't know what to do if I couldn't leave him at Kyun-ho's house. Sung-hee is meeting with someone about her business tonight, and unfortunately, his mother is too unstable to be left alone right now. I took a gamble, leaving to bring him here."

"Uhm, really? Well… well, that's good, I guess…" Chae-won murmurs, scratching his head as Eun-seok beams again, his tone so light and jovial as he says,

"It is, isn't it? I just came to offer you a ride. You're going to the Choi's house too, right?" to which Chae-won, conflicted on whether he should confirm such, averts his attention to Eun-seok's Mercedes to inquire, "Did you switch cars…? You, uh… You're, uh, driving a red one now…" because he had noted earlier this morning, in the notebook he keeps for documenting such information on his friend's caregivers, that Eun-seok left his house driving his white Mercedes right before he left for school this morning.

And yes, of course, it's odd to document such information about your neighbors, but for Chae-won, writing down the things that bother him about the adults he knows is the only way to calm the anxiety that frequently tells him, *'The world is not safe. The world is not safe because the world is full of criminals who live right beside and around you.'*

This is partly because he invests so much time in *True Crime*, and because he's feared the presence of criminals ever since he discovered his aunt was one. And though she's never *truly* acted on her attraction to minors, as I mentioned before, the fact that she is not discreet with her browser history, openly flirts with students, and tells strange jokes regarding sadism and consent, is enough to make him paranoid to live with her.

His anxiety level is so high around her that he's currently filled thirteen notebooks regarding his thoughts and concerns for that lady.

"Red car…? Oh, yeah, Hyeong-cheol's mother is out of rehab, so we left to visit her after I got Hyeong-cheol from school. You know how he likes my red car more… *The Little Prince* rose and all. But, um, yeah, the visit itself didn't go too well, though. She, uh, she's still physically and verbally abusing him, and it caused him a lot of distress…"

An odd silence fills the air, Chae-won uncomfortably shifting because he hasn't a clue what to say, and Eun-seok staring at him expectantly because he clearly thinks Chae-won *should* have something to say.

"Oh, darn…that's-that's bad. I, uh, I thought she would have gotten better with that; Is he okay?"

"Well, you know, obviously, the initial shock caused a lot of meltdowns. Of course, she was yelling a lot, and that overstimulated him, but I think I did a good job cheering him up. He just needed a lot of love to reassure him everything was okay once we left."

"Well… that's nice."

"It is, isn't it?" Eun-seok smiles, seeming quite proud of himself, which only makes Chae-won grow more suspicious of him.

"So, are you heading to the Choi's house? I shouldn't have assumed." Eun-seok says, putting his hands in the pockets of his black leather jacket as Chae-won, not exactly wanting him to know, shrugs.

"You're going to walk all by yourself? I mean, I know you usually do it, but haven't you seen what's been happening to the children on the news?"

"I mean, yeah, I have… but, like… those children were kidnapped from the Serenity center, right? That place is far— plus, the victims, you know— they're pretty visibly messed up. I mean, not messed up, but sick—mentally unwell, I mean," And he awkwardly laughs because he feels he may have offended Eun-seok by stumbling over his words.

"Well, it's actually not that far. Kyun-ho walks there to visit his friend in the adult unit, remember? Or does he take a taxi? Regardless, it's close enough for me to worry about the safety of the children here... even if you all are older than the recent victims, you're still..." Eun-seok emits a deep sigh, smoothing his dark chestnut-colored hair away from his concerned eyes as he continues, a bit softer, "You're all still young. Maybe I'm just overly paranoid because of Hyeong-cheol, and how trusting he is. I don't even feel comfortable taking him to school now, even if he does only go three days out of the week. He's just so vulnerable, I'm always worried someone will hurt him, and he'll be too confused and scared to tell me."

"Did you hear about the police officers getting killed? It was on the news, but I didn't get to look into it."

Chae-won knows he should have said something else, knows he's coming off as insensitive, merely tossing aside Eun-seok's worries and presenting a different conversation, but Eun-seok has always made him feel so terribly uncomfortable, he's unable to place his thoughts.

"Oh, yes. It's... terrible, really. The deaths, the riots... it seems like everyone's losing a bit of their humanity." Eun-seok sighs, shaking his head before inquiring, much to Chae-won's dismay, "So, are you still going to walk? It just doesn't seem right to let you walk these streets alone with everything going on..."

"Yeah, I'm fine. I wouldn't know what to say to Hyeong-cheol right now regarding his, uhm, current situation. Thanks, though, Mister Na." Chae-won doesn't wait for a response. He steps into his house after saying goodbye and quickly shuts and locks the door, rushing to his bedroom and pulling the thick, sorrel-colored notebook from under his bed, using the fountain pen from his pocket and hurriedly jotting down a brief description of what just happened, tapping his lips seven times to ensure Eun-seok hadn't noticed how anxious he was, and jumping upon feeling his aunt's hand on his shoulder.

"You're not recording my bad behavior again, are you, Ahn...?"

Chae-won sighs, shutting his journal and sliding it back up under his bed as he says, "Uhm, no, I've moved on to someone else, and can you please stop calling me by my last name?" to which his aunt merely shrugs before saying simply, "Listen, *Chae-won*, I know my choice of TV makes you uncomfortable, but you don't have to stay here. You have lovely friends, don't you? Maybe you should live with them for a couple of days."

"Yeah... but I also know there are tons of other 'shows ' you could be watching... things that aren't... uh, illegal, even if you do have a thousand locks on your door..." Chae-won shifts a bit before blinking expectantly at his aunt from behind his wide-rimmed glasses, noting she's dressed as though preparing for a formal party and thinking it's odd his grandma looks so much prettier than her when she's so much older.

Perhaps because his grandmother looks kind, and his aunt looks as though she'd rather not look at you at all.

His aunt, with a narrow nose and high cheekbones, gives him a hard stare as she plays with an inky black coil of hair, twirling it as though a ribbon around her finger and pursing her lips at her deceased sister's child.

"Well, you won't be back until Sunday if you're doing another sleepover with *that* particular family… So we won't have to deal with each other for a while."

"*That* particular family is the only family I do sleepovers with, I'm afraid."

"I know, but I do wish they didn't have to be so controversial. I guess that's why you're so intrigued by them, though… the Choi's have more secrets than me."

Chae-won shrugs, unzipping his bag to ensure his most important notebook is present before sealing it back up and heading out the door again, not wanting to dwell on his aunts secrets and ignoring whatever else she tries to tell him when he bids his grandmother a final farewell.

He peeks out the window to make sure the red Mercedes has vanished before rushing out the door and into the darkness.

- Seven -

Perhaps We Shouldn't Keep Secrets After All...

Min-ho shifts uncomfortably on the couch, trying not to feel so anxious about the decisions he's made today as he stares down at his Nintendo, unease tormenting his mind.

Perhaps Hyeong-cheol should not visit today.

Perhaps he should have told his uncle the truth about his day so he wouldn't have to feel as if he's doomed his entire family to death, because that's what it was: a death threat.

Ryu-han whispered while all the children were getting seated in the morning, *"I'm going to come over soon and fix what Haven didn't. There are too many broken toys at your house, so I'm going to do you a favor and take them out."*

He had unzipped his backpack to showcase the gun sitting atop his study books, had stared at Min-ho from beneath side-swiped, ebony bangs, and said, *"This is my dad's gun. He wants to fix what Haven didn't, too, but he wants me and my little sister to do it instead because we're still kids, so there's more we can get away with."*

He still remembers the way his stomach seemed to drop to his feet.

Still remembers the seriousness written all over Ryu-han's face as he zipped his backpack up before placing it beneath his desk.

Still recalls the way his teacher scowled at him when he wrote her a note about Ryu-han's gun after all the others went to lunch.

"Ryu-han may have gotten a better score than you on today's test, but that's no reason to try to get him expelled. His parents are very good and generous people, they would never allow him to carry such a weapon."

He was told to be nice.

He was told to behave and not burden anyone else with the lie before Ryu-han's parents decided not to cater next month's trip to Lotte World.

And for the remainder of the day, Ryu-han harassed him.

He drew morbid pictures, sent crude texts, and recruited other students who bore prejudice against those with mental disabilities and illnesses, and that only made everything worse.

"We should burn them. Shooting them would be too easy."

"We could cut their hearts out."

"We could hang them from that stupid church."

"My dad wanted me to shoot at least one, though. And besides, the easier the kill, the more we could do after. Our country is practically drowning in broken toys. That's what my dad says."

All day, anxiety has been eating Min-ho, and now that he's sitting here, feeling like flesh and bones, he wonders if perhaps he shouldn't hope to gain any sort of rapture tonight because perhaps he doesn't deserve it.

He has been harboring a dangerous secret, after all.

One that has the potential to kill everyone but himself in this house.

Maybe I should have told uncle, but he's been so stressed these days, if Ryu-han was just putting on an act, that would kill him. Figuratively, of course, but still. Maybe we just need to not be alone.

"Hey, mister! Can we play Little Big Planet when Hyeong-cheol comes over?" Choon-ha proposes, hanging upside down beside him on this soft, cerulean-colored couch and earning an odd look of uncertainty from his cousin, who sounds a bit hesitant when he says, "I… I'm not sure. Do you think, uhm, do you think Eun-seok will stay if we ask him to?"

"What in the world, mister? Why would we want that? Mister Eun-seok is a nice man who buys us nice things, but he's not like… sleepover quality. He's a man, a caretaker, a guy. It'd be weird to have him stay." Choon-ha slides off the couch and onto the floor with a small 'thud,' rubbing his rear while wiping his nose with his other hand to add, "And besides, Chae-won comes over tonight, and he's weird about that guy."

Min-ho's cheeks drain of color, and he blinks several times before he's able to form any words at all.

"Chae-won…? Why would he…?"

"Are you feeling okay, mister? You're acting weird."

Oh, dear.

Min-ho had forgotten that a friend would come to sleep over on Fridays, and now he wonders if his visit would make this house even more desirable to Ryu-han because Chae-won's another *'broken toy'*…

He looks down at his Nintendo to save his game in Pokémon Yellow, clearing his throat and saying, as calmly as he can manage with all this anxiety sickening his heart,

"Well, I've been kind of stressed these days because of school, so I thought it'd be fun to invite Hyeong-cheol as a fun sort of distraction. He's good at coming up with random games."

It's mostly true.

Hyeong-cheol, recognized for his habitual escapism into his imagination, is truly the only friend Min-ho has known not to frequently question an abrupt invitation to play.

And he has been stressed.

Just not because of school.

"Eh. *'Fun'* is a word that really depends on his mood, like a lot. Why didn't you just ask me and mister twin buddy to do something with you?"

"Is it wrong of me to want to engage with people that aren't inside this house? Sometimes, I don't want to do things with you. Oftentimes, really. And Yoon-ha has put me on a variable schedule for human interaction, much like Tae—"

All at once, the doorbell chimes, and instant dread pale Min-ho's cheeks as every possible thing that could go wrong with this visit churns his stomach.

Min-ho's eyes dart instinctively down the hall, as Tae-kyun will usually associate doorbells with his brother coming home, but oddly enough, he remains in his room.

Strange… Tae-kyun always runs to the door when someone rings it. Min-ho frowns, listening to the hurried sound of Tae-kyun's piano playing before deciding he's simply too engrossed to notice.

The doorbell rings again, but Min-ho cannot convince himself to move.

It's as though he's become molded to the couch he sits upon.

What if Ryu-han is planning on doing something to us tonight? He said he'd be here 'soon,' but when is 'soon'…? And what are we supposed to do when his dad's a police officer, and his mother's a lawyer? They have so much power and our family has nothing. No one loves us enough to defend us, no one would care if we went missing or—

Choon-ha jumps up to run to the door, startling both Min-ho and Yoon-ha when he shouts, "Oh, it's Mister Chae-won! The *one* and *only* expected friend of tonight!" which causes the house of cards Yoon-ha had been quietly perfecting to fall.

"I-idiot…! W-why… wh-why would you st-startle me, brother?" he fumes, hurrying to rebuild his fallen masterpiece as Min-ho scrambles up to ensure there's no one else behind Chae-won, who looks as though he's run one thousand circles on a record player.

"Mister Chae-won, do you want to—"

"You didn't happen to see any stragglers around, did you?" Min-ho cuts in, trying to mask his anxiety behind an expression he hopes is neutral as Chae-won stammers, glancing this way and that, "I-I what? What, uhm, can I come in? Eun-seok, I-I knew he was coming here, but he was driving behind me the whole time, slowing down when I slowed down, speeding up when I—"

If Chae-won finds out about my secret, he's going to detonate from anxiety, and that means Yoon-ha will too, and if that happens, there's no way one of them won't tell uncle, and uncle can't even know because of his mental health sucks right now, and also what if Ryu-han was just trying to scare me? What if that gun was fake, and...

He needs an escape, a distraction.

He doesn't know what to do about Ryu-han, so he must try to forget about him entirely in hopes a serendipitous idea will grasp him.

"Min-ho, why-why did you lie and say Kyun-ho was going to be home tonight? Hyeong-cheol's unhappy. Eun-seok told me that before I came...!"

"Oh." Min-ho finds himself frowning, and he does think this may put a rain cloud above his plans, but then he remembers Hyeong-cheol is often unhappy, and that's never caused him to decline to play before.

So now he shrugs and says, "Quite honestly, I thought it would be beneficial to forget about my day at school through means of pretend with Hyeong-cheol." And then, because he doesn't want Chae-won to grow suspicious, he adds, "It's all the homework that's been stressing me. I just wanted to take a break and have some fun."

"Take a...? That... Whatever... Just-just let me inside." Chae-won says, jumping at the sound of Eun-seok exiting his car and darting inside, visibly trembling as perspiration fogs his glasses and flushes his cheeks.

"I wouldn't be so worked up, but..." He inhales so violently it's like he's never breathed before, running shaking fingers through his damp blond hair as he takes several steps back from the door, his behavior making Choon-ha laugh.

"Stop that, Choon-ha! I-I was already stressed with this guy that was loitering around the corner because I wasn't sure if he was crazy like the protesters or not, and so I had to walk more carefully and-and—!"

"Mister, maybe that's why Eun-seok was driving so weird. To make sure the guy didn't attack you or something."

"W-what? I-I mean..." He quickly apologizes and bends to tap the floor five times, still breathing rather heavily as he turns to Min-ho to quietly exclaim, "Anyway, Hyeong-cheol can't be here tonight—it's the rules, remember?"

"Uncle won't even care that much, and besides, Hyeong-cheol isn't always violent." Min-ho insists, swallowing deeply before peeking his head out the door and smiling when Hyeong-cheol emerges out of the car, the moon above them shedding no light on his expression as Min-ho lifts a hand to wave, what little hope he had for rapture gradually fading as an odd stillness fills the air, and Eun-seok, who sounds quite jovial, takes the hand not currently captured by the boy's teeth while saying, "You're okay, Hyeong-cheol. We're going to be with your friends, and then you won't have to worry about Miss Song."

Hyeong-cheol isn't saying anything.

He's allowing himself to be walked to the door, his favorite story tucked beneath his arm, as silent tears fall as though large raindrops from his reddened eyes and onto the soft material of his yellow scarf, which the moon does seem to illuminate.

He's wearing his Little Prince outfit, with the long shamrock coat and crimson coloring inside of it.

Golden stars adorn either shoulder, and the snowy jabot-collared shirt beneath it is tucked into loose white pants that would surely fall without the thick yellow belt's support, while his boots are colored like midnight.

He's usually very happy to show off this outfit, as Sung-hee made it for him several years ago, but tonight, there is a certain sadness veiling him, so he won't be doing any showing off, at all...

"Hey everyone," Eun-seok smiles, not at all seeming to share a single ounce of Hyeong-cheol's disconsolate as he says, holding out a large plate of perfectly round hotteok cakes, "Hyeong-cheol's not feeling too happy tonight because of his mother, but we made you these yesterday and forgot to drop them off. Of course, they'll taste better if you warm them up, but they're really delicious!"

Choon-ha, easily won over by food, gleefully snatches the plate before running off into the living room, forgetting, or simply not caring to remember, his manners, which makes Min-ho flush and stammer apologetically, "Oh, sorry, Mister Na! Choon-ha's a brute—everyone knows it. I'm sure he's thankful, though, we all are."

Eun-seok only smiles, and those bright caramel eyes of his seem to study Chae-won and Min-ho religiously as Hyeong-cheol begins biting harder at his fingers, the band-aids his care-taker had applied before leaving his mother, tearing.

"I'm really thankful to know people like you guys. I wouldn't know what to do with Hyeong-cheol if you hadn't said Kyun-ho was home today. Sung-hee can't watch him because she's doing some work with someone on a clothing collaboration, and his mother is treating him terribly, that's why he's so sad right now. Right, Hyeong-cheol?"

The friends avert their gaze to Hyeong-cheol, but Hyeong-cheol seems as though he's not with them at all, pale eyes glazed and unblinking as he stares past Min-ho and Chae-won as though caught in a trance.

It's odd that Hyeong-cheol is so quiet.

Even when this boy is weighed down by depression, he voices it.

Hyeong-cheol, as Chae-won likes to put it, is not easily silenced by his emotions, and so Min-ho tilts his head and says,

"Why's he not talking? I'm not used to him being so quiet."

"Oh, he's been like this ever since we left his mother. She really scared him…" He looks down at Hyeong-cheol, continuing a bit softer, "I was scared too… I didn't expect her to start hurting him again after she spent so much time away from us."

"It-it must have been awful to make him this, uh, this unre-sponsive." Chae-won stammers, still trying to normalize his breathing as he runs a trembling hand through his blond bangs, struggling to keep his notebook inside his backpack as the urge to document his friend's behavior itches him.

"Yeah, I… goodness, I'm sorry." Eun-seok blinks rapidly, and it's only when he lifts a hand to swipe at his eye that the children realize he had erased a tear, those plump, cat-like lips of his smil-ing sadly as he says, "I thought I did a good job making him happier, but he started shutting down the moment we left his mother's house, and, well, I just really hope the court denies her custody over him after everything she's done.

We had so much fun this morning, I took him to the park before school, and his teachers said he barely gave them any trouble. But once I reminded him about visiting his mother... well, it all went downhill from there."

I thought you said you did cheer him up earlier... Chae-won thinks, furrowing his brows beneath his bangs as Min-ho pats Eun-seok's arm sympathetically, blinking lazy hooded lids up at the man to say, "That does sound awful. You can always come inside for a bit and make yourself some tea. Uncle has a lot, and most of them are stress relieving."

Eun-seok, still smiling, shakes his head, looking back at Hyeong-cheol to admit, "No, I really shouldn't. If I stay any longer, I'm not going to want to go back and help his mother. I really don't like leaving him so unhappy, but his mother can get suicidal when she blows up the way she did tonight."

A thin trickle of blood slides down Hyeong-cheol's hand, causing Eun-seok to gasp before swiftly removing his fingers from his teeth, alarm lacing his usually serene voice as he softly exclaims, "Hyeong-cheol, you bit through your band-aids, and you made your middle finger bleed...!" though the boy shows no signs of this bothering him.

He continues his silent weeping just as he continues to stare into the ether, completely out of touch with the world around him, perhaps because his desire to dissociate has cut him too deeply.

"Can one of you please tell Kyun-ho to replace his band-aids and clean his wound? Oh, and to redirect him to use his necklaces if he puts his hands in his mouth again? I should really get going." Eun-seok says, gently guiding the boy inside and hanging his book-shaped Little Prince backpack by the door.

Min-ho nods, trying to ignore the swell of anxiety sickening his heart as he begins rocking on his heels, coming to terms with the fact that this night might simply be unredeemable.

This is strange. Hyeong-cheol has never been too sad to pretend, but he's like a zombie right now, and once Eun-seok leaves, we won't have any adults to protect us if Ryu-han comes to hurt us. I won't be able to stop thinking about Ryu-han because Hyeong-cheol won't be able to distract me, and uncle will be disappointed in me for having him over unless everyone is dead, in which case, I suppose he'll just be mortified.

Min-ho watches as Eun-seok gives Hyeong-cheol a loving embrace, and he can't help but feel a slight twinge of irritation prick him when the boy doesn't do the same because he's never received such treatment from his father, no matter how sad he's been.

"I love you, buddy. I won't let your mother hurt you again, okay? Be nice to yourself and your friends. Me and Sung-hee will be back later. Bye, Hyeong-cheol."

More tears race to dampen Hyeong-cheol's scarf, and the slightest sign of discomfort is written across his face when he furrows his brows, blinking as though he's never blinked before when Eun-seok lets go of him and shifting his eyes to watch the man turn and walk out the door, his tone so sincere as he says, "You guys are such wonderful people for being friends with Hyeong-cheol. I know he can be difficult at times, but truthfully, we all can be at times."

"Oh, yes…" Is all Min-ho can say as Eun-seok emits a pleasant sigh, fingers lingering on the doorknob, just as his eyes linger on the weeping boy who's refused to move from where he stands near the couch, looking as though sorrow has completely swallowed him up.

"Oh, Hyeong-cheol might start scripting some odd things involving mistakes and blood, but just change the conversation. He's still trying to process what's happened with his mother, so he'll most likely be associating this bad event with others that have happened with her."

Choon-ha's head pops up from the couch, a wide grin adorning his syrup-coated lips as he says, "What happens if I don't change the conversation and tell him to keep going?" to which Eun-seok, who seems to find Choon-ha's question amusing, emits a small laugh before admitting, "Well, the last time he got like this, he summarized a whole afternoon of being locked outside in the snow with a concussion, so I assume you would just feel sad listening to things like that. I'm sorry, it's not funny, but you always find ways to make me laugh, Choon-ha."

Choon-ha grins again before averting his attention back to his half-eaten hotteok, more sugary syrup sticking to his face and fingers as Hyeong-cheol says, more to himself than those around him, "'Oh, Hyeong-cheol, you're so sad, would you like to play a game to make you happy…?'"

"Hyeong-cheol, if you want them to play with you, you can just ask, silly. Anyway, hopefully, I'll be back without any stitches," Eun-seok jokes, adding, because he'd almost forgotten, "Oh, and he's not wearing any training pants, but he used the bathroom before we left his mother's. Bye!" He waves goodbye then and dismisses the odd look he earns from Chae-won, closing the door and unknowingly darkening Min-ho's mood.

"Okay, I can't be the only one who thought that was weird, right?" Chae-won asks, mousy eyes flitting around the room as Yoon-ha nods and whispers, still perfecting his house of cards, "I-I found E-Eun-seok t-to be a bit too-too chipper, but he's-he's always odd, like that…"

"I just like his cooking."

"Of course you do." Min-ho sighed, going over to taste one of the many hotteok Choon-ha's hoarding while looking at Hyeong-cheol, who's standing as still as a garden gnome.

"Hyeong-cheol, is there anything we can do to make you feel better?"

Hyeong-cheol steps wordlessly into the kitchen to watch Eun-seok drive away, brows still furrowed beneath his tousled waves as his hand finds residency in his mouth again, and he murmurs after the car disappears, "'Me and Sung-hee will be back later… bye, Hyeong-cheol…'"

"We could always play pretend or make more houses for the bugs outside." Min-ho tries not to sound too hopeful as he goes to stand beside Hyeong-cheol, but it doesn't matter because the boy has slipped into another spell of vacancy, his tears finally coming to a stop as his eyes continue to stare out the window.

"Each one is amazing!" Choon-ha exclaims, jumping off the couch and running to wave his hotteok in Hyeong-cheol's face, his tone so elated as he asks, "Did you make these, mister? Did you make these sugar-filled dreams?" Though Hyeong-cheol dismisses him entirely, and instead makes his way to the living room, pale eyes scanning his surroundings before he settles gingerly onto the couch, clutching his book and not bothering to wipe remaining tears from his face as Min-ho, still trying to be optimistic, hurries over to say, "I could be the pilot again if you want, we could even pretend to be…" He trails off as he watches Hyeong-cheol, lips forming quite the bitter frown because Hyeong-cheol is blanking again, chewing his injured finger and staring, once more, into the distance with red and swollen eyes.

For a brief moment, Min-ho wishes he had a different set of friends entirely.

He hates that Hyeong-cheol is like this tonight.

He's never been too smothered by his mind or sorrow to play, and he's certainly never been this quiet.

He's so bothered by this friend that he refuses to even consider why he'd be acting like this at all.

"Min-ho, aren't you going to change his band-aids?" Chae-won asks, hanging his backpack by the door and saying, "You did invite him, after all. It's up to you to be the Kyun-ho that never was."

Min-ho doesn't respond to Chae-won; he finds his comment too infuriating.

He simply leaves the living room to retrieve a stack of Pokémon band-aids from beneath the kitchen sink, dropping onto the couch beside Hyeong-cheol and wordlessly removing his hand from his mouth, expecting him to protest or pull away, and noting how odd his compliance is, before dismissing it entirely.

"What happened to make you so stressed, anyway, Min-ho? Homework can't be that bad, you're good at it."

I'm actually not as good at it as I'd like to be. Min-ho thinks, tearing the damaged band-aids from his friend's fingers and rolling his eyes when Chae-won, sitting in the white armchair across from them while gingerly nibbling at a hotteok, says, "I mean, home-work can be stressful, it's just you've never acted this way before about it."

Min-ho heaves a sigh before admitting, as truthfully as he can, while he wraps Hyeong-cheol's fingers, "I may have lied a bit about homework earlier. I am stressed, but it's because the state of our neighborhood has me thinking uncle's dad is going to come out at any second and hurt us with his army of Haven, or whatever."

That's an even better lie than before, and as close to the truth as I dare to get to at this point.

"Oh... Oh, I-I guess that would affect you guys. Kyun-ho's dad *could* come here at any moment, and since he is Haven's leader..." Chae-won flushes in embarrassment while nodding to himself like this all makes sense, which makes Min-ho nod as well, because of course, it makes sense.

It was a lie he had crafted *to* make sense.

"Yes, it's quite unsettling to think about, so you can see why I'd be so paranoid about being here without an adult. You can also see why I wanted to distract myself by inviting Hyeong-cheol. He's very good at distracting people with games of pretend." He looks at Hyeong-cheol when he says that and scowls, though Hyeong-cheol's gaze is fixated on his copy of *The Little Prince*, so he really doesn't notice at all.

"Oh, well, I-I wouldn't have been so pessimistic if you had explained, and we can still do something distracting— we can... Why don't we order food and watch TV?"

"Uncle doesn't like us ordering food. He's convinced the delivery man will be someone dangerous. Besides, we have a whole plate of hotteok right there."

"Everyone knows your family at this point, they could hurt you regardless of ordering food. And this isn't really dinner material."

Min-ho shrugs, not really wanting to eat anymore and not in the mood to browse Netflix for hours just to find one thing to watch.

What he wanted to do, and what's available for him to do now, makes doing anything else seem meaningless.

"Well, we can... we can still play a-a video game or something," Chae-won offers, suddenly feeling like he needs a distraction as well, because it's not fun thinking about Kyun-ho's father being free from prison, nor is it reassuring to think that he knows exactly where they live.

"I suppose that could be pleasant. I just feel like I would have better luck pretending to be someone else right now. Even if Hyeong-cheol did make me a lamplighter, again." Min-ho gathers the empty band-aid wrappers and stands to throw them away in the kitchen, and it's only when he bends to retrieve a fallen wrapper that he realizes he's trembling.

Okay, I should actually stop being so ridiculous now. If anything were to happen, it would have already happened because Ryu-han hates waiting. Besides, I'm sure the Lord would protect us, right...?

Min-ho wishes Kyun-ho would answer at least one of the many questions Christianity has given him, but even though it was him who taught them all, he never seems to have the time to answer any questions at all regarding their religion. And though it's disappointing for Min-ho to admit, even if Kyun-ho were to *magically* have the time now, the more Min-ho studies his uncle, the more he notes how tired, depressed, and visibly anxious he is, the more he wonders; *Does uncle even believe in what he taught us, anymore?*

Despite all Kyun-ho's told them of the abuse he and his siblings suffered from those mistreating Christianity, his faith, Min-ho had thought, was an inspiring example of religion not tainted by those who abused it.

But if even Kyun-ho seems doubtful, now…

Would the Lord protect us…?

"D-do you guys want to… w-wan't to play Little-Little Big planet…?" Yoon-ha whispers, noticing his brother and Hyeong-cheol have been sharing the same sort of eerie silence and thinking it rather odd, considering Choon-ha loves interrupting conversations, and Hyeong-cheol, though quieter than some, has never gone this long without voicing a reiteration or opinion of some sort.

"Huh? Oh. I don't really want to." Choon-ha admits, leaning back against the couch and emitting a loud yawn as Yoon-ha, unsure of what to make of this, rapidly blinks while shifting his gaze to Chae-won, who looks just as perplexed as Yoon-ha, and says, "Really? You don't want to play Little Big Planet…? That's like your all-time favorite game. Is everyone just acting weird tonight?"

Choon-ha shrugs as though rejecting his favorite game is more normal than accepting it, and flips the TV on to simply browse the news, something else that disturbs his friends.

"B-brother, you don't... y-you don't like the news. N-none of us do besides-besides Chae-won," Yoon-ha reminds him, his stomach churning when Choon-ha huffs, cheeks flushing with irritation, "I can watch what I want, *goodness!*"

Choon-ha looks and sounds rather cross.

He never looks or sounds this way unless something's wrong... unless an unannounced visitor has infiltrated his mind.

It's been so long since Choon-ha's had any mood swings, though.

Almost half a year, which, compared to last year, has been more than heaven for everyone living inside this house.

And he was so euphoric just a moment ago; the sudden change seems cruel.

"Y-you aren't acting right, b-brother. I-I think... I think you should take... y-you should take y-your medicine again."

"I'm literally fine, and you aren't even supposed to talk about that in public, mister, *'the world is always ending.'*"

"I-I'm not always like that, but you do-do weird things before-before you start to-t-to spiral, s-so I'm just warning you, which also means... I-I'm worried about you."

"Well, stop worrying." Choon-ha sighs, a sudden wave of dysphoria coloring his demeanor as his eyes grow heavy, and he wonders, as he watches the weather report came in, had he ever felt this tired of existing, or is this something new...? Has he ever been so discontent with those around him...?

Perhaps this is happening because of his medication.

But, no, he's not on any medication right now. He ended that weeks ago, didn't he?

He yawns and then absently watches as a burning police car is shown on the TV while a reporter says, *"These crimes are not random. They are repeat offenses towards law enforcement, and the government will be addressing the public safety concerns of these crimes."*

Yoon-ha has not shifted his gaze away from his brother.

He's raised a hand to bite his nails, blinking rapidly while a tuneless chortle escapes him.

Choon-ha dares to look at him and swears he hears him say, *"Y-you're spiraling after all, brother.... Th-this is the tiring part of having a mind y-you can't control."* and pales because Yoon-ha's lips never moved to voice those words at all.

This is when they hear Tae-kyun scream, and the thread of rapture Min-ho had fantasized about weaving, disappears entirely.

- Eight -

Dangers of The Mind

(What happened before the scream.)

Every night Kyun-ho leaves for work, Tae-kyun wanders off to their shared room and tries to fight the anxiety that always hugs him while Kyun-ho's away.

It's difficult work, given the severity of the unpleasant emotion, but he does it all the same, sitting behind the four bookshelves, forming a cube beside his bed and the wall and using his electric piano in a desperate attempt to distract himself from the absence of his brother.

It's often when he's alone that the whispers will begin to bother him, though, and despite being able to disregard them around Kyun-ho, without him, the whispers, combined with his ebbing anxiety, make Tae-kyun undeniably miserable.

Perhaps because he can barely make out what the whispers are saying…

Perhaps because they overlap too much.

Laughter.

Audible tears.

Vocalizations of pain, and hushed words all muddled together in a cacophony of sounds that refuse to disappear even with the plugging of his ears.

They get quieter with medicine, yes, but the whispers have been something his medicine has not yet been able to conquer.

It's been able to erase the disgusting sight and feeling of bugs crawling inside and out of him.

He hasn't seen his *'father'* for more than three months.

Hasn't tasted blood on everything he puts into his mouth, like he'd been struggling with before his medication changed.

His stars, though he dearly misses them, have not been around to cause what Kyun-ho calls *'a loss of touch with reality'* in what feels like forever... and though he's been told those stars are often the warning of a future hospitalization, he's often mournfully reminiscing about those yellow friends, because they truly only hurt him when he was unable to please them with his music...

He forgets those stars were hard to please, though, just as he forgets how scared his brother looked every time he would unintentionally hurt himself trying to stop those stars from burning him.

We have gotten sidetracked, though, and I must apologize because Tae-kyun had moved on to play a different melody a while ago, one he's probably already forgotten the name of, which means we'll never know what to call it other than an anxious oddity.

It's such an odd way to create music, translating words and noises into melodies, but it's also a very important job that only Tae-kyun can do, because you must remember that he's not from this world, but another one trapped very far in an odd, *futuristic past* that deals with this music quite often.

Such music is the only thing that keeps his world from losing gravity and collapsing into utter nothingness, so he's very serious about his work.

He plays recordings from his day, and the tuning app on his tablet scatters different notes across the screen, notes he swiftly memorizes and uses to create different chords and tunes, spinning them into one melody.

But this week… his music hasn't been helping at all because he's been unable to distract himself from the whispers that frequently plague him despite his piano.

And though he's been unsuccessful in expressing this to his brother, this has been the source of his irritable moods, unwillingness to listen, and general restlessness.

"It's okay…it's okay…" he softly reassures, removing his hands from the keyboard to press his voice recorder to his ear in a desperate attempt at replacing what's in his head.

"*Kyunie, Kyunie~ love Kyunie.*"

"*Ah Tae-kyun, stop trying to guilt me. We can't go to the park. It's too full today.*"

"*Park with Kyunie~ let's go.*"

"*Ahh, no, Tae-kyun, there are too many people, and we have to get Min-ho soon. We aren't even allowed over there when it's like that, remember? We'll get reported again for whatever they can think of. Our neighborhood is mean like that. Maybe tomorrow…*"

AAAH!

Dropping his voice recorder, Tae-kyun blinks rapidly before looking around his room in search of the sudden scream, fingers trembling as the cacophony of sounds in his mind grows louder, and another cry, more piercing than the last, causes him to scurry out from behind the bookshelf cubicle and into the center of his room, where he stands, shaking, waiting for someone, or *something* to appear.

"Kyunie… Kyunie home, home for… h-home for…!" Tae-kyun inhales sharply as another scream startles him, his still eyes darting around the room as an unsteady smile doodles onto his face despite the fear gripping him.

The whispers in his head are starting to sound like shouting, and his hands, though they hurry to cover his ears, fail to reduce the noise within him.

He tries to soothe himself by teetering, legs trembling each time he sways, but the voices are no longer just a mess of cacophony.

They're speaking to him.

Harassing him.

Accusing him of Kyun-ho's depression.

"You're making him worse!"
"You deserve to die."
"This world is not for you!"
"You can't stay here."
"My goodness, you make everyone unhappy.
"Dad should have just killed you."

Tae-kyun's heart seems to be still, and for a while, he's unable to move, because, for a while, the voice of his brother refuses to let him.

He's never heard Tae-ho's voice before.

He's never been able to identify any voices at all besides his father's.

And so now he's frozen.

Forced to listen to his brother's unamused tone because he's unable to turn it off.

"If I were dad, I'd take you to that church and let them burn you alive. They want to, anyway. Yet all you ever come away with is minor char to your bruised and battered skin. Maybe I should be in charge of extracting your demon from now on. That would really bother Kyun-ho, wouldn't it...?"

A violent shiver runs through Tae-kyun, and he struggles to inhale the air around him as a hand slides over his shoulder, and Tae-ho's breath warms his neck.

"Maybe I already am in charge... maybe you should start R e m e m b e r i n g."

This is when he feels Tae-ho's hands shifting towards his neck. This is when he screams.

And now he is forced to run, racing towards the bathroom and dropping inside the tub after slamming the door, his breath strained as he frantically rubs his neck and shoulder to confirm his brother is gone, to confirm he's truly here alone and therefore acquired safety, despite the voices telling him he hasn't.

"Tae-ho's coming."　　　　*"Run."*

"Kyun-ho can't protect you."　　　*"You're not safe."*

"The door isn't locked."

"He's going to hurt you.

"You're not safe."

"You're not safe."　　　　*"You're afraid of fire."*

"YOU'RE NOT SAFE."

"K-Kyunie…! Home for Kyunie… ho-home time! HOME TI—!"

A knock on the door instantly silences Tae-kyun, and within seconds, he's crying, squeezing his eyes shut and pressing his head against the cold porcelain beneath him as several hands begin to grab him, extracting breathless cries from his throat as his skin bubbles with the blood their fingernails draw out.

"You're afraid of fire."　　　　*"The door wasn't locked."*

"Tae-ho's found you."　　*"Should I burn you*

here, or

inside daddy's church…?"

Another hand grabs Tae-kyun's chin once he's forced into sitting, and he screams as something foreign is forced into his mouth, more hands hindering him from escaping as cold water is dumped onto his face, right before the world around him vanishes behind closed lids.

- Nine -

No One Else is Smiling

Min-ho can not stop shaking once the medicine enters Tae-kyun's mouth.

Cannot stop obsessing over whether he's going to choke after he passes out.

The long sleeves of his Tai-chi chasers hoodie are drenched in water, and the glass that Chae-won had tried to hold to Tae-kyun's lips is shattered on the floor beside them.

The house is deathly silent, and none of the children are sure of what to do.

Kyun-ho isn't home, and Tae-kyun just had a psychotic break.

Tae-kyun just passed out.

Tae-kyun was just given medicine none of the children are sure should have been given at all.

"What…do we do?" Chae-won's voice is tremulous as he stares, wide-eyed, at the slumped-over form in the bathtub.

Tae-kyun's Kakao Friend's pajamas are spotted with crimson, and his neck is adorned with multiple scratches, all of which are red, all of which look as though a cat has attempted to kill him.

"He hasn't freaked out like that in years..." Choon-ha observes, staring down at Tae-kyun with eyes that appear rather distant.

"I think... we should call—"

"No!" Min-ho turns around to glare at Chae-won, who stumbles backwards against the bathroom door as though he's been slapped, round glasses slipping down his nose as visible fear pales his face.

"We gave him a sleeping pill and more of his medicine— he should be fine!"

Hyeong-cheol has not left the couch.

He's covering his ears while leaning over the side of it, trying to gauge what's happening down the hall because the fear that had startled him upon hearing Tae-kyun scream is forbidding him to move.

Min-ho looks as though he's about to cry. Yoon-ha observes, biting his nails from where he stands pressed against the wall in the hall-way, as he tilts his head to wonder, *Why...? This is frightening, there's no denying that, but to cry, what exactly is sad about this situation...?*

Choon-ha looks exhausted from simply standing here, and Chae-won is struggling to hold himself together, a task that currently seems more difficult than forcing that medicine down Tae-kyun's throat.

"So... should we start cleaning Tae-kyun up?" Choon-ha asks, the usual mirth in his eyes clouded with something else, something more intoxicated by an unexplained sadness.

Min-ho swallows deeply, taking in the scratches on Tae-kyun's neck and watching the spots of blood spread on his clothes.

He really didn't register any of the pain he was inflicting on himself, or maybe he thought someone else was inflicting it. Regardless, how am I supposed to know if the medicine I gave him will make him worse when he wakes up…?

How will I explain my actions to uncle if this ends up sending him to the hospital…?

"I-I don't think an extra pill will overdose him on his medicine, if that's what you were thinking…" Chae-won offers quietly, adjusting his glasses as he hesitantly says, "I do think we should call your uncle, though, because…"

"Uncle has enough to worry about! All we have to do is patch Tae-kyun up and give him more sleeping pills if he wakes up psychotic again. Then at least he should be too drugged to cause too much trouble when uncle gets home— he'll be happy we helped him!" He's confident in his words, Min-ho, at least, as confident as he can be in this headspace.

"Min-ho, is there, uhm, a reason you think we'll know what to do without Kyun-ho…? Because once Tae-kyun wakes up…"

Yoon-ha emits several shrieks while Min-ho busies himself, ensuring there's no more glass on the floor, ignoring both the trembling in his fingers and the voice inside his head that cries, *'You should let them know! Let them know about Ryu-han and the threats so you can calm down!'* and instead, replacing it with, *'It will freak everyone out if you tell them something that's not confirmed like that when so many weird things are already happening. Look at how uncle is already with all the riots that are happening. Look at how Yoon-ha is, how Chae-won is… You don't want to cause unnecessary panic, do you?'*

Min-ho finally decides to say, after closing his eyes, "I'm just not having a good day, and calling uncle will just make it ten times worse."

"But… it could be ten times worse for… for everyone if Tae-kyun…"

"Ngh…!" Tae-kyun stirs from his crumbled position in the bathtub, and Min-ho stumbles backwards into Choon-ha, who decides to cause a domino effect and fall against Chae-won, who falls into the hallway beneath Yoon-ha's disapproving gaze.

"W-was that-t-that supposed to be funny, b-brother…?" Yoon-ha's tone voices no emotion as his eyes flicker over to stare at Choon-ha, who's frowning because he hadn't felt the joy he thought he'd feel upon doing something so impulsive.

"N-nai fwo- s-shin…!" Tae-kyun groans as he shifts into a sitting position, eyes unfocused and drained of energy as he tries to sort through everything happening around and inside of him.

He's in pain, so much pain throbbing in his neck, arms, and head.

And he's unable to decipher the muffled whispers as those belonging to the children on the floor or something else in his mind entirely.

His vision is fuzzy, and his heart is racing as an unknown panic wraps around him, causing quiet tears to drip from unblinking eyes.

174

Min-ho is the first to scramble up into standing, staring at Tae-kyun in an almost feral way before rushing to grab the sleeping pills he'd left on the counter and...

"Min-ho, he's not doing anything that would require more pills. He looks like we—"

"I forgot uncle makes him take two. He never stays asleep unless he takes—"

"Min-ho, most people only take one. That's what it even says on the back of the bottle."

"No, Chae-won, I see uncle medicating him every night—he always gives him two pills."

"Tae-kyun has prescribed pills, though. It's a stronger dose."

"I'm not waiting for him to run out of the house and into oncoming traffic. He did that before and almost died. And that was with uncle. We're alone. He's psychotic. Anything could happen. Someone might even try to hurt him if he gets out. That's happened before, too!"

Ryu-han could find him. Ryu-han could...

Tae-kyun screams abruptly, jumping out of the bathtub and running out of the door as Tae-ho chases after him in his mind, fire licking at his feet and hands grabbing at his body as he stumbles into the living room before exactly doing what Min-ho feared he'd do: try to escape the house.

He runs straight for the door and fumbles to undo all the locks Kyun-ho's installed over the years, fingers shaking as a shrill scream causes him to abandon the lock entirely to cover his ears at the ferocity of its volume.

The hands are all over him now, grabbing, yanking, and tearing at his skin as muffled whispers turn into words, and words turn into shouting, shouting he doesn't realize is his own because everything is all too disorienting now.

"Older brother, you need to stop screaming! No one is hurting you! Stop scratching yourself and take this medicine!"

Min-ho doesn't want to force it in Tae-kyun's mouth again, but he's scared, and Yoon-ha keeps asking if he should call the police.

Hyeong-cheol is hiding beneath the kitchen table, covering his ears while panic starts to choke him, and Chae-won is stuck between wanting to help Tae-kyun and not knowing how to help at all.

There's too much crying and talking over each other, and it's terribly overstimulating.

Tae-kyun's hands go for the door again, but this time, Min-ho doesn't stop him.

He takes advantage of Tae-kyun's focus on escape to tighten his grip on the syringe he'd previously filled before shoving it to Tae-kyun's lips, shooting out the gritty mixture of water and hurriedly crushed sleeping pill, and clapping a hand over his mouth when he tries to spit it out, realizing, when he begins to thrash, that Choon-ha has been wordlessly helping restrain the older one without being asked.

He opens his mouth to thank him, but Choon-ha isn't paying him any mind.

His attention is solely on Tae-kyun, and his expression is disturbingly unreadable.

He should be fine. That's two sleeping pills. Min-ho thinks, loosening his grip on Tae-kyun as he feels his movement weaken, watching as the drugs fight to take away his consciousness.

The first pill should already be starting to take effect. Everything's fine. You handled it. Tae-kyun will be okay. Uncle will be proud, and we won't have to call him about anything. This night has the capability to recover now, to get better along with Tae-kyun.

He smiles, first to himself and then to Chae-won, and that's when he realizes no one else looks relieved at all.

He's the only one that's smiling, and that ignites a small fire within him.

- Ten -

The Weight of Saving Everyone

"Hey, I called you three times! It's been super busy, but you weren't answering your phone! Did the kids let you get enough sleep last night? Wake up, okay? You've been running late a lot this week, right?"

Kyun-ho pales significantly as the glass doors close behind him, a gradual silence icing over this once lively store as a large majority of people stop their chatter to turn and stare at him, causing a painfully familiar churn inside Kyun-ho's stomach as he averts his eyes to the floor while stepping hesitantly over to Yong-rae, failing to ignore the whispers that follow him as he stammers, "I-I'm sorry. I didn't really sleep last night, and Tae-kyun wasn't listening today. I-I'll try to do better. It's no one's fault but mine—sorry, Yong-rae…" H swallows deeply while fidgeting with his sleeves, because he doesn't have anything else to say, stealing a quick glance at his manager before forcing himself to move toward the bookstore's clock-in system.

He hadn't meant to be late. He never means to be late, but then again, he never means to be debilitated by anxiety, though he's been beaten by it, time and time again.

Poor Kyun-ho has struggled to come to work consistently ever since he started working at nineteen, and has been fired multiple times from multiple jobs before because of this, and the controversy surrounding his family.

There's too much paranoia that occurs once he leaves his home.

There's too much time to worry about who could enter and harm those he loves.

And now that he's finally made it to work, he's suffocating in anxiety.

Too many people are watching him worry.

Too many whispers are exchanged.

Books are being put away, footsteps are rushed and audible, and a woman takes her child by the hand and walks out the doors.

It's me... it's because of me, again... no one is comfortable being around the son of a murderer... what would they do if they knew the truth, though...? How much faster would they hurry away...? Would I even be able to step out of my house...?

Today, he's late by an entire hour.

Yesterday, he was twenty-five minutes late.

He knew Yong-rae was calling him, was startled by the sudden vibrations in his pocket, but was unable to answer, unable to move at all from behind that large cherry blossom tree that sheltered him from the many stares and whispers of those around him.

He was, essentially, petrified at the thought of venturing to any place other than home.

It's not a healthy way of living. He knows this, but it's so hard to dissociate from something that's embedded so deeply into your heart, so difficult to function in a society that wishes you ill every time you're seen.

While most of the people who lived through the downfall of his father's church, his brother's descent into schizophrenia, and his father's imprisonment have gone, there are still some who remain and remember, and those who remember have done everything in their power to ensure everyone around knows Kyun-ho's family is still worthy of being avoided.

And now that Kyun-ho's father has escaped from prison, the stares, whispers, and visible avoidance have only gotten worse.

"It's his father that's causing all these crimes. I'm sure of it."

"Do you think the crimes would stop if everyone in the Choi family were locked away? I'm sure they're influencing it."

"Perhaps we'll hear of another murder very soon… his son, he'll probably off one of his own children any day now or sacrifice them to his father's church."

Kyun-ho's anxiety has always been terrible to live with, but it's gotten progressively worse over the years, and ever since news of his father's break from prison surfaced, he hasn't once felt peace even briefly touch him.

What if dad finds me and makes me kill myself for framing him?

What if he finds Tae-kyun and my children
and sells them off to someone in his cult?

Does his cult even exist anymore?

Would he still have ties to it?

Why haven't they tried to hurt us if they are around?

Sang-ho was a terrible father, and his abuse, combined with Tae-ho's and Hae-sol's, has damaged him an insufferable amount.

"H-Hae-sol, wait…! Maybe we should just end Haven…! Maybe we shouldn't try to blame everything on my dad!"

"Kyun-ho… why would we ever end Haven…? And why would… you be so afraid of bringing a monster like him to light?

If we end Haven… Tae-kyun will never get better… because your father will keep hurting him… and all those rituals will keep occurring… over and over again, until Tae-kyun is dead. Without Haven… we have no chance of stopping anything the world will do to eliminate those like Tae-kyun from society. You… Kyun-ho… you say you're a Christian… you're supposed to be ready to make a difference, right?"

There was so much stress then, such heaviness from the way Hae-sol would manipulate his thought process through reiterations of safety, the twisting of his faith, and swift acts of violence.

"I can't rule over Haven by myself... If you were to ever abandon me, I'd just kill myself and fall into hell's abyss... forever tortured by the presence of my father and the ghost of my innocent brother..."

"Kyun-ho...? Wow, you're as spacey as a cadet today!"

Yong-rae grins, gently tapping his friend, who blinks rapidly as though awakening from a trance, eyes glistening because tears were very close to falling...

"It's your dad, right...? Your dad is troubling you again? He broke out of jail and committed another murder, and you're having nightmares about it, right? Because that's what you told me yesterday, too, and that's why you aren't sleeping, right?" Yong-rae's carefree tone grounds Kyun-ho back to reality, his expression looking so concerned that Kyun-ho almost lies in agreement just to drop the conversation as he rubs his eyes while lifting his shoulders in a weak shrug.

It is true that he hasn't been sleeping, but he never sleeps well, even with the aid of medication, because his past will often resurface in the form of nightmares, and the suffocating panic that catches him when he wakes has never made it easy to close his eyes again.

Sleep has been troubled ever since the rituals started with Tae-kyun, and it only got worse after violence colored Haven.

"Because if it's your dad, and he's... trying to hurt you again or something, you should let the cops know. You would do that, right? Because you know cults like his will do anything to..."

"N-no, no... it's-it's not... it's not..."

What else is it, if it's not...?
What else would it be if it can't be the truth...?

182

Kyun-ho winces a bit as he looks at Yong-rae, forcing a voice he hopes isn't as panicked as he's feeling right now as he says, "You know, I-I guess it is, really… I-I'm just worried because I don't know what to do, and the police haven't been very helpful when it's me or my family, but, uhm, Min-ho always says I worry too much, so we're probably fine. I-I'm fine… I'm fine, sorry." He swallows rather hard then, glancing about the store nervously because he's felt the eyes of so many others staring at him, heard the quiet whispers with each word he speaks to Yong-rae, and is not at all comfortable because such atmosphere is churning his stomach.

"Hey, if you ever need help with your family or whatever, you can tell me, okay? I think the only one who didn't like me the last time I watched them was Yoon-ha, but he doesn't really know me that well, so maybe next time I can be his friend. You'll let me do it again, right? Or maybe you need help with that Night Owl? Because I know he's been calling you when he's not allowed to visit, and…"

"I-I don't need help with him," Kyun-ho quickly stammers, feeling his heartbeat stutter at the mention of Hae-sol and trying not to seem as bothered as he is by such, as he adds hurriedly, "Hae—Dong-shik is just lonely— we're fine. He just doesn't like being alone in that hospital."

He's never liked hospitals, especially that one, and he still thinks I hate him for not letting him live in my house. He still thinks I'm a terrible friend, saying he's not mentally stable.

"Oh, that's his name!" Yong-rae exclaims, snapping his fingers as a wide smile spreads across his ingenuous, oval-shaped face, unaware of the way Kyun-ho has paled at his words as his eyes dart anxiously to and away from his manager, fingers burning with the suppressed desire to scratch his skin.

"Night Owl suits him better, though, right? Yeah, I don't really mind you taking his calls, but goodness, when he's mad, everyone knows it! I mean, the other day, I guess a couple of our customers heard him screaming at you, and everyone, I mean everyone, disappeared! I honestly think it's better when he visits with his therapist because at least then I get to give him food from our café— he's kinda sickly, right?" He waits for Kyun-ho to respond, but when he realizes he's said too much because of thinking too little, his smile drops, and he blushes at his mistake while scratching at his loose, messy curls, the inky black coloring of them causing his wide, timid brown eyes to look a bit pale behind his purple-rimmed, round glasses.

"Oh, I shouldn't have said that, huh? I talk too much, sorry. Well, just know I'm here, and I don't mind helping you, so don't think I'll treat you like everyone else does. You're a good friend, and I'll help you no matter your situation, so just let me know if..." Yong-rae pauses before scratching his head again, standing awkwardly beside Kyun-ho before turning to shuffle silently towards the various boxes of books by the door, wide mono-lid eyes flickering to and from Kyun-ho while he nearly whispers, "I'll just go ahead and shelve these..." as Kyun-ho nods before beginning to carry his own stack of books from the counter to the nearest aisle, a familiar sickly feeling spreading within him as Yong-rae's words replay in his mind.

"No matter the situation... no matter the situation... no

matter the situation..."

Would he still help me if he knew I should be in jail instead of my father? Would he still be my friend if I told him my past and present? Or is my situation too far from hope and too corrupt for any sort of intervention?

"Oh! I can cook dinner— you would have to eat then, right?"
"I never told you I haven't been eating..."

I haven't been, though, and Hae-sol hasn't been either. He thinks they're trying to poison him. He only eats when he's with me. You can die from not eating, right? Maybe... we'll both die before anything with Haven can resurface or happen again, but who would take care of my family? I can barely take care of them myself.

Looking a bit dazed, Kyun-ho blinks rapidly, only to nearly fall backwards when Yong-rae rushes forward abruptly, talking even faster than he usually does as he insists, "You did because you aren't cooking anything for your family because you keep buying the quick, nasty stuff, right? And on the days you let me over, Choon-ha says you hardly eat anything but tea, and that's not even edible, so you kinda have told everyone you've been too down to enjoy life, right?" He fingers the ID dangling from the cloud-printed lanyard around his neck as he leans over to try to force Kyun-ho to look at him, lips forming an expectant 'o' shape as Kyun-ho swallows deeply before forcing their eyes to meet, something that makes him feel a bit ill, for he's too gullible, Yong-rae, believing all his lies when half of them don't nearly make sense.

"I just… I'm not feeling very well these days. M-maybe my medication's off. I-I dunno…" He trails off then, picking up a book only to set it down to scratch at his wrist, agitating the wounds he had previously left before.

"But I thought your panic attacks and PTSD were only triggered by your dad because he caused it, right? So that means you really are getting scared of him being out of jail, so I should…"

Yong-rae's words are getting harder and harder for Kyun-ho to hear as the sound of his own heartbeat begins to drown them out, violent tremors shaking his body as perspiration meets and gathers beneath his bangs, moving faster against his skin as he continues to stare at Yong-rae.

He's trying not to let his anxiety churn to panic, trying not to blink so much to force away the tears threatening to fall, but he's so afraid of all the lies he's told to Yong-rae, so ashamed of standing here and being his friend when he knows he should be incarcerated with Hae-sol for everything they've done and everyone they've hurt, knows it was his idea to blame his father and send him to jail, and fears the Lord's punishment for such will be so much greater than any other form of pain he's ever felt before.

"Hey, are you okay?" Yong-rae takes Kyun-ho's hand and lowers it from his wrist, frowning when Kyun-ho jerks away and begins to hurriedly sort through the stack of books before him, swallowing nausea as he thumbs through a novel about gardening only to drop it upon catching the blood he's left on the pages.

"You're super anxious right now, right? Plus, you're—whoa, you're bleeding! Hold on, I still have band-aids from last week." Yong-rae's glasses nearly fall off his face with the swift motion he makes ducking behind the counter, retrieving the small box of band-aids he keeps for this friend alone and applying them without hesitance as he says, "Your anxiety is super high, maybe you should get home. Want me to phone a taxi? It's slow today. Well, it wasn't before you got here, but it's slow now, so you can just—"

"N-no, I'm fine," Kyun-ho choked, his voice strained by the hurriedness of his breath as he watched the thin streaks of blood get hidden beneath the many band-aids Yong-rae plasters to his skin.

"Hey, I've been paying you more than enough for your half day's work. You can go home. It will barely hurt your check! But you probably don't want to do that, right? So you should go sit down instead, okay?" Yong-rae smiles brightly at Kyun-ho's troubled face after discarding the band-aid wrappers, trying not to let his worry for his friend show too much as he adds, in a rather jovial manner, "Hurry, before I change my mind! Go sit down. What kind of best friend would I be if I forced you to do your job when you're looking so horrible? I've known you too long for that kind of cruelty! Best friends don't do that, right?"

Kyun-ho winces at Yong-rae's words, and an abrupt wave of unease and sorrow colors him as his mind whispers, *Can you even have any other best friend besides Hae-sol? Are you even deserving enough for one…? Let alone any others after everything you've done…?*

He swallows harshly, biting his tongue to keep his thoughts from being voiced while resisting the urge to tear off the band-aids irritating his skin.

He would like to consider Yong-rae and Eun-seok both as friends, as they've known each other for quite some time, and most people would rather avoid any affiliations with him and his family, but there's so much danger injected into that word, so much caution that must be taken with friendship, because with Hae-sol, that word is only meant for two.

And he mustn't forget what happened when he met *her* because it was her death that made him paranoid about *him*, Shreiyne, the whimsical oddity he met in high school.

Her death that made him begin avoiding that friend, forced to lie when his whereabouts were questioned because he was told the truth wouldn't make any sense to Shreiyne, though in reality, the truth Hae-sol was referring to only made sense to himself.

"That boy will not understand... because that boy is not meant to become one with Haven... We can only become one with Haven because we're two people—two doctors who were chosen. So, no, there will be no additional friends because Haven only needs us, which means we only need each other."

Hae-sol would say that anytime he saw Kyun-ho walking to or from school with Shreiyne.

Anytime Kyun-ho would dare mention his name, until eventually, he added, while staring out the window at their treehouse, *"I can do what I did to her again, Kyun-ho. If it's too hard for you to abandon that boy, I can untangle his heart from his body, and then you won't be tempted to make any other friends."*

And that was the last time Kyun-ho ever mentioned Shreiyne and the first time he vowed to never see him again.

Hae-sol didn't use to act so violently towards those Kyun-ho considered close, but then again, he was never the same after burying his brother and leaving his father to bleed on the living room floor.

The friendship he and Kyun-ho had before was free from abuse and manipulation, because life had not yet unraveled him to insanity.

"Tae-kyun, look! Hae-yon is with Hae-sol, today!"

Kyun-ho, eight years old and dressed in brown corduroy shorts with an oversized, blue, collared sweater, had been holding his four-year-old brother on the porch, looking as though he was having a pleasant time reading the Bible when the reality of that situation was he wasn't.

It had been another Sunday when his father got mad at him for forgetting the Bible verse he and a few other children at church were required to recite.

His father always tasked them each with a verse from the same chapter of the Bible, one that he would base his sermon on. He would have them each say them, one after the other. When it came to Kyun-ho, the boy who was afraid to even stand in front of the congregation, he would fall silent. Right after he opened his mouth, the other children beside him would laugh while Tae-ho cursed at him beneath his breath or announced something to further embarrass him, such as, "My dear brother has a memory problem when it comes to the Bible. We should all assume it's because he has too much sin in his life to hold such valuable words in his heart."

His father would laugh while they were in public, dismissing Tae-ho and lightly scolding Kyun-ho, while his anger grew silently throughout the service, where it would later be released in the form of violence once the door to their house was locked.

And so, after being beaten and yelled at for forgetting the verse that was assigned to him, he was given the Bible and told to read the entire book of Leviticus until he could recite it chapter by chapter, a task his father knew would be impossible and one Kyun-ho knew he would be beaten for, again.

So while it looked pleasant enough to the neighbors, poor Kyun-ho had been panicking inside while his mind strained to retain the words his eyes were scrolling over.

"Yes… it's me… and Hae-yon…" Hae-sol had nodded, walking slowly up the driveway with Hae-yon at his heels, both boys dressed in loose-fitting ebony suits because they, like most of their neighborhood, had gone to church today.

"Should we go and play in your treehouse…? I assume your father was cruel to you because you forgot another verse… on another Sunday." Hae-sol had an interesting way of stringing silence throughout his sentences, even then, and his voice, though much higher than it would be in the future, still held that same feathery tone.

Kyun-ho had glanced into the window of his house, fingers trembling as he held both his book, and a squirming Tae-kyun tighter, while he took note of the closed curtains and lack of noise around them.

He thought to himself, 'Dad will still hate me regardless, so I guess it doesn't matter if I stop reading,' and stood up, along with Tae-kyun. He left his Bible on the porch, and followed Hae-sol and his brother towards the woods behind his home.

"Dad's always mean to me about everything, but Tae-ho gets away with murder…"

"Murder, really?" Hae-yon, who was five at the time, looked up at Kyun-ho with wide eyes that matched his brother's emerald ones. "Is he really good at hiding the bodies, then?"

"Oh, that's just a…"

"A saying, I know. It's just funny how something so dark could be used so freely in a conversation." He had laughed then, and his waist-length black hair had bounced in the wind's breeze when he ran ahead to catch a large butterfly, which he kept in his hands the rest of their walk to the treehouse, which was mostly silence because they were often quiet around each other.

Not because there was nothing to say, but simply because they didn't mind the silence.

Kyun-ho could complete an entire seven-hundred-piece puzzle without saying a word, and Hae-sol would sit content beside him, occasionally placing a missing piece or bringing something to do next to his friend instead, which would usually be drawing, a skill he'd been working on perfecting, as everything he'd drawn so far had consisted of various stick figures in various hospital settings.

And the odd thing was, Tae-kyun, unlike Hae-yon, would be satisfied sitting with the two as well.

They'd bring him toys, of course, but Tae-kyun was more interested in observing the older children. He would rub a fisted hand beneath his bangs while they busied themselves in the quiet of their treehouse, each at peace with one another.

Sometimes, they would watch Tom and Jerry at Hae-sol's house, as it was mutually understood Kyun-ho's home was a place he'd rather stay away from, but that didn't happen too often, despite it being Hae-sol's favorite show, because Hae-sol would often say, "My father isn't feeling well... I think... the disease he has... is getting worse," though neither he nor Hae-yon would ever specify the disease, even when asked, and so eventually Kyun-ho stopped asking altogether.

'Maybe his dad is like mine... Maybe the disease is just another word for 'cruel parent,' and he's too ashamed to admit it...'

They were quiet days, the ones spent with Hae-sol, but they held a certain amount of serenity and fulfillment Kyun-ho couldn't find in his own home or with anyone else at his school or in the neighborhood, because to them, he was only his name and Tae-ho's weird younger brother, who crocheted instead of pursuing a sport, read books instead of watching television, and busied himself in his mother's garden instead of trying to make friends.

Hae-sol never thought of him like that, though, perhaps because no one cared for him either, perhaps because he was homeschooled along with Hae-yon, talked in a way that most children found odd, or because he spent a lot of time searching for dead animals or bugs in the woods, analyzing their cause of death before he allowed his younger brother to perform taxidermy on them, a hobby the five-year-old disturbingly excelled at.

Whatever the reason, Hae-sol and Kyun-ho were drawn to each other.

They hadn't needed permission from one another to become friends; they simply were…

"Kyun-ho…?" Yong-rae starts to laugh, but he sounds a bit nervous as he reaches over to lightly knock on Kyun-ho's head, saying, once Kyun-ho startles from his thoughts, "Knock, knock, are you there anymore? You're super spacey, and you're pale.

That probably means you don't feel well, right? You should sit down."

Not wanting to try to argue with Yong-rae, Kyun-ho quietly agrees with him and goes to sit at the round table in front of the large, circular window near the door, hands shaking as he slides them underneath his thighs in hopes of keeping his nails from scratching, knees bouncing with a noticeable sense of urgency as he glances repeatedly out the window while sweat trails silently down his temple and past his ear.

I need to leave. People keep looking at me. Do they know something? I need to leave— I want to leave!

He's not sure how long he's been sitting here, drenched in anxiety and perspiration and staring anxiously out this window, but suddenly, a terrible realization strikes him, one that makes him audibly gasp.

"You okay…?" Yong-rae's voice is laced with hesitant concern as he stares at Kyun-ho while inserting another book in the shelf, wide eyes flickering over to the window as Kyun-ho shakily inquires, "Has-has Dong-shik visited at all today…?" to which Yong-rae, checking his watch before rolling his eyes to stare thoughtfully up into the pale blue ceiling of this store, frowns a bit before slowly shaking his head.

"I'm not sure because my mom opened today, but no, I didn't see him when I clocked in. That's weird, right? Night Owl hasn't visited but once this week. Maybe you should call him?"

"N… no, I don't— maybe he's heavily medicated or something…" He tries not to sound as disquieted as he feels, but Hae-sol's allowed to leave his hospital room with one of the staff three days a week, and he's never missed a single one of them, perhaps because something has changed.

Perhaps because something is wrong.

His eyes have been looking more and more fervent with each visit, and he rants excessively about loneliness and why Kyun-ho should *'work with him'* instead of keeping his job, unable to reveal themselves as Haven's doctors because he's too paranoid about the nurse that accompanies him, despite how lackluster the staff at the Serenity center are about truly watching those assigned to them.

"You say you can't sleep at night… yet you never come to visit, even though… that means you have the time. You say we can't visit… because somehow you're very tired and want to sleep… even though you rarely do because you have insomnia… and dreams you call nightmares. Have you not been wanting to spend time with me, Kyun-ho…? Are you already failing again at this friendship when I've given you so many chances to get better…? Do you really want to end our friendship? Do you really want me to hang myself… on the last thread of hope I have for our future?"

Yong-rae sidesteps a passing customer as he stands beside Kyun-ho, scratching his head again, as confusion will always force him to, before asking, once more, if his friend feels alright.

"If you're feeling sick, you really can go home. People are staring, and I know that's not helping, right…?"

Kyun-ho looks away from the window right as everyone who was previously watching him pretends they weren't, shuffling further towards the back of the store and nearly tripping on dropped books as they whisper noisily about him.

"N-no, it's not helping, but I left early yesterday…"

I was worried if I didn't, Hae-sol would think I hated him because I missed his call, and when he thinks like that, it's so much harder to calm him down, so much harder to not panic under so much stress and so much yelling… so much blood.

"You sure did leave early yesterday, huh? Three hours, right? I don't mind if you're sick. It's not like you're my only closer. We still have Hee-chan, Kang, and Na-ri, remember?"

194

Kyun-ho nods quietly, bringing a shaking hand from beneath him to wipe away the perspiration wetting his skin as his heart stutters loudly inside of him.

"Anyway, just don't make a habit of it, alright? Because my mom already hates you for it." Yong-rae tries to smile, but it looks a few shades duller than his usual one, which makes Kyun-ho feel worse, not only because he knows Yong-rae knows he's consistently lying about his situation, but because he's already formed a habit of leaving early because it's already his second week.

No… maybe it's his third.

He keeps worrying about upsetting Hae-sol.

Keeps feeling like he *has* to spend more time with him or else the entire world will detonate.

He wants to refuse Yong-rae's offer and ignore his anxiety, but it truly is troubling him to know Hae-sol hasn't arrived at all today when it's an hour past the time he usually visits on Fridays.

"Maybe you need to take some time off and get checked out at the hospital. You've been really sick with worry these days. You could even ask your brother to take you…" Yong-rae doesn't end his sentence with a question as he usually does, and the blank expression he wears nearly startles Kyun-ho when he meets his unblinking gaze.

"It's–it's just my medication and my dad. I-I don't like having him out of prison— Tae-ho's too insensitive to that. He-h-he thinks I'm w-weak…!" His voice breaks as he pushes away from the table and pulls his vest over his pants, feeling suddenly very out of place in this store and very uneasy standing before Yong-rae, who slowly clasps his hands behind his back while forcing a very strange and small smile before saying, "Mental illness isn't a sign of weakness. He's wrong about that, you know."

Mental

...ill

ness...?

"I-I... I'm not—Yong-rae, I have to go home now." Kyun-ho clocks out before stepping swiftly out the door and towards the Serenity center, Yong-rae's smile bothering him almost as much as Hae-sol's absence, as a gale of autumn wind whispers through the trees around him and ruffles his hair.

- Eleven -

Nothing Ever Feels Right

Tae-kyun threw up right after Min-ho and Choon-ha moved him to the couch.

He looks and feels feverish, and has been slipping in and out of consciousness, reality still alluding to him.

"We really should call, Min-ho. Tae-kyun is *really* sick," Chae-won warns, a deep frown adorning his face as he looks up from his phone.

"No. Tae-kyun's fine—stop googling stuff on your phone that generates anxiety."

"Okay, but you know you're not *actually* supposed to crush sleeping pills, or—"

"Listen, Chae-won. Tae-kyun will be asleep for a good long while. He's all bandaged up now. He can't be psychotic because he's sleeping, and I'm sure the sickness will go away once he wakes up."

Chae-won shifts uncomfortably, slipping his phone into his pocket and glancing over at Min-ho before hesitantly saying,

"Uhm—I know you had a bad day, but not telling Kyun-ho is really not like you, Min-ho. I'm sure you know this."

Ignoring Chae-won, Min-ho slides off the couch and looks around, smiling when he finds Hyeong-cheol, who's been hiding beneath the kitchen table, rubbing his fingers beside his ears and looking very, very frightened.

"Hey, should we play a game now, older brother? I know you were too sad to play earlier, but now seems like a good time to have some fun. Your mother's not going to bother you anymore, remember?"

Hyeong-cheol flinches when Min-ho drops to his knees to meet his gaze, expression quite disturbed as wide hazel eyes carefully search his friend's brown ones beneath sorrel waves.

He pauses in his stimming and blinks at Min-ho, but refuses to say anything.

"Older brother, come out from under there. Tae-kyun's fine, your mother isn't bothering you, and you don't have to be sad anymore."

Hyeong-cheol looks visibly bothered by Min-ho's words, and despite opening his mouth, nothing comes out, so he purses his lips before roughly patting his ears, shivering as though it's very cold.

"Eun-seok said he would be like this. Might as well leave him alone before we have to drug him to sleep, too," Chae-won advises, looking nervously at the silent boy as Min-ho emits an exaggerated sigh before standing, sweeping his eyes around the living room before going over to Choon-ha and his brother, the ones sitting on the floor, whispering behind the couch.

Yoon-ha notices Min-ho's shadow and passes a look to his brother, bringing a hand to his mouth to chew stubbed nails while blinking rapidly.

"Do you and Choon-ha want to do something now? Tae-kyun won't be waking up for a while now, so we can finally do something fun. Come on, the night is miserable right now."

Choon-ha looks and sounds very, very tired, still lacking mirth in his wide eyes as he massages his temples while saying,

"I don't feel like doing anything right now. I think this night has given me a headache. I would actually like to take some pain reliever."

"Y-you'll take that, but–but n-not the medicine that helps your mind…? It's not-n-not a good idea, you know this…"

Choon-ha's cheeks flush a violent red as he glares at Yoon-ha, his tone almost a hiss as he whispers, "For the last time, I don't need my medicine like *you*. I stopped taking them because *I didn't need them*. And you don't need them, either. I'm telling you, we never needed them before '*daddy*' decided we did…!" to which Yoon-ha shakes his head and says, that monotone voice of his sounding almost pained in Choon-ha's mind, "S-so what? You're suffering from-f-from delusions now, like me, now? Y-you're spiral-ing, after all, brother…"

"You already said that before."

"I-in your mind, maybe… but–but n-n-not out loud, I'm afraid. Wh-what if you end up like Tae-kyun? What if… w-what if we have t-to subdue you because of negligence?"

Shocked by Yoon-ha's words, Choon-ha swiftly regains his composure by pursing his lips together and stating, "This whole conversation is dumb. I'm not even listening anymore," and then, because he sees Min-ho looks rather skeptical, he adds, crossing his arms and forcing what he hopes is a humorous tone, "And if you mention any of this conversation to outside forces, you'll die."

He's being quite unserious, Choon-ha, so why has Min-ho's mind turned so dark?

Die… Death… If Ryu-han came here right now to harm people the way Haven did, how would I be able to stop them when I'm the only normal person here? I would be the only one they wouldn't hurt unless I interfered… That's what he said.

Min-ho looks at each one of his friends, past their eyes and straight into their souls, as he studies each one carefully.

Would it truly be better to tell them they may die because someone threatened them and risk paranoia, or say nothing and risk death while avoiding paranoia?

For a brief moment, Min-ho and Chae-won lock gazes, and the atmosphere seems to still as a single unspoken question stands between them: *Why are you letting your secrets trouble you when we could all be troubled together?*

And to that, Min-ho responds: *Because there's nothing we can really do about it, even if I tell you. It's not a secret that's capable of being fixed with the knowledge of others.*

An odd and selfish feeling of dysphoria begins to color Min-ho, and he's thinking, as he drops his gaze to Tae-kyun's sleeping form, that if everyone was taken out together, perhaps there would finally be time for him.

Perhaps his uncle could end his mental suffering and become the father figure he always longed for.

It's the stress of his family that triggers his PTSD, right…?

Maybe he wouldn't cry so much in the kitchen at night, failing to gain solace from a cup of tea because his world revolves around those who remind him too much of his past.

His father would torture Tae-kyun with the sole purpose of extracting whatever demon he believed had taken refuge inside of him, and Kyun-ho still thinks that's his fault because he couldn't stop him.

The majority of his childhood was centered around mental illness and the terrible things people did because of it… Even now, he can't escape it. Is it wrong to want to give him peace? Is it wrong to think they might deserve some peace as well?

He thinks back to Tae-kyun: how they found him, bleeding in the bathtub with no recognition for them at all, that silly smile of his trembling on his tear-streaked face even after he was screaming, even as he cried and fought to escape. He was being tortured mentally, and the only thing they could do was be terrified of him before drugging him, just like they do at the hospitals.

He thinks of Hyeong-cheol, how he's constantly trying to soothe himself, not just because his mind is a mess of emotions and the inability to properly regulate them, but because he's bothered by things most of us wouldn't be bothered by at all because of how he processes things.

He thinks of Chae-won, who's spent hours counting blades of grass and relocking doors, trapped in an unforgiving cycle of obedience to compulsions whenever his mind finds it necessary, because without that obedience, anxiety will refuse to let him go.

He thinks of Yoon-ha, vividly aware of his schizophrenia yet silently obsessing over who's poisoned his food at school and refusing to eat it despite his evident hunger, trashing his and Choon-ha's room with leaves because he's afraid his mental creations won't protect him if they're not near.

And finally, he thinks of Choon-ha, the one who's looking a bit dysphoric himself sitting here behind the couch, resting his chin on his knee while staring absently down the hall.

Choon-ha, despite his cheerful and playful demeanor, has scared his family many times with attempted suicide, self-harm, and isolating moods of depression, and he hates himself because of it.

He hates being that vulnerable.

He hates taking the medicine he swears makes the suicidal thoughts and tendencies stronger, and he has had more than eighteen changes to his medication in the past ten years because of it.

"Your uncle wouldn't be so stressed if he could just put his brother and kids away, don't you think? I know you people claim to be Christians, but really, why would a God that's supposed to be so loving inflict so much mental agony on a human being? Why would a God like that not use any sort of healing power when the sick people and those around them all agree they should just die? Isn't that cruel...?"

Those were Ryu-han's words, so why does he feel as if they're his own now?

It is true; he's wondered countless times why the mind can be so easily tormented by illnesses and disabilities.

Why prayer seems completely worthless when it comes to those who are mentally different, or even why it's so easy to become spiteful towards ones unlike yourself just because they're different.

Just because that difference requires so much more care and compassion than you're willing to give sometimes...

It's not fair the way they live, the way we live because of them. Maybe Haven was trying to make us understand that. Maybe Ryu-han and his friends will make it painless. Maybe I should try harder to make things fun here because there might not be another chance for us to all play together.

It should disturb Min-ho how easily he was able to come to such a grim conclusion, but instead, it begins to melt away dysphoria until there's no unhappiness within him at all.

He grins and is about to announce the start of the greatest Pokémon battle ever when Hyeong-cheol suddenly exclaims,

"'Oh, no! He is so sad about all this pain, it's s-so dumb!' 'I'm so sorry, Hyeong-cheol. Here's some medicine. I'm so sorry...'"

Before sticking his tongue out and emitting a sound of disgust while shaking his head, tears gradually trailing down his cheeks as he sorrowfully laments, "'It's so dumb, and there's so much...!'"

"Hyeong-cheol, do you..."

"Wait! Let him finish...!" Chae-won begs, his notebook already drawn, as Min-ho looks at Chae-won in exasperation and says,

"We were told to change the topic when he said weird stuff.

He's sad enough as it is…! Letting him dwell on a bad memory will just make things worse, something I'd assume *you* of all people would want to avoid."

Chae-won opens his mouth to protest, but decides he'd better keep it closed, instead watching as Hyeong-cheol crawls out from beneath the kitchen table to go retrieve his book on the couch, paying no mind to those around him as he says, aimlessly flipping through the pages of his favorite story,

"'Hyeong-cheol, would you like to make a fort? We can have so much fun…'" before falling into another spell of vacancy, staring straight ahead into nothing but pure atmosphere.

"*Do* you want to make a fort, Hyeong-cheol? That could be fun. I suppose we could still find something to watch if you also wanted to, Chae-won."

Hyeong-cheol offers no vocal opinion on the matter, nor does he show any signs he's heard his friends at all.

"We don't *have* to do anything." Choon-ha sighs, leaning against the back of the couch as Chae-won says, "Well… if we do nothing, we'll be… doing nothing…?" and awkwardly laughs while fumbling to put away his notebook, which sadly only has three more pages left to fill.

"I think we should make a fort because that will make *anything* fun—even doing *nothing*, right, Hyeong-cheol?" Min-ho asks, looking back at the boy and frowning when he whispers, to no one, I suppose, but himself, "No, no, put them away… Put them back into his mind. That was a thoughtless mistake, and Hyeong-cheol should not assume every fort will have such a bad day…" before allowing his fingers to meet his teeth.

Chae-won shifts his gaze to Min-ho, who blinks back at him imploringly, before they both mutually decide that questioning Hyeong-cheol right now simply won't do anything but possibly aid in his distress in the event he does answer.

So Min-ho says instead, "I guess we're making a fort. Would you like to come to get the blankets with me, Hyeong-cheol?" though Hyeong-cheol has already started walking away.

"You guys can look for a movie if you want," Min-ha calls to the others, following Hyeong-cheol down the hall and tilting his head in confusion when the boy begins to weep upon entering Min-ho's room.

"Hyeong-cheol, you don't have to think about your mother anymore. Eun-seok said you're safe, remember?"

Hyeong-cheol stares at the floor, breathing a bit heavily as he bobs his head slowly up and down, reaching out to Min-ho without lifting his gaze to impulsively pull on his sleeve, his voice so quiet and tremulous with tears as he says, "M-Min-ho is here, and-and Hy-Hyeong-cheol is here, and there is no Eun-seok, and n-no... no Miss Song."

"Yeah. Eun-seok will be back later with Sung-hee, and your mother's at her apartment. You're safe. We can forget about our troubles and play games instead."

Hyeong-cheol doesn't respond, nor does he look up, so Min-ho assumes he's still processing whatever's left of his emotional shutdown and gently pulls his fingers from his sleeve before guiding him to his bed, the thick, blue and white checkered bedspread neatly hiding the assortment of bug jars and bedding beneath the frame.

"Want to help get the blankets from beneath my bed?"

Poor Hyeong-cheol. He's so out of it today. I guess I do feel sorry for him… Perhaps I won't hold a grudge against him for spoiling half my plans after all.

"Here—I'll pull them out, and you can hold them," Min-ho says, bending to pull blankets from beneath his bed and startling when his phone begins to vibrate aggressively.

He had left it on the dresser beside his bed after school, firstly because he hadn't figured out how to permanently keep Ryu-han and his friends from harassing him after blocking them failed, and secondly, because he wanted to pretend they hadn't been bothering him at all, and had always been paranoid about breaking electronics by powering them off.

"It's not important," he quickly says, untangling a thin white sheet from the disorganized bundle of blankets beneath his bed and withholding a shout when Hyeong-cheol, intrigued and momentarily distracted by the constant vibrating of this phone, holds it to his cheek despite the wetness from his tears, still looking very miserable.

"Uhm—c-can I see my phone really quick, Hyeong-cheol? It's quite urgent." He holds out his hand for emphasis, perspiration forming beneath his chestnut waves as he waits to be persecuted for his request.

Hyeong-cheol isn't negatively affected by him at all, though.

He simply lowers the phone from his face and drops it in his friend's hand, shifting tearful eyes about the room as his fingers come up to meet his teeth, causing Min-ho to sigh with relief as he drops onto his bed, eyes straining to take in the messages that continue to flood his screen.

"Min-ho is here, and… so is… so are all his friends, and there are no more thoughtless mistakes…" Hyeong-cheol murmurs cautiously, pale eyes roaming the screen of Min-ho's phone as the boy says, "Uh, yes, sure… We can make a fort in a second. Hold on. I just need a minute."

"'I just need a minute…'" His voice is almost a whisper as he tilts his head at the words on the phone's screen, puzzling at a conversation that doesn't make any sense to him at all.

Unknown number: I see you tried to block me. I've switched to using other phones, though, so no luck there. You should really be on our side. You don't have to act like a slave to the deranged people you call 'friends.' I never said I would hurt you, just the ones around you. And not even for no reason.

Min-ho: Are you really serious about becoming a serial killer, or have you just been influenced by True Crime to make baseless threats?

Unknown number: Both. Haven is thought of as a crime, and I have been inspired by the group. A lot of people have, but no one knows how or when to go about it, though.

Min-ho: Who's no one? Are you referring to your friends, or are there others?

Unknown number: Of course, there are others. More adults than children, but when you're older you get away with less than when you're younger.

Unknown number: A serious question for you, though: Do you think it'd be easier to kill your mentally ill people or wait until the government takes them?

Unknown number: My mother says they all deserve to be tortured for ruining our neighborhood. My father wants to be the one to escort your broken toys off to the government's facility, though.
They'll be going there anyway if they live through what I'm planning.
Unknown number: Last chance to...

"Oh—! Hyeong-cheol, what are you doing?" Min-ho says, laughing nervously as he quickly pockets his phone before bending to retrieve the forgotten blankets folded beneath his bed, mentally cursing himself for what he fears Hyeong-cheol saw.

"Why is... why is Min-ho talking to a person with no picture...? Why is Min-ho still shaking...?" He reaches impulsively to touch Min-ho's shoulder, swiftly retreating because it bothers him, that feeling—the sensation of trembling because fear has dared to sit too close to you.

"Hyeong-cheol, he's not a stranger. I-I just didn't give him a profile picture because we're not friends. He even has a name. He's... his name is Ryu-han." He tries to suppress the anxiety stuttering his heartbeat for the sake of his friend, knowing how afraid he is of strangers, but it's near impossible.

He read it. Hyeong-cheol read his messages. What should I do? What should I do? He's focused on the aspect of me talking to a stranger, though. Yes, maybe he didn't read any of those messages at all.

"Oh no, why would a stranger be on your phone...?" His voice is already tremulous, Hyeong-cheol's, those pale hazel eyes of his, regarding Min-ho cautiously while Min-ho hurries to form a response and averts his attention to the blankets beneath his bed.

"Well, as I said, he's not a stranger. He's just someone I don't like from school. You don't have to be afraid—we were just discussing a stupid movie about war. So anything you read that confuses you is only confusing because you haven't watched that movie."

Min-ho pulls out a thick brown blanket, glancing up at Hyeong-cheol, who's standing above him and noting the fear etched into his face, for he's paled significantly, this friend, and his eyes have widened as though he's witnessed something dreadfully heinous.

"Look, I'm not sure why he's bothering me about stupid movies, either, but jerks will be jerks, so let's not worry about him. And he doesn't have a profile picture because I haven't given him one, because he's not supposed to have my number, the jerk..."

He's very scared of that, Hyeong-cheol.

Messaging someone without a profile picture due to the probability of that person being dangerous, because his mother did it so often when he lived with her, and those people would hurt him all the time when they came over. He never once saw their faces, because they always arrived and left when their house was quite dark, and he was never allowed to turn the light on.

"You'll only get scared if you see them, Weeping Willow... They've messed themselves up more than me. Besides, I have a headache, and it's good for our plants—the darkness, I mean. They benefit from hiding away just like you do from me, sometimes. Let's leave the lights off."

"W-why's Min-ho talking to a stranger...?" The words come out strained and small as he struggles to inhale the air around him, which seems thick and heavy, weighing down on his chest as he stares down at Min-ho, the boy who's refusing to meet his eyes.

"He's not a stranger, I told you. He's someone I don't like at school, no one you have to be concerned about."

Maybe you should be concerned, though. Of course, you should be. You're different, too. Should I call uncle? No, I know what I have to do. I have to forget the threat of death and make tonight as happy as possible. Besides, Ryu-han really could just be lying.

"*Min-ho is with a very bad stranger!*"

"Hyeong-cheol, it's okay. Disliking someone doesn't make them a stranger, it just means I don't care to be his friend at all. Now, let's hurry and make our fort."

Hyeong-cheol shivers as several tears descend his cheeks, chewing at his fingers while giving Min-ho such an exasperated expression of fear that he's forced to look away as soon as their eyes meet.

"Min-ho is scared of the stranger, too...?" His inquiry is almost whispered, lifting a trembling finger to point at the boy who sighs deeply before saying carefully, "No, I'm not scared, Hyeong-cheol. And Ryu-han is not a stranger," ducking beneath the bed to withdraw another blanket while trying to pretend the world is not as scary as it's presenting itself in his mind.

"There are so many needles and not enough air to breathe when so many people are lighting the papers inside the dark...!"

"Well... He doesn't do drugs to my knowledge, if that's what you're implying. And he's really not a stranger. At least not to me. There are just some people we don't like that we already know..."

Hyeong-cheol says nothing, biting a bit harder at the tips of his fingers while he continues to gaze at his friend with fear and disapproval in his eyes.

"Hyeong-cheol, don't get like that...! It's fine... I just don't like the guy, that's all. He's not a random stranger, and he's not going to..." Min-ho trails off then, noticing the way his friend is shaking as he drops into a crouch and hating the way it's making him feel.

"Uh, do you want a hug...?"

"'Do you want... a hug...?' 'I understand it's uncomfortable, but y-you can tell me to stop.'"

"What? Oh, I'm not trying to make you uncomfortable, I'm just trying to let you know I'm sorry I scared you. I promise I won't be talking to anyone like the people your mother has talked to. He's not into drugs, and he can't hurt you. You don't have to be scared, Hyeong-cheol. It's okay, really..."

Hyeong-cheol raises his hands to his ears and pats them vigorously, shivering as he tries his best not to breathe so hard, despite the way air seems to be slipping out of him.

"Hyeong-cheol, you're panicking. If you don't listen to me, you're going to have an asthma attack. Everything's fine. We're all okay, and Ryu-han is not a harmful stranger."

I've told so many lies already. You're a part of Haven's problem, too. You're an oddity the world wants to devour. Why wouldn't he hurt you if he got the chance? There are so many people that aren't neurotypical in this world, so many opportunities for too many lives to be stolen because of the way they are. And what was that about the government? What does Ryu-han's family know that we don't? If the government is involved, maybe I shouldn't...

"*Mmmh!*" Hyeong-cheol stims more aggressively with his hands to his ears, tensing when Min-ho moves to stop him, his fingers gripping his wrist tightly as he reiterates while holding his gaze, "Everything's fine. We're all okay."

Why am I lying? We're not okay. Ryu-han really is dangerous. His dad is an officer, and I'm sure he has a gun. His mother wants to hurt us, too. How am I supposed to know what he will or won't do? Why am I lying to you, Hyeong-cheol?

"Everything is fine, and we're supposed to be happy right now. We're going to make a fort to play in, remember? We're going to make a fort and—"

"*No, no, they're taking out paper to make his favorite paper friends…!*"

"What? We never… Okay, fine, whatever. We can do that inside the fort. But right now, I need you to either forget about Ryu-han because he's making you panic, or believe me when I say he's not a stranger, and he's not going to hurt you. Let's get the blankets for the fort."

"'Get-get the blankets from the f-fort…!' *He's s-so sca-scared!*"

"Hyeong-cheol, you don't have to play in the fort if you don't want to, but we all— well, I thought we all agreed to play games inside the fort."

"*Oh, no! M-Min-ho plays them, too? G-games are s-so dumb! S-so bad…!*"

Loosening his grip on Hyeong-cheol's wrists, Min-ho furrows his brows in confusion.

"What are you talking about? Of course, I play them too. Some of them are owned by me because the PlayStation is technically mine, but I guess if that bothers you, you don't have to play…?" He poses this as a question because he doesn't understand this friend, and frowns because Hyeong-cheol looks just as confused as he sounded.

"Oh… oh, yes, the-th-the PlayStation with all the games and the… Min-ho is w-wanting to play games on the TV."

"That's where the games are usually played in a group setting, the TV, yes. What were you thinking?"

He tilts his head this way and that way, pulling away from Min-ho to fiddle with his scarf while blinking several times into the air, sounding almost computerized as he says, "Min-ho is a boy who plays games on his TV. Eun-seok and Sung-hee are grown-ups who do not… 'But that's okay, because everyone does different things, Hyeong-cheol.'"

"Oh, I didn't know that. I thought Eun-seok and Sung-hee played Yoshi with you."

"They do not like to play games on the TV, but sometimes it can make Hyeong-cheol so very happy after so many tears. They will say, we can do reading, we can go to the park, or we can play pretend inside your fort. Then they will say,

'Hyeong-cheol, do you want to play again?' and you will say,

'Oh, no, thank you, I am all done playing that game…' but don't say no again, because Sung-hee will get so very mad at you, and Eun-seok will say, 'Hyeong-cheol is acting *so* shy, but he is having *so much* fun…'"

Thinking that rather odd, Min-ho wrinkles his nose at Hyeong-cheol, lowering his voice as he carefully inquires,

"What… what game is that, Hyeong-cheol…?"

Hyeong-cheol begins biting his fingers, noting the worry in Min-ho's voice and studying the concern on his face, anxiety eating at his belly because he's wondering if he said too much about something he's supposed to say nothing about at all, because he's been told not to mention those games. But it's all so confusing, remembering not to talk about things that trouble you, because they're not supposed to trouble you at all. He can't help but wonder if those children, the ones he sees at his second house, feel the same way, because none of them look as though they enjoy the games they're playing with the adults that initiate them, perhaps because they're forced to play in front of so many eyes, so many cameras, and you should never be forced to have fun.

"Hyeong-cheol, that doesn't sound like a fun game... Why would Sung-hee get mad at you, and what reason would Eun-seok have to say that...?"

"No, no, he doesn't know, so many questions. Let's go play."

"We can play, but you're worrying me because the game you're talking about doesn't sound safe. It sounds scary."

Unsure of how to respond to Min-ho, Hyeong-cheol begins to vigorously pat his ears, anxiety teasing his heart again as his brows knit together, and several tears escape his eyes.

"It's okay to tell me. You won't get in trouble because we're the only ones here," He tries not to sound as though he's pressuring the boy, but he's no longer able to brush off his friend's behavior as he did before, so worried about what Chae-won said is true, it's making him forget to be patient as he continues, moving closer, "You can even whisper it to me to make sure no one hears, or nod your head if you feel unsafe in your environment. I heard a police officer telling someone that before. You have to do something, though, Hyeong-cheol, otherwise, nothing will change…! Unless-unless I'm just not correctly understanding, because you can let me know about that, too."

"Hyeong-cheol, do you feel safe at this house…? Are you happy you don't live with your mother anymore?" Those were the words of the first social worker who came to visit him the day after he was removed from his mother's care and sent to stay with the ones now called his caretakers, because there was nowhere else for him to go.

"It's a relief she went to prison. She won't be able to bother you now. You're safe. And you have so many nice toys, here. This is better for you, is it not?"

She had asked so many questions that day, and he hadn't answered any of them because there was too much to sort through in his mind, too much his caretakers had already done to make the word 'safe' feel foreign to him, for what is safety once it's been violated…? And how can one gain serenity when one is constantly afraid of losing it…?

"Older brother, are you okay…? I didn't mean to make you cry. I just want to be a good friend and make sure you're okay…" He's speaking so softly, Min-ho, carefully hindering Hyeong-cheol's hands from hitting his ears while gently squeezing them to try to ease the visible fear shaking him.

"The Little Prince told the pilot about his complicated relationship with his rose… maybe you have some complicated relationships, too."

215

He won't say anything. Even his tears have no volume as his memories take him further back into his mind and cause a rather blank expression to take over his face, the red blush beneath his eyes looking so much darker because of the way his skin has paled against it.

Maybe I shouldn't have asked. Maybe I didn't have the right to pry into a secret when I refused to expose my own... but those games don't seem like games at all. Why would that be happening, though? Why would Chae-won be right, and what are we even supposed to do about that when he's the way he is, and the police have never helped us before?

- Twelve -

Who are You...?

Kyun-ho doesn't want to open the door to Hae-sol's room once he stands in front of it.

He's visibly shaking; of course, he is.

He's always ridden with anxiety before and after he sees this friend.

You have to visit him. You have to visit him because if you don't, he might hurt himself. He might get sick because he hasn't eaten, or he might try to get the nurses to let him watch the news again, even after I told them not to, and then what if he sees, and what if he knows dads escaped...?

It's okay. You're okay. You have to be for him.

"Mister Choi, is there a problem with patient Kim's room?"

Blinking rapidly, Kyun-ho flushes as he turns to shake his head at the nurse who appeared beside him, struggling to respond as he chokes, "N-no! No, I-I'm just checking to see if he's a-awake...!"

To which the lady, a new nurse who goes by the name of Ha-ru, smiles tightly before stating, "Mr. Choi, patient Kim doesn't sleep so easily without a visit from you. Everyone knows that. Why, right now, he appears to be enjoying the scenery outside."

Biting his tongue in a failed attempt at distracting anxiety, Kyun-ho shifts uncomfortably before impulsively asking, "Has Dong-shik seen the news at all today?" to which Ha-ru nods and simply says, "Why, of course. All the patients watch the news at least once a day. It's the only channel they can all agree on. Was he not supposed to?"

Oh, dear, it's happening again.

That terrible sensation that feels like you're falling, the one that nearly takes your breath away because you're falling at a speed that tells you it's impossible to breathe.

"Is there an issue with patient Kim viewing the news...?"

"I told Nurse Kang I didn't want him watching it three days ago." Fighting the urge to leave this hospital entirely, Kyun-ho tells himself again and again that he's okay, that Hae-sol probably hasn't seen anything regarding the escape of his father or the recent murder rumored to be connected to some fan of Haven.

"Oh, goodness, I'm sorry. No one told me anything of the sort! Patient Kim's regular nurse has also been out for the last few days, so please don't blame her for not relaying your instructions. Again, I apologize about that, Mister Choi."

Kyun-ho can only force a nod at that, biting his tongue again and flinching involuntarily upon feeling Ha-ru's hand on his shoulder, her tone warm as she inquires, "Is it because of what's happening with the government...? It's dreadful, to be honest. I wouldn't want anyone here to discover what's planned for the future just yet."

"W-what do you mean? Did-did something happen...?" Kyun-ho's words push and shove each other as they exit his throat, causing him to sound rather strained as anxiety rapidly runs through his imagination.

"Have you been following the news at all? I'd think, as Sang-ho's son, you'd be all over it."

"N-no, I-I don't. I'm not..."

Oh goodness, Kyun-ho feels his stomach playing tricks on him, the suspense of not knowing what Ha-ru is talking about and the terrible thoughts of Haven dizzying him.

"Well, I feel it's best for you to look into yourself, but they don't feel safe having people like our patients around everyone else. There was another murder last night, and the police claim it was by a victim who escaped Haven years ago, a mentally ill man in his twenties."

The entire world seems to collapse on Kyun-ho's shoulders as his face drains its color, and Ha-ru's words begin pricking his skin.

"That man, the one who claimed to be a survivor of Haven, killed an officer right inside the police station. And before he was killed in self-defense, he shouted about some kind of revolt that would..." Ha-ru stops then; her eyes seem to take in every little detail fear has brought upon Kyun-ho's face as though making a mental note of it, storing it away somewhere.

"You look pale. Perhaps you should visit your friend first before discovering the rest of the story." This is all she says before turning away and disappearing down the long hallway, her footsteps echoing in Kyun-ho's ears as panic swallows him whole.

What... what was she talking about? There weren't any survivors from Haven, Hae-sol. No, no, that doesn't make any sense, does it?

If Kyun-ho had any confidence to face Hae-sol before, it surely isn't here now.

Am I supposed to ask Hae-sol about this? Would he know anything? What if someone's lying, what if…

He grips the doorknob to Hae-sol's room tightly and refuses to look inside the oval window, because he doesn't want to risk meeting his gaze if he's already looking.

God, I-I know I've been absent for a while, but please let everything be okay. If you're even listening after everything I've done, please don't let things get any worse. Please, at least give me peace.

It's a selfish prayer; he's ashamed of it.

But it's the only one he'd been able to send up after spending so much time trying to ignore the Lord entirely, too focused on the scars inflicted by his past to see any sort of healing in Christianity at all.

"That title… Christianity. Do you even own that silly title anymore, or were you just holding onto it for dear old mommy and daddy…?"

Those words were the only thing Tae-ho said to Kyun-ho three days ago before he left on a 'business trip.'

They bothered Kyun-ho because he didn't know what to say.

I… I don't know; I don't know what I am anymore.

Praying won't do anything for me. I'm too messed up to sort anything out, but if I can't pray for peace, how am I supposed to get any without medication or-or drugs?

Oh, dear, he's forgotten not to cry through this inward struggle, and now his tears have gone and run wild down his face, plump cheeks flushed with too many quarreling emotions as his fingers lose their grip on the doorknob and his feet cause him to stumble backwards away from Hae-sol.

"A-agh, I-I can't...! I can't do it! *I can't do anything!*" Kyun-ho sobs pitifully, leaning against the wall opposite Hae-sol's room and trying not to be so audibly distraught as several nurses walk past him while he ducks his head in utter shame.

They won't judge him here; he knows that.

They never have, not even the new hires.

They're a hospital, a hospital that uses medicines instead of band-aids for wounds inside the mind.

But he still can't let go of the embarrassment and shame that comes with this sort of breakdown.

Still refuses to think he's okay being like this here because he's not.

Hae-sol said it himself, time and time again, after shouting at him for crying or messing up on a 'surgery.'

"Kyun-ho! Idiot, get yourself together! There's no lasting trauma.
There are no regrets.
There's no fear, and there are no memories associated with Haven that those stupid doctors could label as 'PTSD'...!

Act like a victim, and they'll take advantage of your mind. Present yourself as a victor... and the only one who can control your mind is you.

Haven did nothing wrong to you.

We did nothing wrong... in Haven.

Gather yourself as a doctor and remind yourself you're not like the patients we're operating on!

You're not broken, and the moment you do break, I'll have no choice but to fix you myself...!"

He's running out of air.

His heart is stuttering so fast it's sickening him.

He is crying, even though he's trying to frantically erase the evidence by scrubbing his eyes.

"You don't even need medicine, Kyun-ho. Everyone who's ever claimed to understand you is lying.

There's nothing wrong with you and nothing wrong with us...! Get me out of this hospital before you end up as my roommate. We're supposed to be fixing Haven's children!"

"Mister Choi, would you like to take a walk outside?"

"H-help me...!" Kyun-ho chokes, dropping his arms from his eyes and looking around frantically before averting his teary gaze back to the tall woman in front of him, her chest-length auburn hair and calm turquoise eyes holding no familiarity at all to Kyun-ho's mind as he continues, his body shaking as though wrapped in snow, *"I-I can't do it— I can't be here, n-n-nothing—nothing's making any sense, a-and I-I don't want to see any more memories— I don't want to hear them!"*

The lady in front of Kyun-ho is someone he really ought to remember, though, and the weight of this shows in her eyes as she turns to whisper something to the small gathering of nurses who had formed behind her before extending an arm down the hall and stating to Kyun-ho, "Mr. Choi, let's go outside for a bit."

"I-I didn't even want to do it, b-but now it's t-too late, and you're st-still hurting Tae-kyun…!" He's no longer directing his speech to those around him; he's completely lost inside his mind as he jerks his head left and right before emitting a pained cry and sinking down into the floor, where he remains for several minutes, eyes full of so much fear-laced disorientation as he stares, unblinking, ahead of him.

She doesn't try to force him to leave or shake him out of his memory; no, that won't be very helpful at all.

She's tried that before. Many of the staff here know Kyun-ho and have tried coaxing him out of his past to no avail.

She merely stands above his shaking form, making note of how quickly his PTSD has worsened throughout the time she's known him and wondering why he continues to come here when it always seems to physically or mentally pain him.

Her name is Ari, and she's worked here for several years, but no… there must be more.

But if you were to ask Kyun-ho, he'd simply stare at you in confusion and reiterate your question back to you.

Who is Ari?

And why does she always seem so familiar, yet so distant, all at once?

- Thirteen -

Her

It was Monday, another day in which 14-year-old Kyun-ho dismissed the existence of school entirely.

It wasn't as though his mother was alive to chastise him, and his father would beat him regardless, so he'd decided for the last few weeks to simply not go at all.

'Besides, what's a few weeks when I'm already constantly missing days...? No one cares, anyway... no one cares...'

That had been his mindset that day.

That had been his mindset for the last few months, because depression griped him tighter with each sleepless night after his father beat him, each interaction with Tae-kyun and the realization that his condition was getting worse, and every single visit with Hae-sol and the falling of Haven.

'I'm so tired... so tired. Maybe... I should just...' His thoughts broke off as though fallen leaves when the wind picked up and rushed through the trees that surrounded him, and he was reminded he was wan-

dering alone in the forest as the sun began to set behind the clouds that gathered so swiftly.

The day had slipped away from him again.

And nothing had changed.

Hae-sol stole the neighbor's cat and forced Kyun-ho to perform a lobotomy that, of course, failed, just as it did when done to the children.

The treehouse floor was painted with crimson, and for the first time in a very long time, Hae-sol had reacted to the sight of it and spent several hours crying, mourning the loss of his brother, and repeatedly blaming Kyun-ho for his death as he tried, again and again, to cut himself with the bloodied knife Kyun-ho had thrown against the wall.

"Hae-yon…! Why didn't you stop me? Why didn't it work? W-why are you such a bad friend, Kyun-ho?"

The knife had sliced effortlessly through Hae-sol's leg because Kyun-ho failed to retrieve it in time.

Hae-sol was bleeding because Kyun-ho messed up again.

'I mess up so much. I should have just thrown the knife out of the treehouse once I saw his eyes change. Now, if he gets an infection because I didn't clean his wound well enough, he's going to die, and that will be my fault too, even though he told me to go away, even though I did go away once I forced him to take that medicine once he fell asleep…'

I'm not sure how far he wandered; he wasn't sure, either.

It's hard to pay attention to your surroundings when your mind is veiled with dysphoria.

Eventually, though, he stumbled upon a small clearing where long blades of grass intertwined with cosmos flowers, and the sun shone a little more brightly than it had before, and in the center of this small universe lay a girl, Kyun-ho's age, tucked away in the long grass with flowers that tickled her face, her dry laughter being the only indication of her presence, the only reason Kyun-ho came so near to peer down at her.

"I know you, Choi Kyun-ho. Everyone thinks you got expelled from school. Your weird friend thinks your dad is caging you again. You don't have many fans, not after what happened with Tae-kyun. Your whole family's on the verge of persecution." She laughed again, and thin and wispy charcoal-colored hair blew into her face as she inquired, after closing cerulean, narrow eyes, "Wanna take some blue angels...? Promise it will make you feel better. They worked for me. They always work for me."

Kyun-ho stared down at her in confusion and glanced around as though to confirm they were the only ones there, before he hesitantly inquired, "Wh-what's a blue angel, and why-why aren't you running away from me or telling me to leave...?"

She opened one eye to stare at him, and a devilish smile slightly parted her lips as she said, "I could say the same for you. I'm known to cause trouble, simply because my mother does. So I don't mind if you do the same. Though honestly, you look more like a victim than a victimizer."

Quite simply, her words scared Kyun-ho, and suddenly he wanted nothing more then to get away from her, perhaps because he wasn't used to people wanting to be around him, so he took a step back and stammered, "I-I don't... I have to go home, Tae-kyun— he should be back from the hospital by now," to which the girl, who had yet to give herself a name, sat up abruptly to agree with him and dusted her pleated yellow skirt off before she followed behind him, as if they'd known each other for quite some time.

"Let's go."

"Oh, well..."

"I knew it. You don't really want to go home. Your home is probably no better than mine, and Tae-kyun's just going to be taken to another ritual.

Everyone knows your daddy's habits by now." She tilted her head, and charcoal colored hair fell across her face as though sheer curtains while she mused after she observed the crimson that painted Kyun-ho's clothes, "I see you've gotten into some trouble today. Would you like to elaborate?"

"N... no." Is all Kyun-ho could manage as he pushed past the discomfort that happened when her hand grazed his cheek, for she had noticed the dried blood and murmured, in a curious sort of way, "Tell me... Just what do you and that strange boy do in that treehouse that would cause so much blood to mark your body?"

She looked at him and searched those frightened eyes while she waited for his response, but only the wind answered.

It's very hard to form a response when so many of your words have vanished.

He'd been uncomfortable, terribly uncomfortable because he wasn't used to this.

Why was this girl so intent on talking to him?

Why did her clothes smell so strongly of smoke and perfume, and why were her eyes... why were her eyes so strikingly different?

Not just the color, but the obvious lack of vision in her right eye, the one that'd been lulling about lazily through clouded cerulean, the one with the aged scarring beneath it that looked disturbingly close to a knife wound, something Kyun-ho was all too familiar with because of the many attacks he's suffered throughout his life.

'No...' he decided, and pursed his lips into a thin line. 'Either there must be something wrong with you, or you have other intentions, because there are only three people I know who want to be around me: Tae-kyun, Hae-sol, and shr...' At that, he swallowed deeply and shook his head in a failed attempt at clearing it.

He had startled at the warm sensation of tears that spilled down his cheeks, for he hadn't known he'd been crying, just as he hadn't known he'd been trembling.

He tried to gather the parts of himself that felt unraveled, tried not to appear so terribly pitiful in front of someone he didn't even know, but no matter how many times he inwardly scolded himself for crying while he swiped at his eyes, the sadness stayed, and so did the girl in front of him.

She dropped to the bed of flowers beneath them, lay with her hands behind her head, and admired the setting sun.

She had noted, as a small smile graced her, that perhaps Kyun-ho's life was laced with the same kind of tragedies that adorned her own.

And this is what prompted her to stay, despite all the warnings from the world around her that told her she shouldn't.

IMPORTANT NOTICE

최근 장교 살해에 관한 새로운 법률

(New law Regarding the Recent Murders of Officers Effective October 7th.)

Another officer has fallen victim to a fatal shot dealt by an individual suffering from mental illness and intellectual disabilities.

The perpetrator opened fire at a police station in Hongdae, and severely injured four officers before taking his own life after claiming there were several more survivors of Haven who would work together to overthrow the government.

After the prison break of Choi Sang-ho, the organization's leader, crimes involving officers and the mentally ill have increased in just five days, and mental health facilities are experiencing a concerning amount of missing patients who return with no memory as to why or how they left the hospital, causing citizens to suspect those without hospitalization may become targets as well.

Several police officers have faced abuse at the hands of those believed to have a mental illness, and several citizens of Korea have reached out in concern over the anonymous phone calls and emails regarding Haven and a public uprising against those 'oppressing the mentally ill and disabled.'

In order to protect our country, its civilians, and its officers, the government will be relocating its mental health facilities and requesting families of those with mental illness and/or disabilities to help relocate their loved ones to Hope Ridge and Sang-joon's pediatric facility, which has been converted to fit the needs of individuals with mental/intellectual disabilities.

Until the people behind this uprising are behind bars of justice, it is mandatory to relocate all persons diagnosed with mental / intellectual disabilities to ensure the safety of our country, its citizens, and persons suffering from mental/intellectual disabilities.

- Fourteen -

Undivided Attention

It doesn't take that long for the fort to be made.

No, the process is quite simple, really.

After all, it's only a few blankets tied onto the chairs they've encircled around the living room, a long stick with a small weight secured with rope, stuck in the middle of the fort to heighten the roof.

It's not very fun, though, sitting in a fort when you don't feel enthused about it, and most of these children don't feel particularly enthused at all.

A quiet visit of rainfall had started not long ago outside, softly hitting the windows as Yoon-ha began the uncomfortable game of suppressing his vocal tics to avoid upsetting Hyeong-cheol, something he feels is almost mandatory considering how close they are inside this fort.

Choon-ha is no longer pretending to feel okay.

One moment he was struggling to force exuberance, and the next he was practically drowning in pure depression, no longer caring about what his friends think because why would they care, anyway?

Tae-kyun hasn't woken at all despite his rising temperature, and Chae-won merely wants to maintain his composure, which he feels this night is trying to tear down.

He wants to offer some sort of solution to the obvious lack of mirth around him, but he's afraid rejection will worsen the anxiety so much silence has brought him.

So he says nothing at all.

Min-ho *did try* to entertain his friends by reading aloud one of the many Pokémon manga he owned, but eventually he realized Chae-won was the only one paying attention, so he solemnly returned to the difficult task of unraveling the mystery of Hyeong-cheol's life, tilting his head at the boy who's coloring his paper quite hurriedly.

Has Hyeong-cheol always been so restless, or is he repositioning himself so frequently because an event has left him wounded?

He's coloring his paper dolls, but he's so distracted by everyone around him, that he doesn't look like he's enjoying himself. He keeps stopping to hit his ears.

He's quiet again— is he shutting down, like before? And he looks miserable. Hasn't he always looked that way, though?

What are we supposed to do about you, older brother? What am I supposed to do with what you said before at a time like this? Maybe I should just stop thinking. You say weird things all the time, and we would know if your caretakers were hurting you because you would act scared, just like you do with your mom, right?

It's all very messy at this moment, and I do worry these children won't gain any rapture at all.

"So, how, uhm, what is Kyun-ho doing about... Well, not to...

Actually, never mind." Chae-won sets the remote down and pushes up his glasses, combing a hand through his hair as the low volume of the TV provides background noise in place of the silence.

"Y-you must... you must be referring t-to daddy..."Yoon-ha whispers, his eyes focused on the screen before him as Chae-won slowly says, "Well, it's just that the police will be here to patrol the neighborhood tomorrow and make sure everything's okay, but that's kinda scary, right...? Because that means they really do think he may come here..."

Tearing his gaze away from Hyeong-cheol, Min-ho rubs his eyes and inquires (fighting a yawn because all this thinking has made him feel rather weary), "Yeah, but the police really don't do much..."

He's feeling strange, Min-ho, his eyes traveling slowly back to Hyeong-cheol as he murmurs, forgetting he isn't inwardly speaking, "I wonder if they'll still try to torture you all knowing that..." to which both Choon-ha and Chae-won turn to stare imploringly at him, Hyeong-cheol carefully setting down his crayons before lowering his face into his hands as though sorrow has abruptly beaten him, which I suppose it has because he's been looking distraught ever since he left Min-ho's room.

He's so sad now, what have I done to this night...? Tae-kyun's sick. He's covered in band-aids because he hurt himself. Hyeong-cheol's depressed,

233

and his presence here is illegal. There are people out to kill everyone in this house but me…

"Uhm, Min-ho…? Can you, uh, shed some light on this-this torture?"

Blinking rapidly, Min-ho turns to face his friends while furrowing his brows in confusion, still under the impression he was merely thinking earlier as he says, "What are you talking about…?"

"The torture. You said something about people and torture earlier." Choon-ha says, sounding slightly agitated.

"Well, to be honest…"

Do I really have to be honest…?
Will honesty really make a difference…?

Min-ho glances over to Hyeong-cheol, who's paused again in his coloring, this time to stare at him, the pale green of his eyes seeming to darken a bit as he begins biting his fingers, the band-aids Min-ho applied earlier tearing a bit.

Does Hyeong-cheol know I'm thinking of lying…? Did he really even read those messages? I don't have any indication to say he did, but I also don't really have any indication to say he didn't.

"We're waiting, Min-ho. Torture is-is pretty serious." Chae-won swallows, combing a hand through his blond bangs as Min-ho sighs while rolling his eyes around the fort, deciding he can at least prolong his response by searching for another.

"Hyeong-cheol, be honest with me. Did you read anything on my phone?"

Hyeong-cheol looks at Min-ho for what feels like an eternity before answering, "Yes. 'Did you read anything on my phone?' Yes, yes, Min-ho was so very scared."

"Min-ho, what does your phone have to do with this? I think we're all feeling like you're stalling."

"Did you read what Ryu-han said…? Ryu-han was the one without a profile picture; he's the one who scared me." He already knows Hyeong-cheol is unlikely to respond, but the tension he's woven in the atmosphere has him anxious to weave more, and he's not really sure why.

Perhaps it's the attention.

It's undivided.

Everyone, even Hyeong-cheol, is focusing on him.

He's the center of attention, and he's not hurt.

He's not dying.

He's not in trouble.

And he's certainly not disabled or harboring any mental illness.

He looks around, Min-ho, taking in the uneasy expressions, the frequent shifting of Chae-won, the muffled shrieks of Yoon-ha, who had tried to suppress the noise behind his hands.

"I've barely said anything. Are you guys already scared?"

"It's because you've barely said anything that's making things weird, Min-ho," Chae-won explains, shifting again while nervously raking his fingers through his hair.

"Oh, well, what do you guys think I have to say?"

"I think, whatever it is, is secretly not that important." Choon-ha frowns, rubbing his eyes before crawling towards the exit of the fort.

"Wait! Choon-ha!" Min-ho grabs the back of Choon-ha's school sweater vest and pulls him backwards, emitting a dark sound of irritation from the boy who would normally find the notion quite amusing.

"It is important and super secret!" Min-ho feels as though he's inhaling too much air as he struggles to regain what little spotlight he held before.

Yoon-ha's lost interest. He's examining the leaves he'd withdrawn from his pockets, placing each one carefully on his lap before vigorously wringing out his wrists.

Hyeong-cheol has taken his paper dolls to sit beneath the kitchen table, the frequent exclamations from his friends and discomfort the fort brought proving too difficult to ignore.

Choon-ha is trying to leave as well.

Chae-won is the only one still looking at him.

"It's about Haven! Duplicating their crimes. Ryu-han and some others have started a group that targets people with mental illness or disabilities, and they threatened to hurt you all first! I was already going to tell you, but I couldn't find the right moment, and I guess you could assume that's because I was afraid..."

Choon-ha, unsure of whether Min-ho is lying or not, laughs before saying over Yoon-ha's abrupt shriek, "I thought Haven trafficked children and sold them for rare Pokémon cards or something."

"That's the farthest thing from funny. Haven is a group you should know all about. A group you should be paranoid about recurring because they target people like you and everyone else that isn't normal like me."

"So, but is it trafficking? Because…"

"No, you idiot! They kill people with mental issues because they hate them. That's why you should be worrying about it and not…!" Exhaling slowly, Min-ho pinches the bridge of his nose while trying to soothe his raging heartbeat, closing his eyes as he calmly says, "You know what, Choon-ha? I'm not going to yell at you anymore because I don't want to further agitate Hyeong-cheol. But if you could stop pretending that you know nothing about Haven, that would be great. Terrific, even."

"So they are human traffickers. Splendid! I will make sure I wear my best clothes and hope that they'll be the ones to rip them off and ravage—"

"Would you shut up and be more serious about your life…?"

The amount of self-control it takes to withhold the urge to choke Choon-ha is visibly flushing Min-ho's cheeks as he glares at him, fingers trembling with morbid desire as Choon-ha merely smiles.

And that makes him even angrier, not just because the boy is smiling, but because he knows if he *were* to strangle Choon-ha, he'd never get away with it like one with a mental peculiarity.

Hyeong-cheol has committed numerous acts of violence towards himself and others, yet they're dismissed almost as soon as they happen, dropped into the giant pot of, *'He didn't mean to'*, *'He can't regulate himself like you do'*, and most famously, in Eun-seok's case, *'He's having a bad day, I'm sorry.'*

"Aren't you even a little bit scared? People want to kill you, Choon-ha. Ryu-han's father, who's a police officer, wants to kill you, and you're not even taking this seriously?"

"Well, I'm certainly not Choon-ha, but I-I do find this news disturbing. Could we maybe…"

"Why don't you care?"

"Why does it bother you…?" Choon-ha challenges, sounding and looking a bit cruel as he silently dares Min-ho to answer him.

He needs to leave.

He feels himself sinking.

Sinking into a cold, colorless abyss of discontent.

Lifelessness.

Utter dismay and dysphoria.

But why? Why am I feeling like this when I wasn't feeling anything before? That's so unfair, so ridiculously unfair!

It doesn't matter if I flush those stupid pills or not— eventually, something stupid will always happen inside my mind!

"There are literally people who want to kill you, and you're acting like I'm joking. I'm not joking, Choon-ha."

"I never said you were. I just don't care if you aren't."

Chae-won blinks rapidly, pushing up his slipping glasses as his cheeks drain in color, and perspiration fogs his lenses.

"Min-ho, I-I think we should tell Kyun-ho because we can't really do anything to-to stop them…? I-I mean, how are they planning on…" Chae-won swallows hard, running a hand through his bangs before continuing, "How are they planning on harming us?"

"Does it really matter when the main thing they want is you guys *dead?*" Min-ho snaps, whipping around to glare at the boy, who hurriedly puts his hands up in surrender, stumbling on his words as he says, "O-oh, of course! I… Uhm, how a murderer kills is–is also important, though…!" feeling dizzy as perspiration gathers beneath his bangs and slides down his temple, too many terrible scenarios causing him to bend his fingers against the hardwood floor, one at a time, in a hurried attempt to empty his mind, which feels close to detonating.

Someone's trying to kill us!
I won't be safe when I walk back home tomorrow!
I won't be safe alone in my room!

I won't be safe around the Choi's, or school, or…!

"S-should we call the–the police…?" Yoon-ha inquires, suddenly deciding to be involved in the conversation as he's quite satisfied with the condition of his leaves, which he carefully slides back into his pockets.

"The police have *never* helped us before!" Min-ho shouts, cheeks reddening with anger as he continues bitterly, "All they do is look at us with *pity* and say there's *nothing* they can do! Haven't you heard of all the times uncles tried to go to them for help? We have a permanent stamp of Haven on us because of our uncle's dad, so *everyone* still hates us. We can't even go to the park like regular people because some idiot will always be there to call the police and say they feel threatened or whatever."

"Y-yes, that…Yes, that's true, but we can't d-do much because no one wants us around, anyway."

"You don't believe me."

"What g-gives you that impression…? A-all I s-s-said was…."

"Do you think they'd kill us if we all hid at my house? My aunt's a lawyer, so maybe…"

"No, they know where you live, too. Besides, if we were getting chased or something, we'd all die because you'd keep re-locking the door out of paranoia or whatever. The only way I can think to stop them is if we fight them, and if we do that, it will only make you all look more like violent monsters because that's the first thing people will want to see. They won't see it as self-defense. No one is going to care that you fought because someone set our house on fire or beat us up. That's just the truth of it."

Chae-won has paled so much. I do fear he's turned ghostly, his mouth slightly parted in an 'o' as he stares at Min-ho in disbelief, inwardly continuing to panic because he doesn't know how to respond to any of this.

He would probably get them killed, because the doors wouldn't lock in his mind; doors and locks have been a constant battlefield for him for as long as he can remember, and dwelling on such when he's always panicking is making him feel as though the door to this house, like all the others in his mind, is unlocked and ready to be opened by a killer.

His hands have started sweating, and though he wipes them on his pants in quick intervals of ten seconds spaced five seconds apart, they continue to perspire, and his mind sets out on a course to obsess about how weak he must look in front of his friends, how *pathetic* it'd be to die from over perspiration, which of course has gotten him *visibly* panicking, which of course means he must abruptly leave this space to ensure the door is locked to disarm any possibility of death from himself or others, a risky compulsion that he knows Min-ho will fully judge him for, but one he's unable to resist.

"We're getting nowhere but closer to your death." Min-ho states, releasing a deep and irritated sigh as Choon-ha says, the lack of playfulness in his tone quite unsettling, "There's clearly nothing we can do besides tell dad. It's not like you have some kind of great big plan or something."

"I really don't think that would be good for uncle's mental health. He's barely functioning right now."

"Well, what do you suppose we do if we can't tell him…?"

"We have to stop them by ourselves somehow before they even try to come near us. I just don't know how, especially if the neighborhood is truly on his side."

It's dreadfully silent for what feels like an eternity, not even Yoon-ha disturbing the air as Min-ho bites his lower lip in contemplation.

"We need to draw up a plan. We have to get this sorted before uncle comes home."

Min-ho reaches for one of the papers Hyeong-cheol left behind, when, all at once, he hears a knock.

"Did you guys hear that…?"

"It's r-raining… I-I assume w-we all hear that."

"No…"

There it is again, and this time, Chae-won is frightened out of his trance and falls backwards away from the door.

"Maybe it's–"

Heavy bangs have replaced the knocks, and Min-ho is no longer alone in what he hears.

They all hear it now.

They're all afraid of it now, and the banging refuses to stop.

- Fifteen -

We All Fall Down

When Kyun-ho's past finally resides and lets the present take over, there's an unsettling amount of panic and chaos that causes his heart to stutter.

He can't remember closing his eyes, but he's forced to open them because it's so terribly loud, so what happened?

"Are they taking us away? Are they taking everyone away?"

"What about our families!?"

"Doctor why!? Why would that reporter tell us something so ridiculous?"

Kyun-ho, terribly perplexed by the world around him, raises a hand to massage his temple while glancing about the room, realizing, after several seconds, that this is the lobby of Serenity Center, and he must have been moved from his previous position in the hall.

"Call the police, please call and tell them the government lost it!"

"With all due respect, we can't possibly do that. Let's all calm down and hear what else the reporters have to—"

"They're taking *EVERYTHING AWAY!*"

Kyun-ho hears the sound of wreckage, and immediately after, the chaos gains more volume, and he's forced to cover his ears once the screams of Serenity Center's patients grow too reminiscent of his past.

"Tae-kyun's brother, why are you doing that to my arm? Why are you putting those inside of me? It hurts! You cut open my arm to fill it with bugs, and it hurts!"

"It's okay, s-st-stop crying! I-I'm helping you…! Me and Hae-sol both…! If you don't let those parasites take away your differences from the inside, the world outside will take away everything you could be…! Nobody will even care if you die or get hurt because society won't ever let you breathe! They hate you! They hate everyone who's different, so please, please just st-stop crying so I can feel better about helping you!"

"Mister Choi, you should hurry home," It's Ari, and she's taking Kyun-ho by the shoulders and forcing him to stand and hurry towards the door, her tone so tremulous as they burst through the hospital and into utter darkness and rain.

Rain… darkness… utter chaos…

Why is it all so familiar? Why… why does he feel so veiled in fear?

Perhaps it's because of the rain that hit against the window of that terrible treehouse, the one that holds so many broken pieces of his past.

Perhaps it's because of the way the rain was muted by Hae-sol's screams, the night Kyun-ho realized just how broken his friend and Haven were.

Or perhaps, still, it's the feeling of liquid slipping down his skin and soaking his clothes the same way blood would every time Hae-sol hurt him, every time his father and Tae-ho beat him for crimes he never knew he committed.

Perhaps I've always feared the rain…

"Mr. Choi, I'm sorry for throwing you out, but…" She swiftly pulls Kyun-ho's hands from his ears, feeling him shake beneath her touch as she softly admits through the rain's growing whispers, "Nothing good is going to happen, Mister Choi. Nothing good. You need to gather your family and run away. Nothing good can come of this. Nothing*!*"

"But… run…? What… what… are you talking about?"

"Kyun-ho, this world is about to treat you and your family a lot harsher than you're already used to. I know you're still hurting, and I know there's a lot you refuse to unravel about your past. I acknowledge that as the reason you are the way you are…" She swallows deeply, and Kyun-ho wanders absently while his heart stutters in his chest. Just who is this lady, and what reason does she have to be so near to him?

"Kyun-ho, I still hurt, too, and it's been more than a decade since Soarrarity's death. But you have to stop letting the past take you. You have to protect your family, and right now, I don't think you can do that unless you pull yourself together the same way I was also forced."

Kyun-ho fails to find her eyes in the veil of darkness draped over them, his stomach churning as his fingers curl and uncurl into fists that are shaking…

I'm shaking. Why am I shaking?
And why… why is she saying that name…?
Why does she know that name…?
Why do you…
Why…

It's hard to decipher her face through such thick layers of rain and darkness, and even harder to decipher his thoughts as they run and trip over each other.

His throat feels dry.

Painfully dry, as he reiterates the lady's words in his mind, he obsesses over that *one* name, that one *unfortunate* soul who now lies beneath the surface of the earth.

"S… soarrarity… w-why… why do you know her name…?"

She dismisses his question and says instead, "People like the ones at our center… like the ones in your family… are no longer allowed to live freely in this world. The government is going to take them all away. And as much as you hate to acknowledge it, that means you, too, Kyun-ho."

A terrible churning disturbs Kyun-ho's insides and sends his thoughts spiraling as the rain begins to burn his eyes.

Or perhaps… it's his tears…?

Nothing is making any sense. Things are happening too fast despite the fact that he feels as though the world is moving in slow motion.

He wants to say something, *needs* to say something, but he no longer has any control over his body.

He's as still as a puppet, waiting for its master to lift a finger and direct his movements.

The wind picks up and rushes through their hair, carrying crimson leaves from the shedding Maple trees around them and sending shivers throughout Kyun-ho's body as he struggles to piece himself together.

Is the past really trying to repeat itself in terms of pain and mental agony? Is this something that's happening because of Hae-sol? Is it dad, or is it a repercussion of the things I did in Haven all those years ago? Is this lady someone I should recognize because she knows her name, or not...?

All at once, the alarm sounds in the hospital, and a panicked voice announces over the chaos, "Patient 63 is missing! I repeat, patient 63 is missing!"

The children do not consider breathing a requirement when the banging continues, and so when it stops, all of them gasp for the air that they hadn't realized they'd been missing, faces flushed as frightened eyes jump around the room before looking to each other for answers on what to do.

"M–M–Min-ho, is that–is that..." Chae-won's shaking so much even his words are being affected, his glasses sliding down his nose as perspiration causes his hair to cling to his forehead while he scoots backwards into the fort, the blankets above him threatening to collapse once Hyeong-cheol rushes in after gathering his paper friends, shakily patting his ears as he stares, wide-eyed, at the door through the fort's gaps.

Yoon-ha is torn between hurriedly whispering to himself (or perhaps his leaf creatures) while sporadically cutting himself off to abruptly ask if he should call their father, Choon-ha's mouth frozen in a small 'o' as his eyes flicker between Min-ho's, Chae-won's, and his brother, who holds his gaze so intensely, the gravity of this mysterious situation grows ten times worse.

"I don't think it's Ryu-han. Ryu-han wouldn't knock. H-he's never been that-that polite," Min-ho chokes out, jumping when another loud and hurried bang cuts through the air, causing a small whimper to emit from Tae-kyun, who stirs beside Min-ho while struggling to open his eyes.

"W-who the heck i-is it then, Min-ho…? Because-because I don't think—"

"If I knew, I wouldn't be panicking…!"

In ordinary circumstances, Choon-ha would simply exit the fort to see who's knocking, as he's quite fascinated by danger.

But tonight he's experienced everything but ordinary, so he sits, knees drawn to his chest, while dark fantasies about this intruder fill his mind.

It could be the people Min-ha was talking about… could be someone who wants to kill us.

I want to care, but I don't, and I guess it's because a lot of things just don't seem worth it anymore.

"Maybe it's uncle. Maybe we should all—"

"Hello!? It's–it's Eun-seok! Can someone please answer the door?"

Eun-seok, the children all seem to think in unison, *What would he be doing, banging on the door...?*

Eun-seok bangs again on the door, and again, no one moves to open it.

"Hy-Hyeong-cheol, maybe that–that's really your care-taker. Go answer the door," Chae-won suggests, clearly not mak-ing any attempt to do so himself as he turns to nudge the boy encouragingly.

Hyeong-cheol does not feel encouraged to answer the door, though.

In fact, he's terrified.

Eun-seok sounds panicked, and the only time Hyeong-cheol has ever heard that emotion constrict his voice like that is when his mother is raging and can no longer be controlled.

And oftentimes, if she's raging, Eun-seok will make him go into his room or hide beneath his bed because she's too intent on hurting him.

Or he'll be rushed out into the car, with his mother chasing after them even as they drive away, which will always leave him paranoid for the rest of the day.

So no, Hyeong-cheol will not be answering the door, because Hyeong-cheol is thinking the moment he does, Eun-seok will rush in, all battered and bruised, with his mother right behind him, anxious to do the same to him.

"Let's all go. We're all scared, and we can all answer the door," Min-ho suggests, looking at his friends for confirmation and visibly relaxing when finally Chae-won nods, and Yoon-ha, who grips his phone with the intent of calling the police, slowly edges out of the fort while whispering for his brother to do the same.

"It shouldn't take a million people, people..." Choon-ha mutters, leaving the fort simply because he knows Yoon-ha won't leave him alone if he doesn't, and pausing when he feels a hand grip the back of his sweater vest.

"Wait, wait, it's so scary...! Miss Song can be so scary."

Hyeong-cheol's eyes seem to hold an infinite amount of fear as he withdraws his hand to place between his teeth, and he flinches violently when the banging resumes and Eun-seok calls again for someone to answer the door, the rain outside muting some of his words as it falls harder.

"Your mother doesn't even remember where we live. We're opening the door. It's fine."

He gives Hyeong-cheol all three seconds before deciding to abandon the boy to join the others at the door, thinking he wouldn't mind if there was a murderer knocking at all.

There is a brief session of second thoughts and hurried glances from the others before the door is unlocked, and in comes Eun-seok, terribly pale and drenching the wooden floor with the collapsing of his clear umbrella as he shakily announces, "We have to leave. Right now."

It's so quiet in Eun-seok's car. All that's audible is the violent battle of the windshield wipers against the pouring rain and the stifled shrieks and tuneless chortles from Yoon-ha, who hasn't once removed his hands from covering his mouth after entering the minivan.

Eun-seok will not stop shaking, and he's gripping the steering wheel so tightly, Hyeong-cheol briefly wonders if it will break.

His bright, caramel-colored eyes are glassy, hints of red tracing the corners of them, while his expression is riddled with fear.

"Eun-seok is so scared. Is Miss Song chasing him?"

Hyeong-cheol has asked this question more than five times after being forcibly removed from the fort, and Eun-seok has responded, each time sounding more and more clipped, "No, she wasn't, buddy. Your mother's at home."

"Oh, but he's shaking, and Miss Song will make him do that when she's so very—"

"Hyeong-cheol, this has nothing to do with your mother. Can you please stop leaning so close and sit back in your seat?"

Eun-seok swallows hard, and Min-ho can tell he's trying very hard to calm himself from whatever's scaring him, which both frightens and frustrates him because Eun-seok should be doing everything in his power to make them, the children, feel safe in whatever situation this is.

"So, uhm, what is the situation, sir? If-if you don't mind me asking, anyway…" Chae-won slowly inquires, shifting this way and that while Eun-seok says, gently moving Hyeong-cheol away from his seat, "The situation… You would you all like to know about the situation, yes?"

"Eun-seok, was Miss Song chasing him all the way into the rain? Is—"

"Hyeong-cheol, buddy, can you please not lean so close? You're stretching out your seatbelt. It's-it's not safe, and we can see each other just fine. I will continue to look scared no matter how close you lean, so please sit back."

"Oh no, Eun-seok is shaking. Was Miss Song chasing—"

"Hyeong-cheol, I'm not feeling too great right now. Sit back in your seat and let me process some things, okay?"

This response only agitates Hyeong-cheol's anxiety, and he's unable to sit still now, twisting and turning to look out the windows while biting at his hand and kicking at the glove compartment, emitting several sounds of agitation, which in turn intensifies the emotions Eun-seok is struggling to contain.

"Eun-seok, it would really help to know who or what we're running from. Did uncle call for you to get us?"

"D-does daddy-d-daddy know we're w-with you?"

"I told you we should have called Kyun-ho earlier, Min-ho...! It's probably something involving Ryu-han! He's probably already formulated a plan. He's probably already—!"

"Chae-won, shut up!" Min-ho snaps, paranoid he's already said too much and turning to clap a hand over his mouth right as Hyeong-cheol begins crying, loud, guttural tears over the fingers he's aggressively biting despite the tearing of his band-aids.

"Stop it, Min-ho! H-hey guys, maybe driving around without a-a plan isn't such a good idea? O-or I mean, I'm assuming you know where we're going, but we-we don't know anything at all, and to be honest, my aunt doesn't even know—"

"I've already contacted your aunt and Kyun-ho. We're all going to the same place. Stop biting your fingers, buddy."

Eun-seok moves to withdraw Hyeong-cheol's fingers from his mouth, and for the first time ever, Chae-won and his friends see the man lose a bit of that eternal gentleness he has with Hyeong-cheol, all because the boy bites him.

"Hyeong-cheol, *stop it!* Sit back in your seat and *stop upsetting your body by hurting it!*"

It wasn't anything physical he did, but it was his tone and the sharpness of his words when he snapped, and Eun-seok, a man practically made of serenity, has never been heard snapping before.

Eun-seok has never been heard raising his voice like *that* at all with Hyeong-cheol.

So now the car is silent.

And Hyeong-cheol, who looks as though those words have struck him, is no longer voicing his tears at all.

It's as though he's petrified.

He's no longer biting, twisting, or kicking at the glove compartment.

He's still.

Utterly and terribly still, once he raises trembling hands to cover his ears, and Eun-seok almost runs into oncoming traffic because of this.

"Goodness… I–I'm not in the best of moods right now. I'm so sorry, Hyeong-cheol. That–that wasn't very nice of me. I shouldn't have reacted so cruelly. I–I'm really sorry." He reaches to try to reassure him with a touch, but Hyeong-cheol has already moved away from him, withdrawing into himself as though a turtle frightened into his shell.

All the children are wondering what to say now, yet no one dares voice anything in such a thick and dangerous–feeling atmosphere.

Eun-seok swerves again, and this time, the bright lights and loud sound of car horns blaring cause Min-ho to shout, "What in the world has messed you up so much you're trying to kill us?! You're supposed to be an adult, reassuring us that everything is going to be okay regardless of the situation! But you haven't even told us where we're going or why—!"

The car stops abruptly, jarring everyone from their seats because Eun-seok has jerked out of traffic to park on the side of the road, shoulders shaking as he brings a hand to his mouth and simply stares straight ahead of him, rain pouring down on the windshield wipers as he softly utters, "They're trying to get rid of different people. Anyone who's medically diagnosed with something the government deems as a threat towards society. Tomorrow, tomorrow morning, maybe even tonight, they're doing a whole sweep of the neighborhoods to escort those they feel threatened by to a new hospital, o-one that they won't be treated right at. Anyone who doesn't comply will be deemed a threat as well, which means..." He swallows deeply, eyes reddening as though the tears within them have already fallen several times before.

"Anyone who doesn't allow their family or friends to be taken will be marked as unredeemable."

Chae-won blinks rapidly, all color drained from his cheeks as Eun-seok continues, the tone so much softer now, "Unredeemable, from what I've heard, means the government can do whatever they want to you. If you're not for society, society, in the government's opinion, has the right... to silence you."

"W-wait... So what are we going to do if they find us? And who-who even told you this? Is it... Was it on the news...?"

It's Chae-won who's spoken, hands shaking despite being clasped in his lap as he stares at the back of Eun-seok's seat through glasses fogging from perspiration.

All the children are waiting for a response, but the only one they get is a long and terribly shaky exhale from Eun-seok, who has yet to let any tears fall, despite how they linger in his eyes.

The rain outside begins to fall more violently, the strain of the windshield wipers against the window briefly waking Tae-kyun from his restless slumber as Eun-seok closes his eyes.

They exchange a look, the friends…

Choon-ha to Min-ho.

Min-ho to Chae-won…

Chae-won to Yoon-ha, whose face undoubtedly says, *'I'm terrified of this situation because I don't know what to do about it.'*

Anxiety is often manifested when the great unknown wraps around and squeezes your mind, because it's what we can't see or figure out how to grasp that truly drives us mad, unable to cope with what's to come because you haven't a clue about it yourself.

"Mister Eun-seok, are you going to get in trouble for running away with us…?"

A soft, unsteady laugh tumbles out of Eun-seok's mouth, and Min-ho swears he sees him swallow rising bile before he says, "It's not really running if we're in a car, right?"

Anxiety begins to shift to paranoia for these friends, and thoughts begin to lose logic as *'what if?'* begins to shape them.

What if the police kill all of us?

What if Eun-seok gets killed, and the police take us somewhere daddy won't be able to find us?

What if uncle's dad is after us, too?
What will I do once everyone I know
is dead or taken from me?

What if Eun-seok is secretly
the murderer on the news,
and we're all about to die?

What if everyone but me gets taken away
because I'm normal...?

What if everyone is
about to go to war because half
the world has lost
their minds?

There are so many reasons to be afraid, so many reasons imaginations are sick with the unknown, and so, of course, the children continue to be afraid.

Hae-sol was missing.
No, Hae-sol *is* missing.
To everyone but Kyun-ho.

And he's terrified because of that.

They're here, behind the hospital.

Surrounded by trees and secluded in an area the staff had already searched before…

Just Kyun-ho and Hae-sol… under the blinding downpour of rain and the soft glow of the moon.

"Kyun-ho…" Hae-sol's voice is hoarse, as though he's been crying for a thousand years, though the reality is just that he hasn't been using that voice when he's away from this friend, the one his fingers latch onto, in a grip that says, 'I refuse to let go,' as his emerald eyes stare into Kyun-ho's mocha ones.

"Take me… You have to take me. Keep me safe, otherwise… the world will end without me, which means it will end without you, too…"

The rain is blurring Kyun-ho's vision… or maybe… no, is he crying…?

"I'm only missing… because I wanted you to find me… so that we could run away… and go back to the way things were before."

'Back to the way things were before…'

"Hae-sol, you're hurting her!"

"She's filth! Worthless, ruining everything we do for Haven!"

"N-no she's not! And regardless of what you think, sh-she's still a person! A-and you're hurting her!"

'Back to the way things were before.'

There's blood, so much blood, all over the floor, decorating the walls of this treehouse and littering the pale ivory of Hae-sol's skin, dripping from the body of…

'B a c k

t o

t h e   w a y

t h i n g s

w e r e

b e f o r e.'

"H-Hae-sol, she's-she's my friend! Sh-she's my friend, and you're killing her…!"

"She's not your friend, she was using you! Couldn't you see that? ALL SHE WANTED WAS MORE TIME BENEATH THE COVERS OF YOUR BED! SHE NEVER LOVED YOU! YOU NEVER LOVED HER! PEOPLE LIKE HER ARE MONSTERS WHO WANT TO RUIN YOU!"

Soarrarity…

Hae-sol's *fingers were* **tearing** *at the deep wounds he'd made on Soararities neck with his knife; more crimson was spilling, and more nausea churned what little food was left in* **Kyun-ho's** *stomach before it was all over the floor.*

Dizziness forced him to his knees as the sickening sound of Hae-sol while he mangled his friend grew louder and louder in his ears.

His fingers were spread **apart** *to desperately scratch at his throat because he knew his bile had tried to choke him.*

*"I'M SAVING YOU! **I HAVE TO KILL** HER! AND WHEN I FIND THOSE STUPID BABIES, I'LL KILL THEM TOO!"*
"H-H-Hae-sol, St-stop! Stop! S-stop!"

'BACK TO THE WAY THINGS WERE -

It was Monday, November 23rd.

Kyun-ho was walking home from school, and he'd been heading straight to his treehouse.

Elation had drawn up the corners of his mouth because yesterday, he'd gotten a whole year older.

Yesterday, he turned nine, which meant he'd celebrate his birthday with Hae-sol today because the actual celebration he had with his family was simply not enough to make him happy.

Perhaps that's because the only one who remembered was Tae-ho, who gave him nothing but a reminder that their parents no longer cared to celebrate his existence.

Tae-kyun, though old enough to remember, had been practically overdosed on various medications their father was forcing him to take, and was, just as the week before, in a catatonic state.

It was the same at school, too.

For Kyun-ho, it seemed the universe had not yet wanted him to exist, let alone be celebrated.

No, yesterday was not a happy birthday, but it was okay because after he lamented to Hae-sol, the boy agreed to make it better.

"We don't need your family to have a happy birthday... We can celebrate all by ourselves... and momentarily forget they exist."

Tae-kyun had gone to a doctor's appointment with their mother, and Hae-yon, Hae-sol had said, wasn't feeling well.

So it was just the two of them.

Or it would be... very soon.

When Kyun-ho reached their treehouse, he was astonished to see it had been decorated with lights.

An odd assortment, no doubt, but a euphoric sight for Kyun-ho regardless.

There was a banner, colored entirely in crayon, and on it, Hae-sol had printed, in his best lettering, 'Happy Birthday Rewind,' with hurried drawings that Kyun-ho supposed were supposed to be him and his best friend, though Hae-sol only drew in stick figures, and the stick figures never had any descriptive features aside from height, so he was only assuming.

He had laughed then, already elated, and hurried to climb the rope ladder to the treehouse, where large handfuls of leaves were instantly thrown atop his head.

"Confetti, confetti..." Hae-sol said, and he tossed another handful of leaves at his friend, who fell on the floor of the treehouse and laughed.

"Hae-sol, those are leaves!"

"No... today, it's organic confetti." He smiled, emerald eyes glinting with satisfaction while Kyun-ho, cheeks rosy, stifled another chortle before he admitted, "You didn't have to celebrate my birthday, Hae-sol, or redo it.

No one's ever done that for me."

"I guess that's because no one's ever cared..." Hae-sol mused and turned to retrieve a large box from beneath the windowsill before sliding it in Kyun-ho's direction.

"I got you a gift... Hae-yon did too... but we put them both in the same box."

Oh, what joy Kyun-ho had felt when he received that box.

But more than joy, he felt a great deal of warmth, a great amount of love, and a boundless amount of gratefulness as he opened the box to stare down at his gifts.

Here is what they were:

An assortment of soft yarn, along with a worn yet beautifully bound blue dictionary, and a neatly stitched leather notebook that said, in equally small and neat lettering,

'Here is where you will place all your sad thoughts.

And this is what you'll use when they get too big.

I have a theory that burning them up may just make them disappear.

– Hae-yon

There was a small box of matches across from the last sentence, and Kyun-ho laughed at the child for thinking he'd be brave enough to burn any pages of a book, sad thoughts or not.

"You and Hae-yon are so amazing!" He had gathered the yarn in his arms as though a giant kitten, placed both his dictionary and notebook on his lap and gave Hae-sol the biggest, most genuine smile the boy had seen Kyun-ho wear in a very long time, for depression was a common friend of Kyun-ho's, even then.

"I wish everyone could treat me like you guys do! You guys and Tae-kyun are the best people around!"

"We have to be... We're your best friends... It's only natural we'd be the best people around." Hae-sol had smiled proudly at that, *and then they had both settled into the corner of their treehouse to play Legend of Zelda on their Game Boy devices, and no more words were needed to confirm the presence of euphoria.*

No words are needed at all to say to one another,

'Today and tomorrow you're my haven, because yesterday and all the days to come, you've become my refuge.'

- Sixteen -

Whispers of Manipulation

What am I going to do?
What am I going to do?
What am I going to do?

Hae-sol hasn't let go of Kyun-ho's arm.

His jagged fingernails have probably already left bruises, and he's unsure if the warm liquid sensation trickling down his skin is blood because of Hae-sol's grip or rain because it's relentless in its falling.

Where are we going? I can't take him home. I can't take Hae-sol home with me, but I need to go home. I-I have to go home. Something's happening. I-I need to go home...!

They've been wandering around the streets for a while now.

And oddly enough, the rain has warded off most of the protesters that had littered the streets before.

263

Hae-sol must have already planned on escaping, for he wasn't wearing his hospital clothes when Kyun-ho found him; no, he was wearing clothes that looked like they were stolen from somewhere else.

Someone else...

A deep blue turtleneck and an inky black leather jacket...

Smoke-colored jeans that hardly fit him because he's refused to eat anything at all if it's not from Kyun-ho, paranoid of the poison he believes the staff sneaks into his food.

As Kyun-ho leads his friend aimlessly through the streets, he can't help but wonder, *Whose clothes are those? Where did you get them? Did you have to take someone's life again just for your own selfish gain?*

"Kyun-ho, my friend, where are we going that has you so quiet...? Are you thinking we should go back to our treehouse, too...? Why are you silent when your heart is beating so loudly?"

The rain is starting to sting Kyun-ho's shoulders; perhaps it's beating down too heavily...

"THEY'RE GOING TO TAKE OUR CHILDREN! THE GOVERNMENT IS GOING TO ROB US OF OUR CHILDREN JUST BECAUSE THEY'RE DIFFERENT!"

A young woman is shouting that, over and over again, as she waves her ruined sign in the rain, marker dripping from the colorful letters that have already started to fade as Kyun-ho quickly pulls Hae-sol past her, past the police officers that have pulled up beside her to yank her sign from her hands and shout, *"ENOUGH! You already had your warning! The government is removing threats from society in order to stop the killings!"*

"No, that's not true! You hate them! You've always hated them! Nothing good is going to happen to our children once you've—!"

They hear a scream, and Kyun-ho can't help but turn, eyes widening because from what the rains allowed him to see.

They're beating her.

They're beating that woman when all she's done is speaking the truth.

It has to be true.

Kyun-ho's lived through it.

Countless times, over and over again.

The government and the society itself have failed to care.

"He's not being tortured if your father's trying to heal him."

"We don't care if he's mental. He's a disturbance to your neighborhood, and if we get called for him again, he will be detained."

"Your father is doing the best he can for Tae-kyun. Tae-kyun's sick. He's only covered in bruises because your father claims he's violent."

"If people like them are going to live in this neighborhood, all of us that are normal should simply find somewhere else to be."

"You should really consider putting him down."

"He'll never be normal, there's no point in medicating him. Leave him at the hospital this time and let them deal with him."

"The whole neighborhood hates being afraid of your family, Mister Choi. Everyone who's called has said the same thing. They're terrified because you have a demon in your house, and they're worried you might be one, too."

"Kyun-ho... it's still raining... We should continue walking and should return to our treehouse before we're taken away. They still think I belong there. Don't you know? They don't realize I'm not a patient."

"Those officers... the ones who are supposed to protect us... they're beating that lady, and no one can stop them because they're the law... right...?"

Hae-sol tilts his head at the blurry silhouettes of the officers in the rain, emerald eyes slowly blinking before he returns his gaze to Kyun-ho, who refuses to stop shaking.

"Would you like someone to defy them...? 'Officer' is just a title, Kyun-ho. Beneath that uniform, they're just people... and people are capable of being victims or perpetrators any day... It's circumstances that separate us."

Kyun-ho's heart feels as though it's momentarily stopped beating, and his breath hitches as Hae-sol stares into his eyes, rain pouring on their heads and dripping off their lashes.

"H-Hae-sol, n-no...! That-that's not what I meant, n-no, please no...!"

To that, Hae-sol smiles, an instant and stomach-churning smile that refuses to leave Kyun-ho's mind even after it leaves Hae-sol's face, because he's seen that smile so many times before.

It's rooted in his memory because of all the fear he's felt because of it.

It's the same smile that happened when Kyun-ho first hurt a child in order to stop Hae-sol from hurting himself.

The same smile happened when Kyun-ho found him sitting in the blood of his own father with Hye-yon's dark blue shirt in his hands, the one with the white stripes and embroidered yellow stars adorning it.

The same smile that happened when he squeezed the last ounce of air from the girl who had birthed Kyun-ho's children right before he started to mangle her.

And he hates that.

Kyun-ho hates that Hae-sol's ruined so much of him, a simple smile can shatter him in an instant.

"Kyun-ho, you know they're going to take us away, right...? Tae-kyun too... your children, the ones you've never introduced me to, and anyone else the world deems as broken... all because you refused to help me fix them... so long ago... and had me committed to a hospital instead."

He's trying to manipulate him, Hae-sol, wrapping a thread of guilt and responsibility around him just because he knows he can and just because he knows how to torture Kyun-ho.

"If we escape now... together... we can still gather what we need to perfect a cure... a remedy before everyone's dead... because you know... that's what's going to happen if they go to that hospital... We need to act before they do..." His grip tightens if that's even possible, and Kyun-ho feels his arm going numb as Hae-sol whispers through this rain, "In a world where everyone craves normality because they fear what's different... those who are broken are destined for hell unless we save them, turning into their haven..."

"Haven doesn't work, Hae-sol…" Kyun-ho forces out, swallowing the bile threatening to surface as he continues shakily, "Haven… Haven broke us. Y-you… you… broke…"

Me.

My happiness.

My brother.

My life.

My lover.

My mind.

My faith.

Our friendship.

Those children.

Y o u r s e l f.

The loud sound of approaching protesters rings in Kyun-ho's ears as Hae-sol glares at Kyun-ho from beneath his dripping bangs, emerald eyes colored with so much fury as he growls, "You hate Haven because you messed it up. It was *you* who failed to doctor our patients. *You who* failed to stop the bleeding. *You* who made us kill so many because you couldn't fix them like you were supposed to…!"

Kyun-ho's legs feel weak, and he's not sure when it happens, but he's on his knees, kneeling on the wet asphalt and pressing shaking hands to eyes that won't stop crying as he begins to writhe in mental agony, the volume of the surfacing memories restricting the air around him.

"K-Kyunie, no more for Hae-sol, n-n-no more for medicine!"

268

"If you don't hold him down, all the medicine I injected will refuse to travel to his head."

"B-but Hae-sol, he's bleeding, and h-he's crying…!"

"He's only crying because of the way we've hung him over the edge… Keep holding him down. If you let go, he's going to die. We're too high up… You'll kill Tae-kyun, and we'll never know if the medicine worked or not."

"K-Kyunie! Kyunie!"

"He needs one more dose."

"W-what if it kills him?"

"What if you kill him…? You're scaring your dear brother, Kyun-ho. An older brother like you should try comforting him through this process… Instead, you're creating far more chaos inside his heart than he ever had before."

The ground beneath them looks so far from atop this treehouse. Tae-kyun's torso is hanging off the side of it as Kyun-ho struggles to hold him still while Hae-sol advances with the needle.

Inversion therapy, but for your head.

That's what Hae-sol called Tae-kyun's treatment.

That's why he's hanging off the side of their treehouse.

That's why Hae-sol keeps medicating him because he's convinced this is the only way the concoction will flow to his head.

"If we don't fix Tae-kyun now, someone else, in the future, will break him beyond repair… and you will be responsible for his heart once it stops beating."

Kyun-ho can no longer control his breathing.

His throat feels constricted by his past, and I do fear his heart may just burst from such frantic beating.

"Once we take away what makes them different, the whole world will shift beneath us... and we will no longer be ignored by society. Success gives people power... and power makes people scared... Power makes the weak strong. Power means we won't even be controlled by those who mock and abuse us..."

"Kyun-ho, it's still raining. We should go home, back to our treehouse. We need to focus on a remedy for saving Haven."

*"The whole world would love us if we could rebirth the fallen angels of distraught families... Maybe even your dad... your mother... and maybe people would stop hurting you. Maybe... people would acknowledge and truly care about you due to Haven's success... because as it is now... we could kill each other today, and the world would just keep spinning... Humans without success are very insignificant in the eyes of an officer... That's why it's so easy for perpetrators to find victims over and over again without consequence. We've had **thirteen** failed surgeries so far, and yet only **three** families have started to mourn..."*

"We can finally become doctors... real ones. The world will grow to fear and admire this nightmare. This tragedy of a situation the world is putting us in... is exactly what we need to perfect Haven."

"You really don't make any sense, do you, Kyun-ho? Not you, not your silly little religion..." Tae-ho was underneath the treehouse, and he sat on the swing that creaked every time you moved it. He had been smiling at the boy in front of him despite the blood that adorned his clothing, despite the visible tremors and tears that dripped from wide and bloodshot eyes.

"'You're a monster. You killed mom!' No, no, to be perfectly honest, you're the monster because I know what you've been doing here with that boy. You and Hae-sol, the son of a faggot and the son of a saint, running around gaining pleasure from hurting the weaker ones around you, yet I'm the monster for aiding our dear mother in a suicide she'd been planning for years because life just wasn't worth all the suffering…"

He smiled again, Tae-ho, brighter as he tilted his head to ask, inky hair curtaining his eyes, "So tell me, Christian Kyun-ho, why have there been so many missing children? Why do you leave these woods painted with blood without any regard for those you've brutally slaughtered? Why do you continue to play such violent games with that pervert's son?

What exactly do you think will happen if you continue to be Hae-sol's friend?"

It's chaos inside his mind, and yet Kyun-ho is unable to tear himself away from the past and into the present.

- Seventeen -

Unraveling of The Mind

"Hae-sol, where are we going?"

They were nine years old, these friends.

Nine years old and wondering through the forest with small hands clasped together, past their treehouse and further away from civilization.

Hae-sol was smiling.

Kyun-ho was smiling, and he was not afraid at all of where his friend was taking him, even with the black scarf that veiled his eyes and tickled his nose.

Today had been a good day.

Kyun-ho's father hadn't been home to beat him yet.

Tae-kyun finally adjusted to his new medicine, and Hae-yon, Hae-sol's brother, had actually requested Tae-kyun to stay and play with him, despite his usually avoidant behavior with him.

"Just keep walking… We're almost there…" Hae-sol said, and his tone was so low for a child of his age, yet so soft and warm in Kyun-ho's ears.

'I've never been so deep in this forest. Perhaps I should start feeling afraid, but Hae-sol's been really nice to me today, just like dad, so I'm okay... right...?'

He stumbled on a stone, Kyun-ho, and laughed because he assumed Hae-sol would catch him.

But he realized too late that Hae-sol was no longer holding his hand, was no longer near him.

How did he miss the feeling of letting go...?

And so he fell, and his knees, despite the velvet bed of moss that caught him, still ached from the impact.

"Hey, Hae-sol, where did you go? Did you find a frog or something...?"

Kyun-ho stilled as the wind picked up and whispered through the trees surrounding him, and his heart stuttered with unease as his long bangs fell over his veiled eyes.

"Kyun-ho, are you going to be my friend... forever...?"

Startled by his voice, Kyun-ho turned in the direction it came from, and he stood to stumble towards it, only to knock into a tree and hurt his head.

He laughed, because oftentimes he would laugh when he was unsure of what to say, but the warm trickle of crimson that dripped from beneath his bangs and into the scarf that disabled his vision had actually made him feel quite afraid.

"Ouch, this must be a tree," Kyun-ho stated and reached out to touch the rough bark of the oak tree while a wave of fear violently shook his body.

Something had told him not to let his fear show, though. There was something inside of him that said, 'Do not admit you are afraid...' and so he swallowed deeply and laughed again in a failed attempt to lighten his heavy heart.

273

"Of course, we'll still be friends. I think once you're best friends, you-you have to stay with that person forever. That's what I think, anyways, and that's what I've told Tae-kyun. He—"

"You can't have two best friends. Only one."

Kyun-ho felt the claws of fear had scratched him too deeply, and with every word Hae-sol spoke, he tried to appear as though he wasn't wounded at all.

"Oh, well, if I think best friends are forever, I can think two best friends are okay instead of one, right? It's more fun that way anyway, it—"

A sharp blow to the back of his head caused Kyun-ho to drop to his knees, and for a while, he felt nothing but swift, aching pain and the warmth of blood that greeted his fingers when he dared to reach behind him.

"That was a stone… That stone is meant to represent the world… Do you think you'd be able to navigate the world without me…?"

Another burst of pain erupted on his arm, and he cried out as dizziness began to mingle with his fear.

"O-ow, Hae-sol, I never said we weren't friends! We are best friends, I-I promise!"

"That was my knife… The cut I made on your arm represents the cruelty of society… Would you be able to withstand the pain society gives you all alone…?"

Kyun-ho's stomach churned as blood puddled beneath his knees, and the air around him seemed to evaporate each time he tried to inhale.

"H-Hae-sol that hurts! Best friends don't…!"

"And this…" Kyun-ho tried to rid his eyes of the blindfold before Hae-sol could hurt him again, but the moment his fingers enclosed around the material, he screamed in agony, trying to back away from the one who'd struck his knee as he murmured, "That was the strength of a tree branch, a big one. It represents the people in your life that are going to turn their backs on you and leave you with nothing but pain…"

Kyun-ho was unable to form any words because the pain had started to spot his mind with white.

'There's too much blood! Am I dying? Is Hae-sol going to kill me…? He's my best friend though! He's been so nice to me this week, so nice to me…!'

"Kyun-ho, everything you're feeling right now is not because of me… It's the world… society… and cruel people you thought you could trust. It's the pain of going through life… alone."

"B-but I'm not a-alone-! And y-you! You-y-you…!" It was so hard to stay conscious then; too much blood had slipped out of him, too much pain had churned his insides while he sobbed.

"Kyun-ho… do you want to keep experiencing that pain alone, without any help…?"

Kyun-ho's eyes fluttered as he began to see more spots of white right as Hae-sol stepped in front of him, the red hood of his black shirt blowing in the wind as he repeated, "Do you want to keep experiencing that pain alone without any help…?"

"C-c-can't see… ouch-ow! M-my… Help-help me, Hae-sol…!"

"Are you going to be my friend forever…?"

"Y-yes!"

"You won't let anyone take you…?"

Kyun-ho could only groan in response while more blood slid down his skin and into his shirt.

More blood seeped beneath him.

More blood coated his hands as he struggled to stop his arm from leaking.

"*Tell me that you'll be loyal to me forever, and I'll make all your pain go away... pain from the world... society... those y—*"

"*Yes! F-forever loyal, forever... aghh!*" *He gripped his arm tighter and realized it was not a simple cut, but a gaping wound his mind started to tell him he would not be able to hold together.*

"*And you won't put anyone above me...?*"

Kyun-ho jerked his head in a nod but cried out from the pain that throbbed in the back of his head, and then, all of a sudden...

He felt something sharp pierce his shoulder, and within seconds, all his pain began to numb, as though his body was being put into a deep sleep, as though he was never in pain at all.

And that was so absurd to him that he started to laugh.

Short, breathy laughs that reverberated throughout his body as he fought to maintain consciousness.

As he was fighting, though, his ears pricked at the low whisper of a voice he'd heard quite infrequently in his life, a voice that ignited instant panic in his heart as it said, "He's bound to you for life now. Now you see why I did the same to you and Hye-yon. Our world is cruel and unforgiving, full of many temptations placed to snatch our loved ones from our lives. If you don't own those you love by fear, I guarantee you temptation will take them away, because fear will triumph over temptation any day. Fear is what creates loyalty, and loyalty is a gift from the gods few people on earth are able to obtain. You didn't hurt him, Hae-sol. The world we live in did."

Kyun-ho lifted his head to blink at the man, before he lost consciousness, and fell into the crimson grass beneath him.

Acknowledgements

I would be lying if I said I took this journey completely on my own.

I have found that writing, though often described as a lonely art, has much to do with the collaboration of different minds and ideas and that refusing to share one's work or accept critiques, both constructive ones and the ones you may only find helpful further down the line, has the potential to stunt and even kill a story.

A story is born because an author dreams, but a book is published because an author has dared to step out of their comfort zone, entering the land of beta readers, editors, formatters, and, most importantly, alpha betas.

When I first started writing, I didn't think I'd need to have anyone but myself look over my story and shape it into what it is today. As silly as it was, despite being a Christian, I didn't even think I needed any guidance from God.

Perhaps it was out of fear, or perhaps pride was simply taking up too much space inside my heart, but I abhorred the ideation of sharing what I wrote and often told myself, as I hunched over my notebook, writing sludge I was positive was gold, 'This *is my story; the only one who writes it is me.'*

But Renaya Moore, my best friend, fellow author, and sibling who became my alpha reader so many years ago, has long since shown me how foolish that thought process is, how important it is to not only include God in my journey but also open my heart to different perspectives, narrations, and ideas while still keeping the one that birthed my story whole, and it was her who contributed so much to its core.

It is not that writers are incapable of creating a story but that writers, by default, cannot catch every mistake, plot hole, or pacing issue that ensues while writing the story.

I assumed accepting or asking for help meant I couldn't write my story, and that I only needed to share what I'd come up with once I was swiftly published and out on the market.

It never occurred to me how ridiculous it was to expect an audience of people who didn't even know me to read and enjoy something I'd kept hidden, even though my friend would eagerly hand over chapters or inquire about ideas, with little hesitation in her eyes.

I was, essentially, prideful and quite selfish, but Renaya was, and still is, just as understanding and patient with me then as she is today. When I finally decided to share my story, when I finally decided to pray for courage, she held no animosity towards me, only excitement and a willingness to help, and if not for her and everything she's done to help develop not only Children of Dysphoria but me, myself, and I, I would not have dared to share my work, I would not have dared to be more bold in my writing, and I would not have dared to dream as vastly as she's shown me.

I would have kept my pride and selfishness, and my story would remain unpublished, unread by any other eyes but my own, a dream without any resolution.

Of course, I have my beta readers to thank as well, Hallowedseeker being one that not only filled me with euphoria, but motivated me to keep writing book two of my series, and also showed me that God truly does give us stories to share with the world. Though the whole world may not like it, it's the ones that do that make a book that much more purposeful because you never know whose heart you're going to touch or who will resonate with your story or its characters.

God knows, though, and this is why He's given me, and every other writer, a story.

Not everyone can change the world, but anyone can make an impact.

Thank you, dear friend, for being my impact, and thank you, fellow writer, for changing my world.

And finally, though I don't know you personally, thank you, reader, for picking up Children of Dysphoria.

"Dear stranger,
Thank you for reading
Children of Dysphoria!
Please leave your
thoughts on the book in
a review on Amazon and
Goodreads!
It's readers like you that
make all the difference
in an author's life :) "

www.ingramcontent.com/pod-product-compliance
Lightning Source LLC
Chambersburg PA
CBHW071233250626
47163CB00001B/163